NEW TO NEWPORT

EMI HILTON

5 PRINCE PUBLISHING
5PRINCEBOOKS.COM

Digital ISBN: 978-1-63112-399-3

Print ISBN: 978-1-63112-402-0

Cover design by Marianne Nowicki

Interior design by 5 Prince Publishing

First Edition 042925fv1

For more information about this title, visit: www.5princebooks.com

ALSO BY EMI HILTON

New to Newport

Keeping Kama

Picking Pismo

Leaving Cloverton

For all the children I taught to swim.

ACKNOWLEDGMENTS

First, thank you to my readers. Without each of you, I wouldn't have a reason to write. Thank you for sharing with a friend, leaving five stars reviews, liking my posts, and reading my books. Though I don't know you all personally, I'm grateful for you.

A huge thank you to my talented and amazing editor, Cate Byers. It was a pleasure working with you again. As always, you find a way to help bring my story and words to life. I appreciate your constant guidance and support as I grow in my craft. This story is only what it is, because of your help.

Thank you to my publisher, 5 Prince Publishing. I am forever grateful my story found a home at your publishing house. I am thankful for the entire 5 Prince team, who offer me a mountain of encouragement and support. You'll never know the depth of my gratitude, a million thanks.

To my husband, Tyler. Thank you for supporting me in my dreams. Your love is what has given me the freedom to be a writer. My life is beautiful, because you are in it. I love you now and forever.

To family and friends who are near and dear to my heart. Thank you for your love and constant upliftment. Each of you makes my life better and more complete. My heart is full as I think of each of you, so thank you.

Last, I thank my faithful Father in Heaven, God. Thank you for giving me the gift and ability to write. Thank you for your endless goodness and mercy. I live and breathe every day in your amazing grace. May I praise thy holy name forever. In all things, I humbly devote the glory and honor to thee.

NEW TO NEWPORT

CHAPTER 1

Sweat dripped down Hannah's temples and pooled at the middle of her back. She pounded the air conditioning button in her car then attempted to crank it up to full blast. Nothing. Nada. Zilch. Zero change. Hannah would've even accepted if a soft blow of the outside balmy salt air came through the vent but nope. Figures, the car was older than her. It didn't help she hadn't used the AC since last summer. Even then, it had sputtered and clanked along, but eventually had blown a small stream of cool air. Nah, her AC had finally kicked it.

Great. Just great.

With no choice, Hannah lowered her windows a few inches to let the summer ocean air waft through her beat up gold Toyota Corolla. The light up ahead turned from green to yellow. For a split second, Hannah contemplated speeding through the intersection to make the light. Ultimately, Hannah decided it wasn't worth the risk, slamming on her brakes, the car halted an inch from the intersection.

Seconds later, a car rammed into her from behind. Her body lurched forward, making her head whip back to correct it. As she gripped the steering wheel, Hannah's knuckles turned white. Her trusty seatbelt locked. Hannah's body stayed firmly in place as the car scraped its way across the asphalt before stopping several feet ahead. Blood pumped through her veins as she braced herself for another possible impact. Then to her utmost surprise, the car miraculously didn't move.

Heart in her throat, Hannah rubbed one hand behind her stinging neck. "What in the world," Hannah muttered.

A tremor made her hands jump and jive, she brought her hand from her sore neck back to her steering wheel. Hannah peered over her shoulder through the back windshield. A blue Honda Civic, appearing to be even older than her Corolla, had decided to play bumper cars with her. Cars parted around them, swerving into the other lane. Their accident became a commuter's nuisance. Nobody stopped, and Hannah didn't blame them. They had places to go. So did she.

Honk. Honk. Honk. The sound ricocheted around in her brain, making her temples throb. Those who passed by peered curiously out their windows to view the damage. Once past their cars, they picked up speed, melting into the stream of moving metal.

Hannah glanced down at herself to scan her body for any visible injuries. *You're okay. You're okay. You're okay.* No blood.

Honk. Honk. Honk. She winced at the excruciating sound.

With a tremor in her hands, Hannah flipped on her blinker. A smashed bumper wasn't the end of the world. Maybe the car was still drivable? She peered over her shoulder, waiting for a break in traffic so she could move to the side. The light a block behind her turned red, the two lanes emptied, and Hannah merged over. A loud clank repeated over and over as her car limped over to the side of the road. Up a few yards, Hannah found a spot along the curb and parked.

After she parked, Hannah clocked the time on the dash. *Perfect.* Late for day one of her new job, she was no doubt off to a brilliant start. With a groan, Hannah opened her car door and climbed out.

Hannah slammed her door shut and willed herself to dampen her raging temper. *It was an accident, accident, accident.* Slowly, she rounded her car to catalog the damage. The entire trunk was squashed flat against the back seat. Her shoulders stiffened as she inched to the other side. Hannah sighed when she spotted the wheel well crunched against the passenger side tire. She wasn't going anywhere in this thing. And now she was officially late to work.

For a few seconds, Hannah stared at the tire, willing it to magically transform beneath her gaze. Then in a knee jerk reaction she gave it a swift hard kick. *Ouch.* Her flip flops weren't made for this type of action. She didn't know what hurt more, her head, neck or now foot.

Then out of nowhere someone asked, "Are you okay?" The words broke her spiraling thoughts.

Hannah snapped her head in the direction of the voice. Her gaze landed on a good-looking guy around her age with dark hair and stunning green eyes. Was this the guy who had hit her? Or a mere bystander? Slowly, she inspected the guy further, taking in his tall frame, khaki shorts, and plain blue crewneck sweatshirt. He looked like an Old Navy model, in the absolute best way. Did all the guys walking around Newport look like him? Everyone joked that California was the land of milk and honey. Whomever pegged the term certainly knew what they were talking about. Her random sampling only made her wonder what the people looked like on the beach. Maybe Newport was right where she needed to be.

Mr. Hottie cleared his throat, plunging a hand through his wind-blown, sea breezed hair. He asked again, "How are you feeling?" He scrutinized her appearance. "Any injuries? Should I call an ambulance?"

Suddenly, Hannah regretted not doing her hair. She had

arrived in Newport Beach late last night. A blaring alarm clock had awoken her much too late, and Hannah had stumbled her way out of bed. With no time, she threw on her uniform, pulling her ratty hoodie on over it. Hannah wanted to blurt out that she normally didn't look this disheveled.

Her knees shook, and she wondered if it was from the rear end or Mr. Emerald Green Eyes. To find her equilibrium, Hannah crossed her arms and leaned a hip against her car. "I'm fine." She forced herself to look at the damaged section of her car. "But my car is undrivable. Are you the person who hit me?" Hannah peered past the man, spotting a crunched-up now empty blue Civic.

Bingo.

He scratched his head then tucked his thumbs through his empty belt loops. For a split second, the fabric of his shirt rose enough for her to see the inch of skin around the waist of his shorts. Whoa, there. Why was she clocking this guy so hardcore?

"Guilty." For a moment, he glanced down at his feet then swung his gaze back to her. "I'm sorry about that. Are you okay?" His tone oozed regret.

His tone melted away the annoyance of her crushed car and being late for work. The guy hadn't meant to hit her, and she had slammed on her brakes at the last minute. He was at fault, but it didn't mean she needed to be a total brat about it.

Hannah double-checked her watch. "I'm fine. How about you?" She allowed herself another peek only to scan for injuries, not to make goo-goo eyes at him.

"I'm not hurt." He exhaled, making his shoulders drop a good two inches. "And I'm relieved to hear you aren't either."

"Thanks." Hannah straightened herself. "But I'm going to need to call a tow truck."

The man sidestepped around her car. He crouched down in front of the bent wheel well. "Again, I'm sorry." He peered up at her. "I shouldn't have been following you so closely." Sweat glistened his brow, and he swiped at it with the back of his wrist.

Hannah shrugged. "That's why they call it an accident."

Dang, she was going easy on him. Is this how hot people manage to get through life? Did everyone always give them a free pass? He stood back up a mere foot in front of her. The man was tall, easily over six feet and towered over her average height. Hannah stumbled a step back until her hip rested against the side of the car.

She peered over his shoulder toward his damaged vehicle. "How about you? Do you think your car is drivable?"

"Nah." The man scrunched his nose. Hannah wondered if he was squinting or thinking. "I could barely see over the dash enough to pull it over to the side. So, I'll need a tow truck too."

Hannah plunged her hands into the front pocket of her oversized hoodie. With the grey sky, goosebumps ran up and down her arms. "Let me call a tow truck." Hannah tugged her phone free. "Then we can exchange insurance information." Without looking up, Hannah typed tow truck into the internet browser.

"I'll go grab my license and insurance information from the car." Then he took off toward his car.

Hannah scrutinized him for a second as he jogged back to his crushed vehicle. His broad shoulders were what dreams were made of. She shook her head, forcing herself to focus on the internet search on her phone. A lengthy list of tow truck companies popped up. With no clue on how to decipher which was legit, she simply selected the first one listed. Hannah hit call, putting her phone to her ear.

She listened as it rang. The man made his way back from his car with papers in his hands. When he came within hearing distance, Hannah remarked, "It's still ringing."

He nodded and shuffled his feet. Finally, he peered out at the steady stream of cars driving by. When the light changed to red, the cars piled up, waiting again for the green light. The tow truck company answered, and Hannah explained the situation along with the cross streets of their location. Then she hung up once the details were confirmed.

"They said they'd be here as soon as possible." Hannah placed her phone back into the front pocket of her hoodie. "But it'll probably be a half hour." The clouds attempted to part to allow the sunshine to trickle through. She squinted for a second against the rays of sun hitting her.

"Sounds reasonable. Do you want to exchange information while we wait?" He arched an eyebrow and paused. Quickly, he added, "I'm Caleb by the way. Sorry I hit you." His eyes crinkled around the edges, making his stunning green eyes pop back at her.

"Hannah, and you don't need to keep apologizing." Unnecessarily, she tugged the bottom of her hoodie down. "Let me go grab my purse."

Hannah pivoted, traipsing to her car without further explanation. After she located her purse on the floor of the front seat, she returned. Caleb had settled on the curb in between their crushed vehicles. Hannah plopped herself down next to him. She pulled out her license and insurance information from her purse.

As she held it out to him, Hannah said, "Here, snap a picture of my stuff, and I'll take a picture of yours too. I think that's the easiest way to do it." She met his gaze. "I believe it's your responsibility to report this to your insurance company since you're the one who hit me."

His gaze dropped to her outstretched hand and papers. For a good long second, he scrutinized her hand. What was this guy's deal? Her nail polish was a tad chipped, but she hadn't had anytime to fix it. Hannah shook the papers in her hands and shot him an *are you still with me?* glance.

His cheeks flushed. Slowly, Caleb gulped like he was waking up from a trance. "Oh, gotcha. Sorry." Caleb took the papers from her, handing Hannah his own in return. Afterwards he placed the documents flat against the sidewalk and yanked his phone out of his front pocket. "This is the first time I've hit someone. I'm sorry I'm out of sorts." He snapped a picture.

"There you go apologizing again." Hannah crouched over the paperwork on the curb next to her and snapped a photo of the documents. "But, on behalf of the other drivers in this world, let's hope this is your first and last accident."

Caleb grunted a reply that Hannah couldn't decipher, but she didn't ask him to repeat it.

Done, Hannah shuffled the papers back into a neat stack, holding them out to Caleb. He snagged them, giving hers back. She shoved hers into her purse, zipping it closed. Bored, Hannah leaned back on her palms and crossed her ankles out in front of her. She stared out at the cars passing by them.

Suddenly, Caleb stood up. Without a word, he strolled back to his car. Hannah ogled him the entire time. The guy did know how to wear those shorts. She shook off her train of thought. After he opened his car door and dumped his paperwork inside, he trotted on back. When he approached, Hannah forced herself to look anywhere but at him. She didn't say a word when he plopped himself back down on the curb. What do you say to the guy who hit you and you'll never see again? Nothing, that's what.

Time passed. Cars came and went. The light cycled from red to green and back again a few times. Hannah cradled her knees and rested her cheek against them. A light morning breeze fluttered around her as the sky continued to push the grey away and replace it with blue.

Out of nowhere, Caleb asked, "Where were you headed?" He leaned back on one palm and scratched his scruffy jaw with his forefinger. When he found her gaze, he added, "I hope I haven't made you late for a hot date or something like that."

Hannah glanced down at her oversized sweatshirt which was so not date attire. "I'm wearing a too big for me, ratty sweatshirt."

She cocked an eyebrow and fought against a smirk forming on her lips. "I'd hope I would dress a little better if I was headed for a," she made quotations with her fingers, *"hot date."*

Caleb chuckled. "You never know these days." Nonchalantly, he shrugged. "I once had a woman show up for a date in her PJs only then promptly tell me she came only to inform me that she wasn't coming."

Hannah threw her head back and laughed. "Now that's something I haven't heard before. There must be so much more to that story." She felt her eyes scrunch up. The sun fully broke through the clouds, warming her up. By noon, Newport Beach would be hotter than hot. Instinctively, Hannah unzipped her purse and dug around for her sunglasses. "And why didn't this lady simply text you to tell you she was bailing?" She found them and put them on.

Her eyes relaxed. They had always been overly sensitive to the sun. Also, she knew her sunglasses made it impossible to see her eyes. It made it way easier to make eye contact with this hottie through the protective layer of plastic across her face. The temperature increased by the minute. Hannah pushed up the sleeves of her sweatshirt.

Caleb tilted his head closer. "Exactly." He motioned at her. "See, you get me."

Hannah waited for him to tell the rest of the story. "Go, on. You're helping me feel better about my own life. So, I want to hear the rest." She had nothing else to occupy her time until the tow truck showed. Plus, she found his voice soothing.

Caleb yanked a pair of sunglasses from his pocket opposite where his phone was stored. As he placed his aviator frames on his face, he continued, "Apparently, she had been up the entire night throwing up. Again, a text message would have been sufficient here. But according to her, she couldn't remember my number. Which I know was a blatant lie, because we had been texting back and forth the day before." Casually, he leaned back on his palms. "Whatever," he muttered. "I've yet to understand the workings of the female mind."

"You and me both," Hannah agreed.

Caleb smiled. Dang, it made his eyes dazzle. Somebody could live off that smile for days. Some lucky lady probably got to kiss that face every single day.

Hannah sped forward. "I mean, you were worthy enough for her to venture out sick. I'd say that's a positive." She picked a stray piece of lint off her hoodie. "Did you ever make it on a date with her?"

"Nah." Caleb shook his head. Deadpan, he said, "She ghosted me after that."

Hannah burst out laughing. A sense of humor too, Caleb was a wonder.

Caleb's lips twitched at the corners. He continued, "I'm glad one of us can laugh about it. In the moment, I was devastated even though I knew we had zero chance of making it work. But never underestimate the sting of the ghosting."

"Now, I'm the one who's sorry." Hannah wanted to hug him, but she knew it was grossly inappropriate to hug a guy you met fifteen minutes ago. She crinkled her nose, pushing up her slipping sunglasses. "I didn't mean to laugh at your bad luck. I have war stories of my own when it comes to dating. It helps to hear about others who are out in the trenches too. It nice to know you aren't alone."

"Thanks. I appreciate your kind words. I'm sorry to hear you've had back luck too." Caleb brushed some dust off the arm of his sweatshirt then leaned back on his palms again. "I do find it helps to laugh about my terrible dates. I know my mom certainly gets a kick out of my online dating stories."

"Ahh, online dating." Her voice trailed off.

A flood of bad, horrible, never to be spoken of again experiences raced through her mind. Every one of her past relationships were dismal. The guy who dumped her then left her stranded an hour from home, the guy from the dating app who told her straight up he wished he'd stay home, or the guy who lived above her in her senior year of college who took her out only to make out with another woman a half hour after dropping her off at home. She stumbled upon them while taking her trash out. No wonder she had given up a while ago. A few beats of silence ticked by. Hannah figured the topic of dating had ended.

"I think it's my profile picture." Caleb sat up, brushing his hands off on his thighs. "I must look better in photos than I do in real life. She probably took one look at me in person and thought, umm, no thank you."

"Oh, this woman really got to you." Hannah shifted then perched her sunglasses on top of her head. "Let me see." She pretended to be scrutinizing him. No way, this guy was smoking hot. He was probably one of those guys who looked *better* in person. Shaking her head, Hannah put her sunglasses back on. "That wasn't it. I don't know why the woman ghosted you, but it wasn't because of your looks."

Where in the world did that come from?

Her cheeks warmed.

A person can't go around declaring someone's hotness when you just met them. Was this some pathetic attempt at flirting? Hannah blamed herself. The last several years of her life were a haze of graduate studies, working nonstop to stay afloat, and being bone-dead tired. Dating, yeah that was the last thing on her mind. Show exhibit A, Hannah had forgotten how to have a conversation with a guy. Once she passed her Physician Assistant exam, Hannah maybe would dip her toes into the dating pool. Maybe.

Caleb smugly said, "Thanks. I appreciate it."

Then her mind became clear. Hannah blurted out, "I'm late for my new summer job. Oh, dear, oh dear." Hannah dug her phone back out of her front hoodie pocket. "I completely forgot to text my new employer and let them know I'm going to be late. I hope I'm not fired before I even start."

"Now I feel even worse about hitting you," Caleb groaned. Meekly, he added, "Maybe explain what happened? I'm sure they'll understand."

"I hope so." Hannah glanced up as her fingers zipped across the screen. "I mean, I guess I'm about to find out." She buried her head over her phone.

Simply, Hannah wrote a brief text to the pool manager who hired her, explaining she had been hit and would be there as soon as possible. Hannah shoved her phone back into the front pocket of her hoodie.

A loud honk from behind interrupted them. Hannah peered toward the obnoxious noise. A tow truck neared then idled next to their cars. Stumbling to her feet, Hannah brushed off her backside with one hand and swiped her purse off the curb with the other. Caleb rose too.

Once straightened, Hannah slugged her purse over her shoulder. "It looks like we're saved."

"Appears so." Caleb glanced at his watch. "And it only took a half hour, like promised."

The tow truck adjusted its angle, blocking a lane of traffic in the process. Cars slowed down and moved to the other lane. Luckily, in the half hour they had waited, rush hour had ended. Soon, the tow truck parked, and a man climbed out of it with a clipboard in his hands.

As he neared, he said, "It looks like I came to the right spot. I need you both to fill out some paperwork before I hook up your cars to the back." He unhooked the pen from the top of the clipboard. "But you don't have to wait around. Once the paperwork is filled out, you can be on your way."

Caleb gestured a thumb toward Hannah. "Let Hannah fill out the paperwork first. She's late for work, and this was my fault."

"Thanks, I appreciate it." Hannah stepped forward, taking the clipboard and pen from the tow truck guy. As her gaze met Caleb's, she cocked an eyebrow and said, "I hope you aren't late for wherever you were headed."

With a shrug, Caleb replied, "I was headed to work, too." He glanced at his watch again. "But I'll be fine."

The tow truck guy pointed out the parts on the paperwork that needed to be filled out and signed. Next, he handed them each a business card with the address for where the car would be towed. Hannah signed each page without reading it. An imaginary clock ticked in her head, making her anxious to take off. Once the final page was signed, Hannah unhooked her papers from the clipboard and handed it to Caleb to complete next. The tow truck guy took her paperwork. Caleb began to initial down the first sheet.

"Is that all you need from me?" Hannah pushed up the sleeves of her sweatshirt to her elbows. A tickle of sweat ran down her spine. "If that's it, then I'll be on my way."

The tow truck guy flipped through the papers. He scanned each page for the appropriate information. Once confirmed, he said, "Yep. That's it. You're free to go. I'll take it from here."

"Great." Hannah glanced down the street and tried to calculate how long it would take to walk to her job versus calling an Uber. Then she remembered she only had a mere twenty dollars in her bank account. An Uber was out. "Okay then," Hannah pivoted toward Caleb. His head was buried over the clipboard. "Caleb, it's been real, but I'm heading out."

Caleb snapped his head up and found her gaze. His pen lingered over his paperwork. "Do you have a ride?" He initialed again then flipped to the next page. "I'm happy to give you one. My ride is on her way right now."

"Nah." Hannah shook her head. "I can walk. My work isn't too far from here, and it'll be faster than waiting for an Uber."

His eyebrow pointed up. "Are you sure? I hit you. I feel it's my responsibility to get you to where you need to go. My mom is the one that's coming. She should be here any minute." Though he had on sunglasses, Hannah saw him squint against the blaring sunlight. "So you won't be alone with me in case you're worried about your safety."

"Thanks for the offer, but I can't wait. I'll see you later," Hannah gripped her purse strap with one hand, "or then again, I probably won't see you again. So, best of luck to you, Caleb."

Promptly, Hannah left and trekked toward the intersection several yards up the street. She heard Caleb yell goodbye. Hannah held up a hand in a wave but refrained from turning to look. Once at the intersection, she pounded the crosswalk button with a closed fist. Her pent-up anxiety pumped through her body. Jittery, Hannah tried to shake off the entire encounter with Caleb, her crushed car, and her lateness for her first day on the job. Sweat tickled her brow as she jogged through the crosswalk when it turned green.

Once back on the safety of the sidewalk, Hannah pulled up google maps on her phone. After she entered the name of the swim club into the search bar, the directions popped up. Hannah groaned. The club wasn't nearly as close as she thought, a mile and a half away. If she didn't run, it'd take a half hour.

The sun scorched her, seeping through her thick layer of fleece. With an abrupt halt, Hannah set her purse down on the sidewalk and stripped her sweatshirt off. If Hannah needed to jog to the swim club, she wanted to be a little less hot. Once off, she draped it over her purse and walked briskly toward the club. Several times she double checked her phone to make sure she was still headed in the right direction.

Hannah had arrived in Newport Beach only last night to spend the summer with her estranged dad, Adam, and his new wife, Trisha, and teenaged stepdaughter, Jordyn. In a moment of weakness, with no other viable options, Hannah had accepted Adam's offer for her to crash at their beach house for the summer. Hannah needed this summer to study for the Physician

Assistant exam and apply for a full-time job. Her mom had passed away while she was in college a few years back. So, Adam was the only parent she had left. Blame it on her lack of funds, combined with a lack of housing that had her saying yes before she thought the whole thing through.

But those dreams of a reconciliation with Adam were dashed when Hannah arrived last night. Instead of finding a loving home waiting with open arms, she found an empty house. When she couldn't get into the house, Hannah called Adam and he gave her the code to the garage's keypad. Apparently he claimed to have forgotten about his offer even though they'd exchanged several text messages to confirm her arrival. The whole thing screamed fishy. His family had decided to spend the summer in Florida. *Of course.* Adam told her to take whatever room she wanted. Hannah selected a room with a bathroom attached to it.

This summer wasn't anything she dreamed of. Once again, Hannah lived in loneliness. Now an undrivable car could be added to her extensive list of disappointments and annoyances. Hannah forced herself to shake off the sinking feeling in her gut. So, her summer wouldn't be what she planned. At least she had a place to stay and a job. She needed to look on the bright side of things. A cloudless blue sky surrounded her, making even the sidewalk glimmer. No wonder people paid ridiculous prices to live here. This place was gorgeous.

A combination of a half jog and a half walk helped her arrive at the swim club a mere twenty-three minutes later. Drenched in sweat, a breathless Hannah stopped in front of the gate leading into the outdoor swim club. In a swift tug, she yanked her sweatshirt off her purse and used it to sop up the sweat trickling down her temples. Once mostly sweat free, she dug into her purse and took out a loose hairband. Hannah threw her hair into a hastily gathered bun.

When her breath evened out, Hannah proceeded through the gate toward the check-in desk. Behind it was a huge Olympic-sized pool, lined with loungers and umbrellas on both sides. Crystal blue water sparkled under the sunny rays. It was far nicer than the community pool she swam at during her growing up years. Apparently, Adam and Trisha were members here, which is how Hannah landed the job as a swim coach for the summer. Again, how did Adam not remember helping her get a job? Hannah would save the question for another day.

In the far, kiddy corner, the swim team stretched. A wave of relief washed over her. The swimmers weren't in the pool yet. She halted in front of the check-in desk. A pretty blonde glanced up from the check-in screen.

Hannah greeted her first. "Good morning. I'm the new swim coach. I'm late. I was hit by a car on my way here." She ran an unnecessary hand over her messy updo.

The blonde with flawless skin in her early twenties replied, "Oh, you're Hannah. The pool manager mentioned you'd be late, and you should just check in with the swim coach when you arrived." Her eyes slid down Hannah, giving her an obvious once over. "I'm Alyssa." Her voice came out flatter than flat. "I'm a lifeguard here too when I'm not covering the check-in desk. Caleb is the head swim coach. He'll tell you where he wants you." Alyssa glanced over her shoulder and pointed toward the swim team. "Caleb's the guy in the blue polo. Do you see him?"

Hannah tracked Alyssa's arm. The sun gave off an incredible glare which took her eyes a moment to adjust. Then her gaze landed on Caleb, as in, the guy who hit her less than an hour ago, Caleb. An unexpected thrill swooped down her spine. Something she planned on fully unpacking later.

Her purse slipped. Hannah hiked it up and smiled back at Alyssa. "Thanks, Alyssa." She cleared her throat. "You've been extremely helpful. I see him. I'll head on over there. See you later." She waved, strolling away.

With sweaty palms, Hannah rounded the pool toward the stretching swimmers. A steady staccato beat sounded behind her ears. Her hands found the sides of her shorts, and Hannah wiped them dry. *Chill, it's only a swim team, and so what if Caleb is the other coach?*

To boost her confidence, Hannah reminded herself she had swum her entire life and competed in high school. Though she wasn't private club material, she had coached the local YMCA swim team to help pay for college. This couldn't be that different, or could it?

Caleb hadn't seen her. When she arrived, Caleb was crouched down speaking to a five- or six-year-old hysterically crying. This gave her a moment to gather herself. Caleb's luscious dark locks were now covered in a baseball cap. Hannah regretted not bringing a hat for herself.

In her panic, Hannah forgot her bag filled with a towel, hat, sunscreen and most importantly, her lunch. Those things were baking under the hot sun in the back of her crunched up car in a tow lot somewhere.

Caleb spoke soothingly to the swimmer, "It's okay. I promise. I don't see one bee out this morning." He pointed toward the pool. "I'll put you in the far lane so it's easy to jump out of the pool if you see a bee."

"But," the girl spluttered between shaky breaths. "I saw a bee. I swear. You can't make me get in. I can't do it. I don't want to get stung again."

"Let's focus on finishing the stretching then we'll see how you're feeling," said Caleb.

Then Caleb paused, noticing Hannah's presence. Slowly, he flashed his gaze up at her. His jaw dropped for a split second when he registered the person before him was in fact Hannah. Then Caleb adjusted his baseball cap and stood. He continued to address the swimmer, "Maria, you're going to be okay. Promise. Please go get in line with your group." He pointed to a group which looked around Maria's age.

Maria swiped under her eyes with her pointer fingers. "Fine," she grumbled. "But, I'm still not getting in." Then Maria stomped dramatically over to her group.

Only after Maria rejoined the group, did Caleb shift to face her. "Hannah, we meet again." He smiled, making his eyes scrunch up in the corners behind his aviator sunglasses.

For a second, he stared back at her. Hannah realized it was her turn to respond. She forced herself to straighten her back. "What are the odds?" She gnawed on the inside of her cheek.

"I'm not sure, but I'm glad to see you again." More staring. Hannah realized his emerald eyes had tiny specks of gold in them. Caleb cleared his throat. "We need to get started and can chat later." Then before Hannah could respond, Caleb blew his whistle and cupped his mouth with one hand and yelled, "Get in your lanes." Organized chaos followed as the swimmers scattered to their respective lanes and jumped in. "Start with 50s of each stroke."

Once the swimmers were in their correct lanes, and the first swimmers pushed off the wall, Caleb returned his attention to Hannah. "I've heard wonderful things about you Hannah. I'm surprised the club managed to snag you as a swim coach for the summer season," Caleb said.

"Only for this summer, once the summer is over, I'm out of here," said Hannah.

With a nod, Caleb said, "I understand." Then he waved her forward. "We can go over everything later. Why don't you shadow me for the first practice? Next practice, I'll assign you half the kids. Sound good?" His demeanor was casual and confident, something Hannah admired.

"Works for me." Hannah tossed her purse and sweatshirt onto an empty lounge chair. With a hand on her hip, she said, "Put me to work."

CHAPTER 2

Caleb didn't have time to reflect on the happy coincidence in seeing Hannah again, not when he had two criers, one child throwing up, and a myriad of different problems. The first practice of the summer, and immediately Caleb remembered the craziness of getting the team off the ground. Especially, since he hadn't coached for over four years. During medical school, Caleb hadn't come home for the summers. Instead, Caleb had focused on job shadowing doctors, doing research, and other internships.

Then three months ago, Caleb's dad had passed away unexpectedly. To add salt to the wound, Caleb discovered his dad had left his mom, Jenna, with a load of debt. Debts, he failed to tell Jenna about. Coming home for the summer became a necessity. Caleb had three months to help his mom fix up the house and get it on the market. Hopefully, the sale of his childhood home would be enough to pay off the debts owed and leave his mom with a little savings. Come fall, Caleb was headed to Boston to start his residency in orthopedic surgery. If Caleb couldn't find a place for his mom to afford in Newport, he knew Jenna would be headed to Boston too.

He blew his whistle again and brought his megaphone to his

mouth. With his finger on the button, Caleb said, "Let's practice diving off the blocks while doing relays."

Hannah stood a few feet from him. When he brought the megaphone down at his side, he shifted toward her and Caleb asked, "Do you mind taking the two far lanes? Lane one is for eight to ten-year-olds, and lane two is for ten to twelve-year-olds. I can do the older three lanes. I think you can handle it. I know from your resume you've coached before."

"Absolutely," Hannah remarked.

Caleb sidestepped to the lifeguard's tower, collecting the airhorn from where he stashed it. He tossed it toward her. Hannah caught it.

"Can you do the airhorn?" Caleb rubbed his jaw and shifted his weight. "I can announce for the swimmers to take their mark."

Smiling, Hannah asked, "Are you kidding me?" Her eyes sparkled with every shade of blue making her dazzle. "I live to squeeze this thing." Promptly, she headed to the other side of the pool without the need for further explanation.

Caleb forced himself to not let his mind wander. As much as he wanted to daydream about kicking it poolside with Hannah the entire summer, Caleb knew that come August he was out of here too. And from his past, he also learned dating a co-worker, especially one he would be working with so closely with was a huge, big no-no. The thought depressed him a smidge, because Hannah was most definitely his type.

The first swimmers took their marks on the starting blocks. Once Caleb confirmed they were ready, he shot his gaze across the pool to Hannah. She gave him a thumbs up.

Caleb placed the megaphone to his mouth and announced, "Swimmers, take your mark."

Crouched over, the swimmers waited in anticipation. Hannah held the blowhorn above her head at the ready.

"On the count of three," Caleb said into the megaphone. "One — two— three—"

Hannah squeezed the airhorn. The swimmers shot off the block, diving into the water in almost perfect timing with one another. Soon, the swimmers made their way down the pool.

Quickly, the next group of swimmers climbed onto their start blocks. They watched and waited for the first heat of swimmers to hit the wall. When the swimmers hit the wall, those on the blocks dove over their heads and into the water.

Round after round of relays continued for the rest of the practice. Caleb signaled the end of practice when he blew his whistle and announced for the entire team to climb out of the water and huddle up. The swimmers circled together, surrounding Caleb. Hannah hung back at the outer edge of the group.

"This season is off to a great start. Our afternoon practice begins at 4:00 pm." He gestured toward Hannah. "Coach Hannah will be joining us this season. For the afternoon practice, she'll be over the two youngest groups again."

A wave of chatter ran through the swimmers. Hannah smiled and waved to the group with both hands.

"Okay, hands in." Caleb put his hand in the middle of the huddle. He waited for everyone to scoot in closer and form a tighter circle with their hands. Hannah put her hand in too. "Go, Dolphins!" everyone yelled together.

Immediately after, the swimmers scattered. They went to locate their parents waiting somewhere along the pool's sides. Hannah stalled in place next to Caleb. They watched the swimmers rejoining their families.

Slowly, Caleb exhaled. "You survived." He twisted to face Hannah.

Hannah put a hand on her hip. "I guess I did." She paused for a second then scrunched up her nose. "Though I believe I'll be sufficiently sunburnt for our afternoon practice. My hat, sunblock, and towel were in a bag I left in my car. I forgot to grab it before I left my car with the tow truck guy." She ran a finger down the slope of her nose. "Yep. Burnt."

Caleb almost remarked it was a beautiful nose, but he thought better of it. "Yikes, I wish you'd had told me when you first arrived. I would've given you some of my sunblock or at least my hat." He pushed up the bill of his hat. The tips of his sweaty hair spilled out. "Come with me to the lounge." He stepped toward it, motioning for her to follow him. "I'll help you find what you need out of the lost and found box. There's always a ton of sunblock and random hats in it. People leave tons of stuff here and rarely do they ever claim it."

With a smile, Hannah said, "I'd appreciate it."

As they weaved around the pool, Hannah swiped her purse and sweatshirt off the lounge chair. Caleb continued past the swimmers and parents still loitering by the pool. On the far left, tucked out of sight of the pool was a small staff lounge. Inside there were two round tables with chairs, an old brown couch, an individual use bathroom, a wall lined with lockers, and another wall lined with vending machines.

When they arrived, Caleb held the swinging door open for Hannah to enter first. "You're welcome to leave any of your belongings in one of the lockers in here, but you'll need to bring your own lock." They found the room empty. Relieved, Caleb wanted a few minutes to chat with Hannah without interruptions. He knew truly little about her, only that the pool manager had hired her on the recommendation of the club president. The club president mentioned Hannah's parents were members here too.

Hannah glanced around the room. Caleb wondered what she thought of the place. It wasn't much, but this club had been his second home for so many years. Many wonderful memories were contained within these walls.

"I'll have to go purchase a lock after work. I don't have one," remarked Hannah.

Caleb looped a thumb around the empty belt loop on his shorts. "I could take you." He scratched his jaw. "Ah wait, I don't have a car either." He waved a hand. "We need to get that sorted out."

"I need to call the insurance company and see if I can get a rental car." Hannah fidgeted with the end of her shirt. "I hope to get that arranged so I can pick up a car after work this afternoon."

"Let me call them right now, and I'll report it." He strutted toward the soda vending machine. Once in front of it, he plunged his hand into his pocket and pulled out his wallet. "But, first, let me at least buy you something to drink. It's the least I can do." Caleb peeled two-dollar bills from it. He peered over his shoulder toward Hannah and asked, "What would you like?"

"Umm, Diet Coke." Hannah set her purse and sweatshirt on one of the tables. After she rubbed her hands together for a second, she pulled out a chair and sat down. "Thanks."

With a nod, Caleb turned back to the vending machine and fed the first dollar through the slot. He tapped the Diet Coke button. The soda dropped into the spot at the bottom. Caleb repeated it and selected another Diet Coke. When both were at the bottom, Caleb gathered them up. With one in each hand, Caleb made his way over to the table where Hannah sat. After he placed them on the table, he slid one across the table to Hannah.

She caught it with her hand. "Thanks." Hannah popped the top of the soda.

"No problem." Caleb settled into a chair across the table from her.

"I was dying of thirst." Hannah took a long swig. Caleb stared on, mesmerized by the gentle movement of her throat as she swallowed. She caught his gaze. With a smirk, Hannah continued, "I wasn't aware of how hot it gets once the June gloom burns off. Lesson learned."

Slowly, Caleb pulled back on the tab of his soda. It hissed

against his finger. "Are you not from around here?" He took a swig then set it down on the table.

Hannah shook her head. "I'm sure not." Caleb waited for her to elaborate by forcing himself to take another sip of his soda. She wiped her mouth with the back of her hand and continued, "I arrived yesterday. I grew up in the Midwest. My dad lives here with his new family. I'm staying with him for the summer while I study to take my P.A. exam to be a Physician Assistant. I take it at the end of summer. What about you? Did you grow up in Newport?" Her finger looped around the top of the soda can.

"I did. My mom still lives in the house I grew up in. It's less than a mile from here. I grew up coming to this club and swimming with this swim team as a kid. I coached the summers during college, but this is my first summer I've been back to coach in four years," Caleb said.

Caleb wondered if he should elaborate more and tell Hannah his last four years were one long stream of hard work as he pushed himself through the bone-tired years of medical school. Now with residency in front of him, his life was only going to get harder. In some ways, being back at the club was a nice respite from his countless days and nights of studying.

The door to the lounge screeched open. Both turned, glancing in the direction of the sound. Alyssa waltzed in. The door swung closed behind her. Inwardly, Caleb groaned. Since his return last week, Alyssa had been trapping him all over the club. It didn't take a genius to figure out she was interested in him. Too bad Caleb didn't reciprocate her feelings.

With a wide smile, Alyssa said, "There you are." Alyssa crossed the lounge and halted in front of him. She leaned a hip against the table, making her nearness suffocating. Alyssa continued, "I've been looking everywhere for you. Are you going to have your lunch soon? I thought we could walk down to that taco place together."

Did she now? Caleb cringed and wondered how to weasel his way out of this one.

Caleb paused, flashing his glance to Hannah. "Have you met Hannah yet?" He turned back to Alyssa. "She's the new swim coach who will be working with me this season."

Alyssa pushed her hair over her shoulder. Her jaw tightened. "We've met." Her voice came out overly icy. Then as if she remembered to act nice, a smile reappeared on her face. "So," Alyssa scooted a tad closer. "Are you up for those tacos?"

Caleb shifted in his chair, leaning toward Hannah. "Would you like to join us, Hannah? Alyssa claims this place has the best tacos. I've been meaning to try it for a while. And I know you don't have your lunch with you."

He figured there was safety in numbers. If Hannah came, then this lunch thing became a group outing instead of whatever Alyssa wanted it to be.

Hannah hesitated. "I don't won't to impose." Her gaze darted between Caleb and Alyssa. "It sounds like you already had these plans. I don't want to be a third wheel."

Quickly, Caleb added, "You won't be imposing, and we didn't have anything planned. Right, Alyssa?" He peered over at Alyssa.

With a huff, Alyssa straightened herself. "Right." She threw her hands down at her side and exhaled loudly. "We didn't have plans."

"Umm," Hannah gnawed on her bottom lip.

Caleb stood, pushing in his chair. "Come on. It'll give us a chance to get to know you better." He bobbed his head toward the vending machines. "And those things only have chips and candy bars."

"Okay." Hannah stood too. "If you don't mind me joining, tacos sound great." She smiled at Caleb. Then slowly, her smile turned to a frown as Hannah caught Alyssa's dead stare.

Alyssa sighed loudly. "I guess you can come."

Caleb chose to ignore her completely. Caleb and Hannah

tossed their empty soda cans into the recycling bin next to the vending machine.

"Oh wait, Hannah." Caleb strode back across the room. "Let's grab you some sunscreen and a hat from the lost and found." In the corner, an overflowing cardboard box contained forgotten items. Mainly, it contained goggles, sunscreen, sunglasses, and hats.

"Wonderful." Hannah strolled across the room to where he set the box on top of a table. "I can already feel the heat radiating off my face." She scrunched up her nose again. It did appear redder than only minutes before.

"Fine." Alyssa stepped toward the swinging door and held it open with her flat palm. "Come get me when you're done. I'll be at the check-in desk." Alyssa left. The door swung shut behind her.

Relief washed over him and the tension in his shoulders loosened. Some of the contents of the box spilled onto the table as he dug around in the box. Hannah came closer and peered into it too. His fingers hit a tube of sunscreen, tugging it free. He placed it on the table and continued to search the box for stray hats.

"Does that sunscreen work?" With his arms deep in the box, Caleb motioned with his head toward the sunscreen.

Hannah swiped it off the surface and examined the label for a split second then shrugged. "I'm sure this as good as any." Her lips twitched. "As long as it isn't that zinc kind that never rubs in. I'd prefer to not walk around looking like a ghost."

Hannah twisted off the cap, squeezing a bit onto her hand. Her hand hovered an inch from her face before she lowered it back down. "I need a mirror for this." She surveyed the room. "Where's the bathroom?"

"Huh." Caleb paused and caught her gaze then slid his eyes to her handful of sunscreen. He pulled his arm out of the box, pointing to the far corner. "There's a bathroom through that door."

"Great, I'll be right back," Hannah said.

Then she sauntered into the bathroom. Caleb used the time while she was in the bathroom to find three different hats that could possibly work for Hannah. He lined them up in a row and waited for her return.

Alyssa popped her head back into the lounge. "What's taking so long?" Her voice came out overly whiny, and it grated on Caleb's nerves. He wished he was going to lunch alone with Hannah. Alyssa held the door open with her back as she straddled inside and outside. "If we don't go soon, I'm going to waste my entire lunch waiting for Hannah."

Ahh, bingo.

He had an out.

"You're welcome to go ahead without us." Caleb put the scattered contents from the box that had slipped onto the table back into the box. "I understand if you're in a big hurry and can't wait."

With a huff, Alyssa rolled her eyes. "No, it's fine." Her eyes dilated a bit. "This was my suggestion, remember?"

How could he forget? The door to the bathroom swung open, and Hannah appeared. She crossed the room and tossed the sunscreen back into the box.

Caleb shifted his attention to Hannah and ignored Alyssa. "Do you think any of these hats will work?" He picked one up and pointed at the other two on the table.

Hannah swiped the blue baseball cap out of his hand. "I could care less. Thanks for finding me one." Quickly, she removed the hairband from her hair and placed the baseball cap on her head. Caleb stared on, mesmerized, as she pulled the long strands of silky brown hair through the hole in the back. Then she secured her hair again with her hairband. Hannah snatched her purse from where she left it, slugging it over her shoulder. "I'm ready."

"Finally," Alyssa muttered.

Alyssa shoved open the door and walked through. It swung back and forth behind her, nearly hitting Hannah in the face. Startled, Hannah took a step back to safety from the swinging door. Hannah peered over at Caleb and raised an eyebrow.

Caleb shrugged and mouthed, "Sorry."

This lunch was going to be all sorts of interesting. He dreaded the next thirty minutes of his life. Poor Hannah, this would be even worse for her, but he was thankful she was coming.

They left the lounge. Alyssa sidled up next to him, chatting to him in an animated way so different from the person she showed only seconds before. The woman gave him whip lash. Once past the parking lot, they turned right onto the sidewalk which passed by little shops and restaurants. Though they couldn't see the ocean, they could hear the waves crashing on the shore.

The sidewalk proved not wide enough for the three of them to walk side by side. Hannah fell behind them. Caleb kept trying to include her in the conversation by peering over his shoulder and asking her questions. Intentionally, Alyssa left her out which irked him to no end. Luckily, the walk only lasted three minutes. The taco place appeared, and they arrived in front of it.

"Here we are," said Alyssa, opening the door. Caleb and Hannah filed in behind her. "Everything is good here." They joined the end of the line.

"Which tacos did you say you liked best?" asked Hannah as she studied the menu up on the wall behind the cash registers.

"Carne asada," said Alyssa in a completely monotone voice.

"Thanks. I like carne asada," said Hannah in a pleasant tone. With a smile, she continued, "I'll probably get that."

Alyssa leaned into Caleb's arm and said, "Do you remember those tacos we got that one summer after that swim meet in San Clemente?"

What in the world? Alyssa thought he remembered something insignificant from years ago?

"Nah." Caleb stepped forward to rid his arm from Alyssa's touch. "I don't remember that, sorry." He shoved his hands into his pockets.

How long was Alyssa's lunch break? He was more than ready for this to be over. The line moved. Alyssa and Hannah shuffled forward. Purposely, Caleb dragged his feet and widened the gap between him and Alyssa.

Alyssa whipped her hair over her shoulder. "Caleb and I go way back." She jutted her chin.

Hannah kept her gaze on the menu overhead. "That's nice."

Alyssa fiddled with the single bangle on her wrist. "I know, right?"

"Very neat," added Hannah, though Caleb clocked how her back stiffened.

Before Caleb could explain their so-called long nonexistent friendship, they arrived at the front of the line. The cashier asked them for their order. They ordered and paid. Thank goodness. Once they placed their orders and filled their drinks up at the fountain machine, they settled into an empty table. Caleb and Alyssa sat across the table from Hannah. For a moment, they sipped their drinks with not much to say to one another.

Alyssa wiped the condensation on her fingers from her soda cup onto her shorts. "So, what's your deal, Hannah?" asked Alyssa in an overly aggressive tone. "Why are you working at the club for the summer? I've never seen you before. How did you even get this job?" The words came out in fast harsh bites. "Usually, the swim coaches and lifeguards were once on the swim team when they were kids like Caleb and me."

"My dad lives here with his wife and stepchild. They're members of the club. He landed me the job when he suggested me to the Board President." Hannah ran a finger in a circular motion across the top of her soda lid. "I'm here for the summer to study for my Physician Assistant exam. I needed a place to stay for the summer, and the swim team is a way for me to earn some money."

"Who's your dad?" countered Alyssa. "My family knows everyone in Newport. I'm sure I've heard of him."

Hannah shifted in her seat. "His name is Adam Colbert. His wife is Trisha. But they haven't been married long, only a few years, and he isn't from here, but his wife is."

Over the loudspeaker, they heard the numbers of their food called. They each rose and picked up their food, bringing it back to their table.

Caleb dug into his beans and rice.

Hannah took a bite of her taco. "Mm." She finished chewing and wiped her face with her napkin. "Alyssa, thanks for the suggestion. This carne asada taco is delicious."

Alyssa didn't respond but instead rolled her eyes and took a bite of her food. Silence followed, making Caleb's skin crawl.

Hannah cleared her throat. "You asked about me." Hannah snagged a tortilla chip from her plate, popping it into her mouth. "What about you, Alyssa? Have you lived here your whole life?"

"Born and raised." She motioned a thumb toward Caleb. "Caleb was friends with my brother in high school."

"Oh, wow." Hannah munched on another chip. "How about that?" She wiped her face with a napkin.

"I wouldn't say we were really friends," interjected Caleb. "But he did graduate the same year as me."

Alyssa's jaw tightened, but she plastered a smile on her face. "Yes, but my family knew your family growing up."

Caleb scratched his head. "I guess my dad worked with your dad in some way. Right?" He took a sip of soda.

Alyssa knew her brother wasn't friends with him. What power game was she trying to play? In fact, that guy had treated him like dirt in high school. Alyssa's family had money, like millions upon millions type of money. Caleb's family did not. His parents only lived in Newport Beach, because they had inherited the home from relatives when they passed.

"Yes, they did." Alyssa shot Hannah, a *there you go,* glance.

"Wonderful." Hannah tossed another chip into her mouth. "Have you two coached the swim team together? Or Alyssa, do you only lifeguard?"

"I only lifeguard." Alyssa licked some salsa from the corner of her mouth. "I don't have the patience to work with that many kids at once."

"It can be a challenge," Hannah added.

"Which is why I won't ever do it." Alyssa tossed her napkin on top of her plate. She leaned back in her chair and folded her arms. "I'm only working at the club this summer because my dad promised me a new car if I did. I graduated a year ago in Public Relations, but I'm still looking for the perfect place to land. A new car will help me with job interviews and whatnot."

"Should we head back?" interjected Caleb. "I know you only get thirty minutes."

Caleb and Hannah had more time. They coached the morning and afternoon practices with a long break in between. Often private coaching sessions became available for the time in between the practices to make more money. In the past, if he didn't have any private coaching sessions set up, he'd go home then return for the afternoon practice. This season he planned on using the extra time in the middle of the day to fix up things around his mom's house. A ton of work needed to be done to sell it, and Jenna needed every penny from the sale she could get.

Since the swim season only began today, neither of them had any private coaching sessions set up. Those usually took a few practices for the coaches to recognize which kids might need a little extra help to improve. Suddenly, Caleb remembered with the invitation to lunch he had failed to call the insurance company to report the accident. He cringed at his misstep and vowed to take care of it when they returned to the club.

"You're right. I don't get a long lunch." Alyssa whipped out her phone from her pocket. Swiftly, she rose. Her chair screeched against the tile floor. "I need to head back. If I don't clock back on in three minutes, I'll be late." Alyssa swiped her trash off the table and dumped it into the trash can. "I better jog ahead. I'll see you later, Caleb." Without further explanation, Alyssa left and jogged past the windows down the sidewalk.

"Tell me more about being a P.A." Caleb sipped some soda. "What kind of practice are you interested in? One with adults or kids?"

"Definitely kids," smiled Hannah. "I love being around them, and I'm happy I chose a job where I can help them."

Caleb liked Hannah already. He asked her a few more questions about P.A. school. Once they finished eating, they left the taco place.

As they ambled down the sidewalk passing the little boutiques, Hannah asked, "Why did you take a break in coaching the swim team?" She caught his gaze. "If you don't mind me asking."

"Ahh." Caleb scratched his chin. "I recently graduated from medical school. During the summers of medical school, I used to work at labs, internships, job shadowing, that type of thing. I didn't have time to come home." By then Caleb and his dad weren't on the best of terms and returning to Newport held little appeal.

"So, why did you come back this summer?" asked Hannah, folding her arms against herself.

"It's a long story." he stalled, rubbing the back of his neck. "I don't want to get into it. But I'm only here for the summer too, then I'll be off to Boston in the fall for my residency. My dad passed a few months ago, I'm here to help my mom with his affairs."

"That's hard. I'm sorry." A few seconds passed. "So, Boston." Hannah nodded. "Impressive. It sounds like you have your future planned out, a bright one at that." Hannah dragged her feet. She glanced out at the cars passing by. "I wish I could say the same thing about myself. My future is nothing but a big question mark."

"I wouldn't say that. You have a plan. You're in an in-between time like myself. It certainly doesn't mean you're doing anything wrong," said Caleb, shoving a hand into his front pocket.

"True." Hannah bit her bottom lip. "So, I'll take my exam, then what? Where do I go next? My dad lives here with his new family. After the summer, I can't stick around, because I'll only be getting in the way. I was raised by my mom, but she passed away a few years ago. Where do I go? Do I simply pick a random place on a map, point, and say here I come?"

"I'm sorry to hear about your mom passing," Caleb commented.

"Thanks," Hannah said. "I'm sorry about your dad's passing."

For a second, he listened to their flip flops smack against the pavement. "Does it get any easier? With time?"

Sharply, she inhaled. "It does. I'll always miss my mom, but at least it isn't an all-consuming thing now."

Caleb nodded. He pivoted the conversation away from grief. "Have you ever wanted to live in any particular place?"

Hannah pushed up her slipping sunglasses with her finger. "What do you mean?"

"Like when you were a kid, did you ever dream of living in New York or Los Angeles, maybe Washington DC?" he asked.

Her nose scrunched up. "No." Throwing her hands down at her sides, Hannah continued, "I wish I had. That would make this whole thing easier. I'd at least have an idea of where I should apply for a job. Did you always want to go to Boston?"

Caleb shook his head. "No, but the residency program I was accepted into was the perfect fit and an opportunity I wouldn't dream of passing up."

"What will your specialty be?" she asked.

"Orthopedic surgery," Caleb said.

"Wow." Hannah's lips twitched again. "Impressive."

The swim club came into view. They slowed their pace, lingering in front of the gate. For a second, they stared back at one another. Caleb remembered how they had met. It was only this morning, but it felt like a lifetime ago, like he and Hannah had been friends forever.

"Let me go call the insurance company before the afternoon practice starts. I want to get that sorted out."

With a smile, Hannah said, "I'd appreciate it."

Then they entered through the gate, meandering back to the pool.

CHAPTER 3

"Watch me," said Ryker, one of the younger swimmers on the team. "I can do a perfect flip turn."

Hannah stepped to the edge of the pool and motioned for the swimmers in the lane to come closer. "Swim over here, everyone." Hannah confirmed they heard her before she continued, "Ryker believes he's mastered the flip turn. Let's watch him." The last half hour of the swim practice, Hannah had been working with the youngest swimmers to teach them the flip turn. "Go for it, Ryker."

Ryker swam under the lane line into the empty one next to it. Swimming several yards from the edge, he turned back around and headed toward the wall. The entire group of swimmers waited as he swam closer and closer to the end. When he neared the pool's wall, he tried his best to flip and push back off the wall. Unfortunately, Ryker missed it completely.

Soon, Ryker popped his goggled eyes out of the water, staring up at Hannah.

"Great try, Ryker." Hannah crouched down next to her group of swimmers. "Everyone, please clap for Ryker. That was his best flip turn yet." She smiled and clapped too.

Hannah appreciated his unfaltering determination to try something new and difficult. It was a quality that would help him go far in life. The swimmers joined Hannah in clapping. Ryker beamed, looking completely pleased with himself. Too bad it wasn't a flip turn and none of her swimmers understood how to do one either. Something wasn't clicking, and Hannah knew there was only one way; to show them.

So, she kicked off her flip flops. Quickly, Hannah tugged her shirt off and wiggled her way out of her shorts. She tossed her clothes onto a nearby lounge chair and adjusted the strap of her swimsuit.

Hannah shuffled to the edge of the pool. "I think I need to demonstrate." She raised her hands above her head and dove into the empty lane next to her swimmers. Once she came up out of the water, Hannah treaded water in front of them. "Listen up, everyone." The swimmers stared back at her, clinging to the pool wall. "I'm going to show you how to do a flip turn. The key is to do it in one smooth motion and to not overthink it. I need everyone to climb out and sit on the edge of the pool to watch. You'll have a better view."

After a bit of grumbling among the swimmers, they climbed out and sat on the edge of the pool with their feet dangling in. Hannah swam to the middle of the pool.

"Here I go, watch," bellowed Hannah.

When Hannah put her face back into the water, she realized she had failed to bring goggles. The chlorine water stung her eyes when she opened them and swam toward the pool wall. Though her eyes burned, Hannah pressed forward, approaching the end of the pool. With ease, she performed a perfect flip turn at the slowest rate she could manage.

She popped back up for air and pushed her dangling hair out of her face.

"See?" Hannah treaded in front of her swimmers. "It's that easy."

Ryker clapped and soon the other swimmers joined in. Hannah couldn't fight the smile spreading across her face. She loved working with kids. They were easy to please.

"Okay, I'm going to stay in the water." Hannah continued to tread water. "Then I can help to flip those who need it. Who's first?" Hannah scanned the swimmers. There weren't any volunteers. "Ryker, would you like to give it another shot?"

Ryker grinned. Without hesitation, he pushed his goggles down from his head to over his eyes. Then he jumped into the pool feet first and swam over to where Hannah waited.

"Ryker, I'm going to go to the end to wait for you." Hannah found Ryker's gaze behind the blue lens of his goggles. "Remember, when you are a few feet from the end you need to dip down and start the turn. I'll help your body complete the turn if you need it."

Ryker gave her a thumbs up. Hannah swam to the end of the pool.

Cupping her mouth, Hannah said, "Go, Ryker."

With a nod, Ryker took off swimming freestyle toward her. As he neared, Hannah knew he started his turn a tad short. Instead of letting him miss the wall a second time, Hannah grasped onto him, tugging his feet to meet the wall. Ryker's feet landed on the wall, and he catapulted himself forward. After he swam a few feet, Ryker's head bobbed out of the water.

Beaming, Ryker exclaimed, "I did it. I really did it!" His enthusiasm was intoxicating.

Hannah high-fived Ryker. "Great job. Thanks for being first." She motioned toward where the other swimmers waited. "Who's next?"

Maria's hand shot up. Each swimmer in her group tried multiple times to do the flip turn while she remained in the water assisting them. Toward the end of the practice, most had mastered the skill. They were buzzing with excitement. Caleb blew his whistle, announcing the end of the practice. Hannah climbed out of the water. With no towel in hand, water cascaded in fast streams down her body.

Hannah drifted, soaking wet over to where the swimmers gathered around Caleb. Sloppy wet strands of hair stuck to her forehead. She brushed them to the top of her head. Even in full sun, Hannah shivered. She folded her arms over her middle and listened as Caleb spoke to the team.

"Excellent first day of practice," said Caleb to the group. His gaze found Hannah's from across the circle, and he smiled. With his gaze still locked with hers, he continued, "And great job to our youngest swim team members who were mastering their flip turns today." Heat rose up Hannah's chest. Breaking eye contact with her, Caleb waved everyone closer. "Okay, gather up." Everyone shuffled in and placed their hands in the middle. When everyone was settled, Caleb instructed, "And on three, let's yell, Let's Go, Dolphins! One, two, three."

Everyone yelled, "Let's Go, Dolphins!"

The swimmers dispersed, leaving Caleb and Hannah alone. Caleb strode a few feet to come close enough to chat. "You're great with the younger swimmers." His eyes twinkled back at her. They were more hazel than green like she originally thought. Specks of brown and gold shone against the brightness of green. "Now, I'm the one who's impressed."

Water continued to drip down her temples, she swiped at it with her pointer finger. "Thanks." Hannah couldn't help but be pleased with herself. She knew she had a talent for working with children, but it was always nice to have it confirmed. "I really do enjoy working with kids which is why I studied to be a P.A. I hope to work in Pediatrics."

"I'm sure you'll be fantastic." Caleb's gaze slid down her frame. "Can I grab you a towel?"

"Umm," hesitated Hannah. "I don't have one with me. It's in

my smashed-up car." She tilted her face up toward the sky. "Luckily, the sun is still shining, and I should dry off fast."

"Nonsense, follow me." He gestured for her to follow, roaming toward a table with folded white crisp towels. With not a stain to be seen, Hannah wondered how they kept them so nice. Caleb snatched one off the pile. "You can use the towels they have here. There's no need to bring one from home. Sorry, the pool manager asked me to tell you all of this." He held it out to her.

Hannah took it from him. "Thanks." She ran it over her face then down one arm. "I wasn't sure if we could use them."

Caleb rubbed the back of his neck. "I should've mentioned that this morning. I can see I did an extremely poor job taking you around." He brought his hand back down, shoving it into the pocket of his shorts. "Use as many as you like, and you can throw the used one into the bin in the locker room and bathroom the patrons use."

Hannah patted her other arm then started down her legs. "Are we done for the day?" Once dry, she straightened herself, tossing the wet towel over one of her shoulders.

For a second, Caleb stared blankly at her. Hannah wondered if she had black racoon eyes from dripping mascara, but then she remembered she didn't have a lick of makeup on. Crisis averted.

"We're finished." He pulled his gaze away from her then waved at someone. Hannah peered over her shoulder, spotting some swimmers waving goodbye. She mirrored Caleb's wave. Once they exited, he shifted his weight and brought his attention back to her. "Next week, the hours will be longer. You'll probably start getting booked for private training sessions. I think you'll enjoy doing it because it's one on one. Plus, it pays well but let me know if it ever gets to be too much."

"Sounds good to me." Hannah paused, staring back at Caleb. When he didn't respond immediately, she took it as her cue, the conversation was over. "Then I guess I'll see you tomorrow." She moved toward the lounge chair where she had left her clothes and flip flops.

Once at the lounge chair, Hannah snagged her shorts, pushing her legs through the holes and bringing them up to her waist. Next, she collected her shirt. Caleb stopped in front of her, making her halt in place.

"How are you going to get home?" Caleb squinted against the sunlight and tilted his head. "My mom, Jenna, is picking me up in a few minutes to take me to the rental car place. Did you find out if you can rent your car there too?"

After lunch, Caleb had called his insurance company. Hannah called hers too, and they said since it was Caleb's fault, everything would go through his insurance. She arranged a rental car with the place the insurance company recommended.

"I was told to go to a place about a mile from here." Hannah tugged the shirt over her head then laced her arms through the holes. "I believe it's the only one within five miles." Her hand glided over her shirt to smooth out the front.

Caleb readjusted his baseball cap. "Bargain Rentals?"

Her hair hung limply, sticking to the back of her neck. Hannah removed her hairband from her wrist. "Yes, that's the place." Swinging her head forward, she gathered up the loosened strands and secured it into a messy bun.

"Perfect, that's where I'm headed too." Another swimmer said goodbye. Caleb waved but kept his gaze locked on Hannah. "Mom can give us a ride."

Hannah gnawed on her bottom lip.

"I insist."

"Fine." Hannah dropped her hands down at her side. "Let me go grab the rest of my things from the lounge."

They agreed to meet by the check-in desk. Hannah retrieved her belongings while Caleb finished up a few administrative tasks. With stuff in hand, she meandered to the check-in area to wait. Stationed behind the check-in desk, Alyssa narrowed her gaze at Hannah as she leaned against the pool gate to wait. It didn't take a genius to pick up on Alyssa's interest in Caleb. Fine by her. Alyssa could have him. This summer Hannah didn't have time for any romantic notions. Her time in Newport was limited. She hoped Alyssa could realize Hannah wasn't a threat. Maybe if she did then her disdain could melt into tolerance.

The air strained with the uncomfortable quiet. "Thanks for showing me the taco place you like," commented Hannah with a smile.

Alyssa scoffed and didn't reply.

So much for trying to play nice. Conversation over. Silence stretched like infinity. Awkwardly, Hannah fetched her phone out of her purse, opening a random social media app to occupy herself. After a little mindless scrolling, she tossed it back into her purse.

Though she couldn't see the beach, Hannah could hear it. The soothing rhythmic sound smoothed out the knot in her middle. Sunshine tickled her skin as she breathed in the salty sea breeze. Newport wasn't the worst place to spend the summer.

From behind, Caleb's voice startled her, when he asked, "Are you ready to go?"

Hannah flinched, peering over her shoulder. He had removed his baseball cap, leaving behind a messy mane of hair, not straight but not curly either. Perfect beach waves.

"Yep." Hannah straightened herself, stepping closer to him.

"Mom is waiting in the parking lot," Caleb said.

As she adjusted her slipping purse strap, Hannah said, "Thanks again for the ride."

Caleb moved through the open gate. He waved goodbye to Alyssa. "See you tomorrow, Alyssa. Have a nice night."

Alyssa flipped her hair over her shoulder and flashed a toothy grin. "You too, Caleb. See you tomorrow."

"Bye," Hannah added.

Alyssa ignored her. Hannah shrugged and followed Caleb out to the parking lot.

"There's my mom." Caleb pointed to the white SUV idling at the curb. "Come on."

When they arrived at the SUV, Caleb opened the back passenger door. "Do you mind sitting in the back? I tend to get car sick."

"Sure," Hannah replied. "The back is fine."

Hannah loaded into the back seat as the woman in the driver's seat shifted to face her.

"Hey, there. I'm Jenna." She smiled widely.

Jenna had the same wavy hair and stunning hazel eyes as Caleb.

"Hello, I'm Hannah." Hannah buckled her seatbelt. "Thanks for giving me a ride." She adjusted the strap until it fit correctly.

"Anytime." Jenna adjusted her rearview mirror as Caleb eased into the front passenger seat.

As Caleb buckled up, he said, "Mom, this is Hannah. I hit her this morning, and long story short, she's working at the swim club this summer as the other coach too."

Jenna peered through the rearview mirror, catching Hannah's gaze. "I'm sorry my son hit you." Then darted her glance to Caleb and proceeded to whack him on his arm. "I've told you to be more careful. What have I told you about that lead foot of yours?"

"Mom," hissed Caleb. "That's so not true. I never drive too fast."

"Really?" tsked Jenna as she glanced over her shoulder and pulled away from the curb. "Wrong. Remember your senior year of high school? You got a speeding ticket on the way to your graduation."

Caleb groaned and pinched the bridge of his nose. "When are you going to let that go? So, once in my life, I was running ridiculously late and was going to miss my own graduation."

"Still a speeding ticket, and it still counts," said Jenna as she exited the parking lot and merged into traffic.

"I promise," Caleb twisted around his seat and faced Hannah. "I'm a very good driver."

"Umm," Hannah scrunched up her nose. "Are you so sure about that? You did rear end me this morning."

Jenna cackled. "Oh, I like her." Teasingly, she tapped her shoulder against Caleb's.

Hannah laughed. From her view, Hannah watched as Caleb rubbed at the back of his neck.

"I'm never going to live this down," Caleb muttered.

"Not a chance."

They drove for a few minutes as the radio played the latest hits. Hannah peered out the window, spotting bits of the ocean in between the little shops and restaurants along the street.

"I see the car rental place." Caleb pointed at the windshield. "It's up ahead, past this next light."

"On it." Jenna flipped on her blinker and changed lanes. Once through the light, Jenna eased to the side, parking in front of the small nondescript car rental place. "Here you both go." Shifting around in her seat, Jenna peered back at Hannah. "I'm inviting you over for dinner tonight. I made a huge pan of lasagna, and we have plenty to share. From what Caleb mentioned, you aren't from here."

Hannah grasped the door handle. "Umm, I don't know." Her gaze flickered to the back of Caleb's head. Would he want her to join them?

Caleb twisted around too. "Please come. If you don't then I'll be eating lasagna for a week." His lips twisted into a half smile.

Jenna laughed then pushed a finger into her son's bicep. "He's not lying. I don't cook often. So, when I do, we eat the same thing for days until it's gone."

"I guess I could come." Hannah fidgeted with her purse strap.

The thought of spending the evening alone in her dad's empty place wasn't overly appealing. Plus, Hannah hadn't run to the grocery store yet. And there was zero chance she would touch even a morsel of food from the cupboards.

Caleb smiled, sealing her decision.

"You're coming and that's that," Jenna urged.

"Ok." Hannah opened her door. "Thanks for the ride, and I suppose I'll see you soon." She slid out.

Jenna raised her hand in a wave. Hannah shut her door while Caleb unloaded from his seat too. Soon, Jenna merged into the oncoming traffic, leaving them at the curb. They filed into the car rental place. A lengthy line of customers weaved around the room. They joined the end of it. Hannah wondered how long the entire process would take.

"I'm sorry about Mom forcing you to come over for dinner." Caleb skirted his gaze from her to the line then back again. "She means well."

With a small shrug, Hannah folded her arms across her middle. "I appreciate her hospitality." The worry lines on Caleb's forehead loosened. She continued, "I'm home alone so it wasn't like I had any other plans for dinner. Most likely I would be eating whatever takeout I picked up, or ramen."

Caleb rubbed the back of his neck. "I think my mom was being more than hospitable." His words dangled in the static air.

The line moved forward. They shuffled to catch up to the end. Only four employees were working at the check-in desk. According to her calculations, with the fifteen people in front of them in line, they were going to be there another twenty to thirty minutes.

Cocking one eyebrow, Hannah inquired, "Really, what do you mean?"

His lips twitched. Caleb shoved his hand into his pocket. "I believe Jenna is trying to set us up."

"Ahh," replied Hannah, glancing away toward the end of the line. "I see."

Honestly, Hannah didn't care. Jenna was barking up the wrong tree. A summer romance was the furthest thing from her mind. Passing her exam, finding a job, reconnecting with her long-lost dad, those were the plans she had. A boyfriend or even a fling were out of the question. Hannah accepted Jenna's invitation because returning to an empty home, eating take-out standing up in the kitchen seemed far bleaker than sharing a meal with a new friend and his mom.

"No offense, Caleb," Hannah cleared her throat, "but I don't care what Jenna has up her sleeve. I'm not dating anyone this summer. Even guys who might look like you." Her purse buzzed from an incoming text message, but Hannah didn't fetch it out to read it.

Caleb smirked, leaning in a few inches. "And how do guys like me look?"

Heat branded her cheeks at her total misstep. The last thing she needed was Caleb, thinking he was the object of her affection. "If I have to spell that out for you then you're not as sharp as I originally thought."

Caleb laughed.

Hannah rolled her eyes.

"Next," yelled a worker from check-in.

Caleb leaned in and whispered, "You're up." He nodded toward the empty space along the check-in counter. "I'll go next."

Hannah plodded to the long check-in counter, trying to forget the entire flirtatious exchange. It took a while for the employee to find her information in their system. If that wasn't enough, there was a mix-up with the insurance company. Many others checked in and out, including Caleb who disappeared twenty minutes ago into the rental lot. After an eternity, Hannah received the keys to a small Kia sedan. The employee instructed her on where to find it in the lot adjacent to the building.

She exited the building to the parking lot, realizing she had zero way to contact Caleb. They hadn't exchanged contact information.

A voice from behind her interrupted her thoughts. "There you are," said Caleb. Hannah twisted, spotting him on a bench in the shade. "I was beginning to get worried you weren't ever going to get your car." Caleb rose and strutted over to her. "I was about to head back in to check on you. Is everything sorted out?"

"Yes. Thanks." Hannah fidgeted with the bulky car rental key and paperwork. "There was a mix up with the insurance company, but they figured it out." She shoved the paperwork into her purse. "Thanks for waiting."

She readjusted her purse strap. "Hey, do you mind if I run home to shower before I head to your house for dinner?" Chlorine and sunscreen mixed with sweat tickled her nose. Hannah knew she smelled, and she'd prefer to not eat dinner feeling gross.

"You don't need to dress up for us." Caleb gaze slid down her frame then back up to her eyes. "We're casual in our house, and you look great by the way."

"Umm, thanks. I wasn't planning on changing into a formal ball gown or anything like that, but I reek of chlorine. It's making my skin completely itchy." Hannah squinted against the sun. She dug back into her purse for her sunglasses and put them on. "But I can deal with itchy skin if Jenna wants us to eat now."

"Let me find out." Caleb freed his phone from his pocket and called Jenna. Hannah heard the phone ringing. Then after four rings, he said, "Hey, Mom." His gaze locked on Hannah. He winked at her while his lips twitched. "Hannah's excited to eat your lasagna, but she's wondering if she has time to go home to shower quickly before coming over." Caleb listened to Jenna's reply and said, "Okay, I'll let her know." Caleb hung up, cradling his phone between his flat palms.

Cocking an eyebrow, Hannah asked, "So?"

"Jenna says it's lasagna, and she can keep it warm in the oven so you can shower."

"Perfect."

"I'll text you the address." Caleb's fingers zipped across his phone. "Just give me a heads up when you're heading over." He hit send.

Hannah's purse buzzed with his incoming message. "I'll text you. I shouldn't be long." She pivoted toward her car. "See you soon."

CHAPTER 4

Caleb swiped at the foggy mirror of his bathroom. Next, he picked up his simple navy henley tee and slugged it over his head. If Hannah was showering, Caleb figured he'd do the courtesy of doing the same. Nothing beats washing off a layer of sunscreen and sweat to make one feel like a human again. The entire day had been one long blur. Was it only this morning he'd hit Hannah's car? Somehow the incident seemed days ago. His phone dinged on the top of the bathroom vanity. A text message from Hannah flashed on the screen.

> I'm heading over. Apparently, my dad only lives a few blocks from you, so I'm walking. I'll be there in five to ten minutes

Caleb smiled as his fingers zipped across the screen.

> See you soon

He shoved his phone into his pocket and flipped off the bathroom light as he exited.

"Mom, Hannah's on her way," Caleb said as he took the stairs two at a time. "She'll be here in five minutes." His feet hit the bottom step, and he strode into the kitchen.

Instead of finding her in the kitchen, he found his mom relaxing in the living room adject to the kitchen reading a book.

"Perfect. I'm starving." Jenna shut her book and tossed it onto the coffee table. Her gaze slid down his long lean frame. "You look nice." She sniffed. "Do I smell cologne?" She eyed him suspiciously as she stood.

Nope, Caleb wasn't taking the bait. His mom could conjure up what she liked, but Hannah made it clear she wasn't interested in anything but being friends. You wouldn't see him putting up a fight. His summer was chock full, and the tension in his neck and shoulders were proof.

"Where should we eat?" Caleb hoped his mom took it to mean discussing his dating life was off the table. "Did you want to eat inside or outside?"

Jenna moved from the living room into the kitchen. "I think outside would be nice. What do you think?"

"Hey," Caleb held his hands up. "This was your idea. I don't care where we eat."

For a second, she stared at him. She blinked then replied, "I want to eat outside." Jenna sidestepped over to the oven. "Go light those candles. The ones that keep the bugs away, and I'll grab the plates and silverware."

"On it," said Caleb, walking to the sliding glass door which stretched the length of the living room.

With both hands, he pushed it the entire way open. The back of the home had a nice patio which faced the Pacific Ocean. A view his mom was sure to miss when she moved. Caleb would miss it too, but he didn't want to dwell on all he'd lost. The only one to blame was the person who was no longer with them.

The sun began to set, and he flipped on the string of lights lining the pergola. Soothing ocean waves broke against the shore, easing the pent-up energy running rampant through him. Why was he jittery over a simple dinner with a co-worker? With Mom in the middle of it? Geez, he was rusty when it came to being around beautiful women.

Caleb dug the candles from the outdoor bin. Then he placed them on the round patio table and lit them. The candles illuminated the intimate space of the patio. It was a spectacular evening. Newport was showing off as the yellow and orange stretched across the sky melting into the sea of blue. He took a moment to enjoy the view that would soon be gone. Chatter in the kitchen broke the serenity. Inside, he spotted Hannah sitting on a bar stool talking with his mom. He wondered how long he had been staring out at the view.

Hannah's hair was still damp, but she wore it loose. The silky, light brown strands rubbed against her shoulder blades. She had changed into a white sundress, making her look extra tan. His heart pounded. And he fought against the rising anxiety in him. She was a co-worker, nothing more. So why did he feel nervous?

After he took a deep settling breath, Caleb passed through the sliding door and made his way over to the kitchen. "Hey, Hannah." Caleb announced as he inched closer. Hannah swiveled on the bar stool to face him. She smiled. His throat went dry. "You found us," he croaked.

"I did." Slowly, Hannah tore her gaze away, shifting back to face his mom. "I was telling Jenna how close my dad's house is to here. Also, she's been recommending a few local restaurants for me to try."

With her hot pads, his mom scooped the lasagna out of the oven and set it on the stovetop. Tomato sauce bubbled on the sides of the pan. A layer of golden-brown cheese made the dish look delectable. The aroma made his stomach growl. Tacos for lunch seemed like a lifetime ago.

"I suggested she try that little Italian place not far from here." Jenna opened a drawer and selected a spatula. "You should take

Hannah there this week." The words slid off her tongue as easy as a Sunday morning.

"Sure." Caleb leaned a hip against the counter a good two feet from Hannah. "I'd be happy to take you there sometime."

"Oh," Hannah blinked then crossed and uncrossed her legs.

"See, I told you he'd want to take you." Jenna pressed her palms against the slick granite countertop. "Caleb can take you there this week." Shifting her weight, Jenna grasped the full breadbasket. "Hannah doesn't know a single person here. I told her you wouldn't mind one bit."

His cheeks flushed while his jaw tightened. Sure, he wanted to spend more time with Hannah but being put on the spot was a totally different animal.

"Okay, I will, Mom." Caleb directed his words to Hannah. "Would you like to go eat there with me sometime this week after work?"

Hannah's gnawed on her bottom lip. "Are you sure? If you're busy, you can write down the address for me, and I'll try it out on my own."

"He's not busy." Jenna located her hot pads and used them to adjust the lasagna in her hands. "Trust me." She moved toward the patio but paused and said, "Caleb, can you grab some drinks out of the fridge for everyone?" Then she continued to the patio.

"What would you like to drink?" Caleb tried to shake off the entire encounter and forced himself to move to the fridge. Peering inside, he reported, "We have Diet Coke, water, Sprite, and lemonade." He popped his head over the top of the door.

Hannah jumped off the stool, pushing it in. "Diet Coke."

"Ahh, yes. I should've remembered that was your beverage of choice." He placed it, along with a few more sodas and water bottles on the counter beside the fridge. When he closed the fridge door, Hannah was a foot from him. His nostrils flared from the sweet, orange blossom scent wafting off her hair. It had dried a bit more making it appear a lighter shade of brown. He tugged at his restrictive shirt collar. "Do you mind grabbing a few of those and taking them to the table?" He nodded toward the drinks.

"Sure." Hannah gathered up the drinks and strolled out to the patio, setting them down.

"I'll grab the plates and silverware."

Jenna returned to the kitchen and snatched the breadbasket. They gathered up their respective items and went out to the patio. After Jenna set the breadbasket down, she purposely took a seat first. This forced Hannah and Caleb to sit next to each other.

Jenna twisted off the cap of her water bottle. "Thanks for joining us, Hannah." Her eyes misted, and Jenna peered out at the ocean. Blue sky darkened to blackness with each passing minute. Soon the moon and stars would glisten across the water. "This might be one of the last times we entertain someone out here. I don't know if Caleb told you, but I'm selling the house soon." Shaking her head, Jenna dabbed at the corners of her eyes with a paper napkin.

Hannah ran her hand over the front of her dress. "Caleb did mention it to me." She scrunched up her nose. "I'm sure it'll be hard to leave." She placed a hand on Jenna's shoulder and gave it a reassuring squeeze.

Jenna regained her composure then used the spatula to cut into the lasagna. "I've lived here my entire adult life." She scooped out a piece of lasagna onto Hannah's plate. Then she moved on to dishing up Caleb a piece.

"Do you know where you're going to go?" asked Hannah as she turned her plate.

"I have no idea." Jenna served herself lasagna then went for the salad. After she served herself, she held the bowl out to Hannah and continued, "I've lived in Newport Beach my entire life. I think about following Caleb to Boston, but I hate the cold. Ideally, I'd love to stay here and try to find a small condo. That's if I can find something that I can afford."

"I understand how difficult it is to completely uproot yourself to some place new. It's hard. I hope you don't have to do that." Hannah served herself some salad then handed the bowl to Caleb. He grasped it from her. "I hope you can find a way to stay where you want to be."

"I know." Jenna speared some salad, taking a bite. "Me too."

"I selfishly want my mom to follow me to Boston so I can look out for her, but it could be a temporary move for me." With salad on his plate, Caleb set it back down on the table. "The residency program is for four years. After that, I don't know where I'll end up."

His mom smiled. Her fork hovered over her plate. "See?" Her gaze skidded to Hannah. "I have the best son. He's been my rock through this entire nightmare of losing his dad." She choked up again, dabbing the corners of her eyes with her napkin. "I don't know what I would've done without him."

Caleb rubbed a hand over his mom's back until she calmed down. For a few minutes, they ate in silence. The few times he stole a glance at Hannah, she meekly smiled back at him.

Jenna broke the pause, when she said, "My husband and I were high school sweethearts."

"How about that?" Hannah's face brightened. "How did you meet?"

It was a story Caleb knew well, but his mom shimmered when she said, "He asked me to Junior Prom. I was shocked, because during the last year we'd been in the same friend group, and I had no idea he was interested in me."

"Where did they hold the prom?" Hannah nibbled on another bite of her lasagna.

"At a country club not too far from here. The banquet hall overlooked the ocean. It was spectacular, and by the end of the night I was in love. The rest was history."

Hannah's eyes crinkled around the edges, softening the lines of her forehead. "I love that story." Hannah wistfully sighed. "I guess some people do stay together forever."

Caleb wondered if he'd ever marry and stay with the same person his entire life. Right now, the idea seemed like a total pipe dream. Like something that happened to other people and not him. He'd like to believe, though, if he met the right person, maybe his perspective could shift.

"And I thought we'd grow old together too." Jenna leaned forward resting her elbows on the table, folding her hands together. "Now, I'm the only one who gets to grow old." Her bottom lip quivered. "But I am thankful for the years we had together. Though I do wish he had shared with me his financial problems, *our* financial problems." She tsked, shaking her head. "That's the hardest part in all this. Why didn't he tell me? Why didn't he trust me enough to help him?"

Caleb leaned back in his chair. "I'd loved to know Dad's reasoning too." Tension formed in between his shoulder blades. His back went rigid.

The truth hurt. He hadn't truly known his dad, neither had his mom, and now they'd live the rest of their lives with a big question mark.

His mom swiped under her eyes with the heel of her hand. "Anyhow," rapidly, she waved a hand, "enough about me and my money problems." Jenna shifted toward Hannah. "Tell me more about you. I know you're here spending some time with your dad and his new family. Did you go to college?"

"Yes, I went to college and then on to P.A. school to be a Physician Assistant. I'm only here for the summer to study and pass my exam to practice. Then I'll start the real work of finding a job in my field."

"I've heard Boston has excellent hospitals." Jenna turned and winked at Caleb. Inwardly, he wanted to crawl into a cave. She added, "You could apply there for jobs."

"Mom," he said in a pointed tone. "I'm sure Hannah will figure it out."

Caleb caught Hannah's glance. Her eyes twinkled mischievously at him. She appeared to be enjoying his mom's less than subtle attempts to get them together.

Her lips formed a tight smile. "Thanks for the suggestion." Hannah brought her Diet Coke to her lips. "I've heard the same thing." She took a swig then rubbed her lips together. "I'm sure that's why he is headed there in the fall for his residency. It's top notch when it comes to medical advancements."

"I'm so proud of Caleb," his mom commented.

"I bet." Hannah winked at Caleb. "You should be. He's a pretty top-notch guy."

Her comment made him happier than it probably warranted.

They finished up their dinner.

Then his mom rose to her feet. "I made dessert. Are you up for it?" She snatched her plate.

"Sure." Hannah smiled. "I'd love some."

With a nod, Jenna gathered the empty plates.

Caleb shifted to rise. "Let me help you."

Swatting him away, his mom placed his plate on top of the others in her hands. "No. You stay here and get to know our guest more. I don't need any help. I'll be right back." Then she disappeared back into the house.

Dark night sky surrounded them making the lights on the pergola stand out. The ocean waves pounded against the shore.

Relaxing, Caleb stretched his legs out in front of himself. "How long do you think you'll need to study for your exam?" Then he cupped the back of his neck with his hands.

Hannah rested her elbow on the table, cradling her chin with her hand. "I've no idea, but I imagine maybe three or four hours a day for the entire summer. I plan on going home between the practices to study."

"I see." Caleb paused. Hannah looked so beautiful, he found

himself staring instead of being an active listener. He willed his brain to play catch up. "I'm glad my medical school exams are over."

Wiggling in her seat, Hannah flipped her hair over her shoulder. "I can only imagine. I picked P.A. school, because it gave me a faster path to working. I've been on my own for a long time. I had to be practical." The sound of the waves became noticeable once more. People walked and biked by on the lit bike path which weaved by the houses lining sandy Newport Beach.

"What about your dad, his wife and kid?" asked Caleb. "Have they not been a part of your life?"

Hannah's jaw tightened, and she kept her eyes glued to the ocean. Her hand traced the top of her soda can in a circular motion. She fell silent, finally she said, "My dad hasn't been there for me, not even after my mom passed. My dad left when I was kid, and we barely had any contact until now. Honestly, I don't know why he offered up his house for me. Then again, I don't even know why I accepted. I haven't even met his wife and stepdaughter yet. I can only imagine they won't be thrilled to have me around for the summer. If I hadn't been completely desperate, I wouldn't have come. Trust me."

"Maybe they'll surprise you," Caleb offered. "Maybe they'll be nice."

Hannah placed a hand on his forearm. His skin warmed under the feel of her fingertips. "I appreciate your optimism, but I know where I'm not wanted." She removed her hand and refolded her napkin, placing it back on the table.

"I'm sure that isn't true." Emotion bubbled up and made his voice crack, "It's your dad."

We never know the future, and unfortunately, Caleb wasted years feeling bitter and resentful toward his dad over his lack of support. Caleb's dad had wanted him to take over his business, but Caleb had zero interest in it. When Caleb went off to medical school, something most parents would've been thrilled with, his dad never called or asked how it was going. Maybe his dad had been deep in money problems by then? Caleb wished he could've told his dad choosing medical school didn't mean he was rejecting him. There should've been a way for Caleb to have both, medical school and his dad.

A look of melancholy washed over Hannah's face. "And most would think that mattered," Hannah said softly.

His mom interrupted them as she came through the sliding glass door with a plate piled high with double chocolate chip cookies, Caleb's favorite.

"I'm back." She placed the platter of cookies in the middle of the table, retaking her seat.

Hannah's face brightened. "And you made cookies." Her eyes dazzled. "My lucky day."

Caleb swiped a cookie off the platter. "You forget, Hannah," shaking his cookie at Hannah, "I hit you with my car this morning." He sighed. "So, it wasn't necessarily a lucky day."

Hannah shrugged, taking a cookie for herself. "It could've been worse." She took a bite then wiped her face with her napkin. "After spending the day with you, and now having dinner with you both, I can say it was a lucky day. I've met two wonderful people." Hannah locked eyes with Caleb, taking another bite of her cookie.

Heat flooded his middle. Caleb polished off his cookie and went for another. "I agree, but I still feel bad about hitting your car. I'll probably spend the entire summer trying to make it up to you. It's one of my fatal flaws."

His mom scooted around in her seat. "He's right." She took a cookie for herself. "Caleb hates being in debt to others. He wants to be the one helping."

Hannah scrunched up her nose. "I don't see that as a flaw."

"It can be," Caleb grumbled. "Trust me."

His past girlfriends were perfect proof. Being a sucker, he gave everything he had to those he dated and often found the other person picking him last. Maybe he was too open with his feelings? Maybe he was too eager for others to approve of him? For once, Caleb wanted to be with someone who appreciated his giving heart and didn't use it as a weapon against him. Maybe someone like Hannah?

Hannah wiped her fingers on her napkin. "I guess I'll have to wait and see." Her gaze bore into his.

Thunder sounded behind his ears. Caleb scratched his chin. "I guess so."

CHAPTER 5

"Grayson, excellent freestyle," announced Hannah from the side of the pool. She traipsed along the length of the pool, watching as Grayson swam closer to the end. For a second, Hannah held her breath, hoping what she had spent the last several days teaching had sunk in. Then Grayson did a perfect flip turn, pushing off the wall before he headed back to the other end of the pool. Hannah clapped then cupped her mouth and said, "You nailed the flip turn. Awesome."

When Grayson made it to her end, Hannah crouched down next to him and gave him a high five. "I'm very impressed with everyone's improvement on their flip turns," she said loudly.

For the entire practice, Hannah forced herself to *not* glance toward the opposite end of the pool at Caleb. After spending the evening eating dinner with him and Jenna, Hannah knew she needed to put some distance between them. Her time here was short. Her life was complicated and her future unsure. As much as she enjoyed Caleb's company, they needed to remain professional with one another.

It wasn't hard to avoid him before and after practices. Alyssa somehow popped out of nowhere whenever he arrived and was heading out. Hannah managed to slip in and out without much more than a hello and goodbye. Once this week while passing each other by the pool, Caleb mentioned he and a few of the lifeguards were walking to a place to eat lunch. Hannah politely declined and explained she needed to head home to study before the afternoon practice.

When every swimmer had completed their set of laps, Hannah said, "Please gather around." The swimmers in her group swam over to her corner of the pool. Once the swimmers arrived, Hannah crouched down, leaning in closer to the pool. "Everyone is doing an amazing job. I'm impressed by each of your flip turns. I want everyone to now swim 50s of each stroke to end practice."

There was a bit of grumbling, but the swimmers swam back to the two lanes they were previously occupying. The rest of the practice passed quickly. Soon, Caleb blew his whistle.

With the megaphone at his lips, Caleb announced, "Climb on out and meet over here." He motioned with his arm.

The swimmers exited the pool and congregated near Caleb. Hannah joined the group behind her assigned swimmers.

Once everyone scooted in close, Caleb said, "It's only been a few days of practice, and everyone is already improving a ton. Keep up the excellent work. Hands in." Everyone put their hands in. "Dolphins on three. One, two, three."

"Dolphins!"

A wild dash followed as the swimmers quickly dispersed, finding their parents somewhere by the pool. Caleb gathered up some of the kickboards. Hannah went to the other end of the pool, grabbing the remaining ones on the opposite side.

The kickboards were stored in a big bin on the far corner of the gated pool area. With an arm full of kickboards, Hannah opened the bin and dropped in the kickboards inside. Caleb approached, carrying the stray ones. Hannah held the top open for Caleb. He tossed his in, and she secured the lid shut. Hannah swiped her wet hands on the sides of her khaki shorts.

A brief pause filled the tight space between them.

Caleb tipped up the bill of his baseball cap then readjusted it. "So," he rubbed the back of his neck, "I know I promised you dinner. Does tonight work? And if so, what time should I pick you up?"

Hannah stared back at him blankly. "What dinner?"

Was Caleb asking her out on a date? Like a real one? Hannah didn't even know if she wanted it to be real. Her mind tried to play catch up.

"Remember?" Caleb shuffled his feet, "I promised Mom, I'd take you to that little Italian place we like."

Ahh, this wasn't a date.

Not even close.

If Hannah didn't care, why did her heart drop a little?

"Gotcha." Hannah gathered her hair, tossing it over one shoulder. "I completely forgot about that. We don't need to go. I'm sure you have other things to do."

"No." Unflinchingly, Caleb stared back at her. "I really don't. Besides, if I don't take you, Mom will never let me hear the end of it."

Her being deflated. There he went again, mentioning Jenna and his obligation to her. Clearly, Caleb didn't have any interest in her. Hannah didn't see the point in forcing him to spend an evening with her.

Hannah forced a laugh. "An offer of dinner from someone who was manhandled into asking." She squared her shoulders and teasingly asked, "How can a lady resist an invitation like that?" Then she patted his bicep. "It's okay, Caleb. You're off the hook. I give you permission to tell Jenna we went even though we didn't."

"I'm sorry." A drop of sweat ran down his temple. Caleb

swiped at it with the heel of his palm. "I'm terrible at this and that came out wrong." His gaze found hers. "Hannah," he inhaled and exhaled, "would you like to go to dinner with me tonight? I want to take you out, and not because my mom wants me to."

Red ran up his neck. Caleb was nervous.

Her shoulders loosened, and a tiny bit of hope wiggled its way into her. Dinner with Caleb would be nice. It beat spending the evening alone, again.

"Sure." Hannah smiled. "I'll go to dinner with you. When? Now?" She glanced down at her sweaty polo shirt and khaki shorts. Her shorts were sporting a stain from where her sandwich dropped on them during lunch. No doubt she reeked of sunscreen mixed with sweat.

Caleb clocked his watch. "It's only 4:30." Then he rubbed the back of his neck. "I thought I could pick you up around 6:30. It would give us a chance to shower and change. I'm sweaty." When Hannah didn't immediately respond, Caleb nervously laughed and said, "Unless you prefer the older dining crowd. I know my grandma likes to eat this early. Maybe secretly you are eighty?"

Hannah laughed. "6:30 works."

His face relaxed. "Great." Caleb shifted a tad closer to her. "Can you text me your address?"

"Yep." Hannah patted down the pockets of her shorts. "I will, once I grab my phone out of my locker."

With her red lifeguard rescue tube and looking perfectly fit in her lifeguard swimsuit, Alyssa sauntered on by, appearing to want to engage Caleb in a conversation before he left. Her timing was impeccable as always.

Caleb didn't even shift his gaze toward Alyssa, but said, "It's a date."

Hannah wondered if he said it loud enough for Alyssa to hear, or if that was wishful thinking on her part. Alyssa's jaw tightened as her eyes narrowed. The hairs on Hannah's arms stood up.

Hannah wanted out of there, fast. "See you soon."

Then she promptly exited, leaving Alyssa and Caleb to chat alone.

Her hand smoothed out the front of her sundress. An unsettled stomach proved that Hannah was more nervous than she had anticipated. Hannah tossed her jean jacket over her arm for good measure. A double check in the mirror, Hannah was satisfied with her appearance and flipped off her bathroom light.

Only a few minutes to go, she decided to wait in the living room for Caleb. Her phone buzzed in her hands. Hannah assumed it was Caleb. Without looking at the screen, Hannah hit accept and put the phone to her ear. "Hello," she said in an overly warm tone.

"Hi, Hannah, it's Dad," Adam said.

Her gut twisted on itself. "Hey," replied Hannah, refusing to call him dad but avoiding calling him Adam too. It was a weird dance she played with nobody but herself. "What's up?" She tapped her bottom lip with her pointer finger.

"I can see from the security camera by the garage you made it into the house okay," Adam said.

Hannah had arrived a week ago, and she wondered why he had decided to call now. If anything, Adam should've called before she even arrived then again after he knew she made it there. But Adam hadn't ever worried about her before, so his lack of interest in her current well-being wasn't a surprise.

"I did." Hannah surveyed the room for cameras she hadn't seen. "Thanks. And I found the right room. Thanks again for letting me stay here for the summer."

A long pause followed. Hannah wanted to scream he was the one who had called her.

"How long is your vacation again?" Hannah asked out of politeness.

"That's the thing. I'm not entirely positive. We were thinking of heading back but Trisha is worried the home might be a little crowded with you there," Adam said. His voice trailed off.

Her back stiffened. "I thought Trisha was okay with me coming." Hannah ran a hand over her hair. "You're the one who invited me to stay with you." Her throat grew tight. Moisture tickled the corner of her eyes.

Did anyone want to be around her? Where did she belong now? If not with Adam, then where? Hannah missed her mom all over again.

"I know, I did." Adam cleared his throat. "But Trisha doesn't want to be leaving Jordyn in the house alone with you while she is attending her various social events. It makes Trisha nervous, because she doesn't know you."

And whose fault was that? Apparently Hannah's?

Adam continued, "And I don't want to make our daugh— I mean Jordyn, I don't want her to feel like her house isn't her own. You know how teenagers are."

"So, you need me to leave?" Hannah asked.

"No, but we might not be back until the end of the summer. Our plans are fluid."

"I can leave." Hannah cranked her stiff neck back and forth.

She had zero clue where she would go, but she'd figure something out. Hannah regretted not listening to her gut. Adam's lack of interest in her life should've been her first clue. But deep down, Hannah hoped this summer would be a chance for her to get to know Adam better, maybe even push past some of the previous hurt.

Hannah pinched the bridge of her nose. "Just give me a few days to figure something out. I'll find somewhere else to go. I don't feel right being here, when it's only keeping you all away."

"No," said Adam firmly. "You can stay for the summer like I offered. We're going to stay at my in-laws' summer home."

Summer home? How rich was Trisha's family?

"Ok, but would you please give me a warning when you plan on returning?"

"Hannah, I know Trisha and Jordyn will come around to the idea of you being there."

Dread entered her being. Come around? Why had she thought she was wanted here? Her naïve, rose-colored glasses came off. Coming to Newport had been her biggest mistake to date.

"I sure hope so," Hannah muttered under her breath.

Adam cleared his throat. The silence from the other end of the phone was deafening. Finally, he said, "Talk to you soon." Then he hung up without saying goodbye.

Her temples pulsated in her ears. With shaky hands, Hannah stared down at her phone screen. Only her solid red screen saver stared back at her. Anxiety pumped through her veins. Hannah needed a new place to stay.

A doorbell rang, but it seemed far and distant. Her scattered brain didn't compute. It rang again, snapping her out of her panicked haze. Hannah stumbled as she went to the door, swinging it open with far too much gusto. Caleb stood on the stoop. His hair was still damp from his shower. He had changed into slacks, a blue button down, and a sports coat over it. A whiff of spicy cologne hit her nostrils.

"Hey," she said breathlessly. Hannah waved him in. "Come on in. I need to grab my stuff."

"Great." Caleb moved over the threshold but waited in the foyer, not following her any further into the house. "Take all the time you need."

"I'll be only a second."

Then she wandered back to the living room in search of her things. It took Hannah a minute to gather her bearings, enough to find her purse and her phone, which was still in her hand. Hannah didn't know what was causing the commotion in her chest; Caleb, or the unsettling conversation she had with Adam.

Once back in the foyer, Hannah glanced down at her dress and smoothed out the front of it with a hand. "I think I'm under dressed." Hannah tugged her gaze from her dress to Caleb. "You said this place was small. I figured it wasn't fancy."

"It's not fancy. Promise." Caleb shuffled his feet. "I'm probably the one who overdressed. It's been a while since I've been out with anyone, and I think you look fantastic."

Hannah appreciated his compliment, but the words skidded right off her. "Maybe I should go grab a nicer sweater?"

"Please don't." His hand shot out to cup her elbow. "You look great just the way you are."

"Well then," Without thinking, Hannah ran a finger over the lapel of his sports coat. She found his gaze. It was entrancing. Slowly, Caleb swallowed, making his Adam's apple do a tantalizing bob. What was Hannah doing? She stumbled a step back. "I happen to think you look nice too."

You are only here for the summer. And this isn't a real date. Back this train up.

"Thanks." Caleb's hand ran over the part of his lapel Hannah touched. For a second, Hannah swore the air grew thick as her heart took a few liberties.

"Let's go." Hannah abruptly moved toward the door. "Before I further question myself and force myself to change."

She pulled out her keys from her purse. Hannah opened the door, allowing Caleb to pass through it. Once he exited, Hannah closed it behind her and locked it. Hannah glanced toward the driveway, spotting Caleb's rental car. They lingered on the stoop. Her purse slipped off her shoulder, and she tossed her keys inside and readjusted the strap.

Caleb scratched his jaw. A fidgeting gesture Hannah was growing to love.

"Are you okay to walk?" Caleb raised an eyebrow. "The restaurant isn't far, and I love the salty summer air in the evening."

"Sure, we can walk." Hannah moved first past his car and onto the sidewalk.

Then she turned and waited for Caleb to catch up to join her. She needed to get away from that house and her conversation with Adam. They walked for a while in silence. Hannah didn't register it, because her mind was going a mile a minute. Her conversation with Adam replayed in an endless loop.

Caleb asked her something, but she hadn't heard him.

"Sorry, could you say that again?" Hannah asked, reminding herself to be a better date.

"Nothing." Caleb plunged a hand into the pocket of his slacks. They moved to the side to allow a couple to pass them. Then Caleb asked, "Is everything okay?"

"No." Hannah exhaled, and Caleb's face dropped. She quickly added, "But it's not about tonight. Right before I came, my dad, Adam, called and let me know his wife is less than thrilled I'm staying at their house. Apparently, Trisha has some concerns with me being around her teenage daughter. I'd hope after she met me, she'd realize I'm a responsible human being and not a total weirdo failure."

Caleb tilted his head toward her. "Did Adam not discuss with Trisha about you coming?"

"Apparently not," Hannah muttered. A child rode their bike on the sidewalk toward them with a parent trailing along behind them. They sidestepped and waited for them to pass before they continued. The ocean peeked in between the long row of houses. "I guess they've decided to stay at Trisha's parents summer house for the time being, because Jordyn, her daughter, doesn't feel comfortable being in the same house as me. We've never even met." Hannah shook her head. "I've made a mistake in coming here. I don't know what I expected, but it sure wasn't this."

Caleb wrapped his arm around her. "I'm certainly glad you came here." Hannah forced herself to meet his twinkling eyes with a tight smile. He continued, "And I'm willing to bet once Trisha and Jordyn meet you in person, they'll see what only took me seconds to see …" his voice trailed off.

"And what did you see?"

He halted, shifting to meet her gaze. "That you're absolutely terrific in every single way." His voice vibrated through every single part of her body.

Her heart galloped.

And she knew whether she wanted it or not, Hannah liked Caleb in the cheesy, Hallmark-loving way. For a second, they stared back at one another. And she felt it everywhere. A light summer breeze fluttered between them, cutting back at the tension.

Hannah gave Caleb a light shove. "Okay," Caleb pretended to trip. Hannah laughed. "You really know how to lay it on thick. Do say this to all your lady friends?"

"Nah." Caleb shrugged nonchalantly. "Just the ones I think are hot."

Heat splashed her cheeks and smeared across her chest. They left the row of homes and crossed over to the street lined with little shops and restaurants. After a few blocks, Caleb stopped in front of a small restaurant packed in between two boutiques.

"We're here." Holding the door open, Caleb gestured for Hannah to enter first.

"Thanks," said Hannah, passing through the door. Without thinking, she ran a hand across his chest as she brushed past him. There she went again, touching him.

What in the world was wrong with her? Stop it.

Luckily, Caleb didn't say anything. Hannah hoped her forwardness wasn't a turn off, and she promised herself to rein it in. Once inside, Caleb approached the check-in counter, speaking to the host about their reservation. Hannah looked around the pocket restaurant. There were only seven or eight tables which faced the ocean. The tantalizing aromas that drifted from the kitchen made her mouth water. The host told them one minute and disappeared back into the belly of the restaurant.

"It smells so good in here," Hannah commented. "There's something about the scent of freshly baked bread that immediately makes my mouth water."

"I completely agree." Caleb leaned a hip against the check-in counter. "The bread comes out warm, and the butter seeps right into it as it melts. It's heaven in your mouth."

Playfully, Hannah whacked Caleb on his arm. "Stop. You're making me so hungry."

Ahh, more touching. Hannah couldn't help herself because Caleb looked so dang good in his sports coat and slacks. This was the first time in forever she wanted a date to go well.

"I like the gnocchi." Caleb smirked. "They bathe it in a creamy buttery sauce. I could lick the plate clean." He put his fingers to his lips and dramatically kissed them.

"Enough, I can't take it." Hannah gripped onto his forearm. "I've realized I've barely eaten today. Suddenly, the wait seems like more than I can bear."

"We're ready for you," said the host, interrupting them.

Hannah removed her hand from his arm, readjusting her dress.

"Wonderful," Caleb replied.

"Follow me." With the menus in their hands, the host waved them on.

They ambled behind the host, who led them to one of the two-top tables near the windows in the back which faced the ocean.

As she slid into her chair, Hannah remarked, "You didn't mention the view." Her gaze flickered to his. "This is unreal."

Caleb smiled. "It's the best part about coming here." He sat down too. "The sunset over the ocean, it's magical."

The host handed them the menus and left.

Hannah opened hers up, laying it flat against the table. "So, you mentioned the gnocchi. Any other suggestions?" She scanned the listed items. Her finger trailing along as she read the selection.

Caleb pointed to an item on her menu. "The chicken marsala is also very good." Once Hannah saw the listed item and read the description. Caleb removed his finger.

"Yum." Hannah closed her menu, placing her folded hands-on top. "I'm going to get that."

"You're certainly easy to please." His lips twitched in an intoxicating way that Hannah was growing to adore. "I like it."

"You can give credit to being raised by a single mom." Hannah gathered her hair, swooping it over her shoulder. She peered out the window at the view of the ocean. "We had no money, and I learned to eat whatever was put in front of me. It made me not picky which I think is a decent quality to have."

Caleb rested his forearms on the table. "I'd agree."

The server came back by with a basket full of various breads. Quickly, they gave their order too, gnocchi for Caleb and chicken marsala for Hannah. Once the server left, Hannah wasted no time diving into the breadbasket.

As the crunchy outer layer along with the soft inner layer hit her lips, Hannah moaned. Heat still radiated off the bread. "This *is* delicious." She tore another piece off and popped it into her mouth.

Caleb had a little more control. Being civilized, he placed the piece of bread on the small bread plate and buttered it before taking a bite. Hannah inhaled the rest of her bread.

After they ate the bread for a minute, Caleb remarked, "This was my dad's favorite place."

Hannah held the knife in her hand. "How long has he been gone?" She dipped her knife into the butter and smeared it across another piece of bread.

"It seems like forever." Caleb exhaled. Deep worry wrinkles stretched across his forehead. His gaze found hers. "A few months now."

"I'm sorry." Hannah furrowed her brow. "Were you close?"

"No." Caleb shook his head and darted his gaze back to the ocean. Slowly, he took a bite of his bread. Hannah didn't want to press him, but after Caleb took a sip of his water he continued, "At one time my dad and I were remarkably close, but we weren't at the time he died. It's something I regret. It makes his passing sting that much more."

Hannah didn't know how to console him or what to say. Instead, she placed her hand on his forearm. "I'm sorry you lost him and that things weren't in a good place between you. That's hard stuff."

Caleb patted the top of her hand with his own. "Thanks." He removed his hand. Hannah pulled hers away, placing it on her lap. "I can't change the past, no matter how much I want to. I've told myself I can only dwell on the things I can control. Those things are as follows: help fix up Mom's house, help her sell it, and find her a new place to live. Then I can begin to think about my upcoming move to Boston and the start of my surgical residency."

"I admire your desire to help Jenna." Hannah wanted desperately to hug his worries away. "You're an incredibly good son. I know you'll figure everything out before you leave. Let me know how I can help."

"Really?" Caleb smirked, meeting her gaze. The seriousness of the mood shifted instantly. "Are you sure about that?" His eyes sparkled with mischievousness. "I know lots of ways you can help *me*."

"You don't say." Hannah scrunched her nose. "And what did you have in mind?"

"I'll let you know." Caleb tore off a piece of bread and popped it into his mouth. "I plan on saving the offer of help for something really worthwhile."

"Should I be worried?" Hannah asked, loving every minute of their flirtatious exchange.

"Nah." Caleb wiped his hand on his napkin. "I promise it'll be fun for the both of us."

Hannah leaned her elbow on the table and cradled her chin. "I'll be the judge of that." Then Hannah picked up her glass and winked at Caleb as she took a sip of her drink.

CHAPTER 6

As dinner finished, Caleb longed to spend more time with Hannah. For once, he wanted to thank Jenna for her meddling and insistence, because Hannah was beautiful, intriguing, and witty all wrapped into one. After he paid, Caleb put his credit card back into his pocket.

"Would you be up for a walk to the pier?" asked Caleb, sliding out of his seat.

Hannah stood, placing her purse on her shoulder. "I'd love that. I didn't even know Newport Beach had a pier." She pulled her jean jacket closer across her body, folding her arms.

"One of the best," said Caleb, motioning for her to go first.

They exited the restaurant.

Once outside on the sidewalk, Caleb pointed a thumb over his shoulder. "We need to head a block this way to get to the path that leads to the pier."

Twisting on her feet, Hannah followed him. They meandered toward the pier as a comfortable silence settled between them. The ocean waves became louder as they competed against the squawking seagulls.

"Did you grow up going to the beach? Any surfing?"

"I did." Caleb had a strong urge to take Hannah's hand into his, so he shoved his hands into the pockets of his slacks to fight it off. "But I haven't gone surfing in a long time. My dad was an avid surfer, but he also loved to fish. I loved spending time with him doing both of those things as a kid. I haven't had much time for anything other than school in forever."

Her hair whipped this way and that, smacking her in the face. Caleb wanted desperately to touch her hair and tuck it behind her ears, letting his hand linger by her cheek. But he knew it would be way too forward and completely unwarranted.

As if reading his mind, Hannah gathered up her hair, tossing it over one shoulder. A whiff of citrus mixed with the salty ocean air nearly knocked him out. How did a woman smell this terrific?

"What was the best thing you ever caught?" asked Hannah as she held the front of her jacket closed with one hand.

Caleb tried to remember what he caught fishing those many years ago. The memories came flooding back, making his heart ache. Those early days of his childhood had magical moments like the summer nights he spent out on the edge of the pier fishing. He remembered watching in awe as his dad managed to pull in fish after fish.

"A lemon shark," Caleb confided. "A close second was a stingray. With the stingray, my dad had to use pliers to get the hook out of its mouth. Then he had to be incredibly careful not to get stung."

Her jaw dropped. "No way. How cool is that? I mean a sting ray *and* a lemon shark. I don't know which one I'd be more afraid of catching." Hannah raised an eyebrow. "How big was the lemon shark?"

"It was a baby." He straightened his back, finding his confidence. "So, you don't need to be overly impressed. I would say it was probably two or three feet."

"What?" Hannah bumped her shoulder against his. "That's

huge." Her eyes sparkled back at him with the reflection of the last stray bit of sunlight.

"Nah." Caleb shook his head. "The great fishers catch things way bigger than that. I've always wanted to go on one of those deep-sea fishing trips in Alaska to catch salmon."

"Alaska," Hannah paused. "I've never been there either, but I've heard it's somewhere you need to go at least once in your life." She leaned into him and gripped his forearm. "Back to the lemon shark; was it difficult to reel in? Sorry, I have so many questions. I'm simply trying to picture the whole thing." Breaking their touch, Hannah moved one step away. "Was it," she spread her arms, slowing her walk, "like this big?"

An excellent opportunity to break their physical boundary, Caleb stopped walking. Hannah did too. He placed his hands over hers and moved them to the correct length. "More like this."

Their gazes caught. He swore the air grew thick and heavy. His pulse galloped, and Caleb hoped what he was experiencing wasn't only one sided. Because Hannah and him had undeniable chemistry, something he hoped to explore more.

"That's—" Hannah hesitated. "I'm still impressed."

His hands lingered longer than needed, before pulling away. He rubbed one on the back of his neck. "Have you ever been fishing?" asked Caleb, desperately trying to regain his equilibrium. He stepped forward, moving again.

"No." Hannah shook her head. Their shoes slapped against the pavement. "I've never been, because someone would need a dad to take them to do things like fishing." She buttoned her jean jacket all the way up.

"Was your dad not around? At all? Ever?"

"My dad left my mom when I was a young child. After he left, he never showed any interest in me." Hannah squinted against the last straggling bit of sunshine. "This summer," Hannah sighed, "I thought it would be a chance to finally get to know my dad. I can see I hoped for something that will never be." She wrapped her arms across her middle.

Desperately, Caleb wanted to tug her close to his side but knew he couldn't. Not now. Not this soon. He shifted his attention to the water. "It might even end up okay in the end." Caleb plunged his hand into his pocket. "You and your dad still have time. I wouldn't completely write him off, not yet. When was the last time you saw him?"

Hannah scoffed. "Geez, maybe a decade. He visited me when I was in middle school. Business had brought him to the Midwest. I remember he took me out to dinner. We shared a very awkward meal and then he left."

"Ahh." Caleb's heart tugged in his chest. He wished he could make everything right for her, but it wasn't possible. The only person who could do that was her dad. "Did he at least call you every so often?"

Their feet hit the wooden planks of the boardwalk, leaving the sidewalk behind. The sun dipped lower and lower as they meandered toward the end of the pier. The sweet summer air danced around them as the water glistened. Caleb remembered why he loved Newport. He'd be sad to leave once summer was over.

"He did." Hannah's teeth chattered as the temperature dipped with the sun. "We texted. Occasionally, he called. But I didn't have a dad, and I always desperately wanted one." Her eyes became cloudy.

Caleb regretted asking. Without a thought, Caleb stripped his sports coat and wrapped it around Hannah's shoulders as they continued to walk toward the end of the pier.

"Are you sure? Then I'll be wearing two jackets while you have none." Hannah tilted up chin up. "Aren't you cold?"

"Nah. You take it," said Caleb.

Hannah halted in place. "Here hold this." She removed one shoulder of the jacket, slipped off her purse, holding it out to

Caleb. He took her purse from her. Readjusting the jacket, Hannah pushed her arms through the sleeves. Luckily, Caleb had broad shoulders which allowed the jacket to fit even with her jean jacket underneath. He hoped the double layers would make her toasty warm. She took back her purse from Caleb. "Thank you. I thought with it being summer, it wouldn't get so cold at night," said Hannah, slugging her purse back over her shoulder.

They drew closer to the edge of the pier. Caleb found himself wanting to stretch out the evening, to make every minute with Hannah last. He couldn't remember the last time he enjoyed a woman's company this much.

"Aren't the winters in the Midwest a bit brutal?" Caleb asked, raising an eyebrow. "I thought that made a person warm-blooded."

"The winters are horrible, and I'm still not used to it." Hannah glanced down at herself. "I'm happy I won't be returning to the Midwest anytime soon. Maybe sunny weather will be forever in my future? I'd rather it be a thousand degrees than slumming it through the snow."

"Then you would hate Boston," Caleb remarked. His heart plummeted. It was odd, and he wondered why it mattered to him that Hannah hated the cold. "But you'll love Newport Beach. It has almost perfect weather year-round." Caleb playfully nudged her. "Though it might be sixty-eight right now so—"

"Though it's in the sixties, you obviously didn't account for the wind chill," countered Hannah as her hair whipped against her face. She tucked it behind her ears.

Caleb enthusiastically cleared his throat. "Pardon me." He placed a hand over his heart. "It is sixty-eight but with the wind chill I believe it feels like sixty-four."

With a grin, Hannah teased, "And sixty-four is practically sixty."

"This might as well be Alaska."

Hannah laughed, though Caleb knew his weak attempt at

flirting didn't warrant any such response. This made him like her even more. They came to the end of the pier. Hannah wrapped her hands on the top of the wood railing and climbed onto the bottom rung. The ocean shimmered beneath the changing sky of day to night. Caleb leaned sideways against the railing, facing her. The dark sky replaced blue. Overhead, the lampposts which lined the pier flickered on, illuminating Hannah with their light. For a moment, Caleb allowed himself to stare at Hannah and not at the ocean.

Luckily, Hannah was unaware of him ogling her. She stepped down from the railing. "Will you be sad to move away?" She leaned her back against the wood railing and faced him. "The east coast is far away and much different from here."

Caleb ran a hand through his hair. "I haven't lived here in a long time. I went away for college, though I did come home for the summer. But I didn't really make it home much during medical school. This is the first time I've been in Newport for any sustained amount of time in years." He moved closer to her. His hip bumped the railing as wind splashed his face with the salty tang of the sea breeze. "I'll miss this." He tilted his head toward the ocean. "I miss it every time I leave. I never knew how lucky I was to grow up near the beach, until I wasn't by it."

"Ahh." Hannah gripped onto the railing with one hand. "Boston has beaches, right? Isn't Cape Cod nearby? Isn't that where all those Kennedys are from?"

"Yes, you're correct." It grew darker, making the moment seem safe and intimate. Caleb inched a tad closer. "I know Boston has beaches, but I highly doubt I'll have time to visit any of them. Also, I think Cape Cod is more of a summer destination. I've heard it's freezing in the winter."

"I'm sure even if they have a beach, it won't be this." Hannah wistfully sighed as she peered out at the dark ocean with the moon reflecting on it. A canopy of stars lit up the sky. "This might be my new favorite place."

For a second, they stared out at the ocean, listening to the rhythmic waves crashing on the shore. Caleb resisted the urge wrap his arm around her shoulders, making their bodies touch intimately. But it was too early to be so bold, and he was far from the guy who had the confidence to do something that risky.

"I should get you back." Caleb pushed his hip off the railing. "I know you have an early morning practice." He straightened himself. "I happen to have the same one." He smiled.

Hannah peeled her gaze from the ocean to him. "Thanks for tonight." They turned, walking back toward the exit of the pier. "And for dinner and," she motioned toward the ocean, "for this."

The pier swarmed with people. It required them to dip and dive around the throngs of those they passed. Once back next to one another, Caleb asked, "Would you like to go fishing with me?" His pulse quickened.

A look of confusion danced across her face, making her furrow her brows. "Fishing?"

"Yes, fishing." Honestly, Caleb didn't care what they did. Fishing was the first thing to pop into his mind due to their earlier conversation. If Hannah didn't want to fish, he'd find something else. This evening had been a welcome respite from his life, the stress of medical school, losing his dad, and helping Jenna. For a few hours, Caleb hadn't thought about any of it. He'd simply enjoyed Hannah's company. He rubbed the back of his neck and sped forward. "I know I'm not your dad, and I can't promise we'll catch something as cool as a lemon shark, but I'd like to take you."

Hannah paused for a second. Her eyes sparkled when she finally replied, "Sure. I'd love to go fishing with you."

Relief washed over him. The tension in his chest dissipated. "We'll have to go early," said Caleb, dragging his feet and slowing his pace.

"Uh oh." Hannah's hand bumped against his. "How early?" She crinkled her nose at him.

"The best fishing is early in the morning, before the sun even comes up," he said.

He wondered if she'd bow out. Doubt wiggled its way into his psyche.

"Do you promise to feed me?" Flirtatiously, Hannah leaned into his arm and gripped his forearm. "I get a bit testy if I'm not fed."

Boldly, Caleb intertwined his fingers with hers. "Promise." He patted the top of her hand. "What do you like for breakfast?"

"Something substantial—not a muffin." Hannah leaned closer to him as they squeezed through a gap of people coming in the opposite direction. "I'll be hungry an hour later. And I assume this fishing thing is going to take a while. Right?"

"Yep. Let me think." Caleb paused for a second to think of what he could purchase. An idea popped into his head. "Would a breakfast burrito work?"

"Perfect." Hannah grinned. Holding a finger up, she added, "And I'm requesting it with a Diet Coke, ice cold."

Hannah looked so dang cute. It took everything within him not to lean in and kiss her. Instead, he simply replied, "Your wish is my command."

Hannah tilted her chin up, catching his gaze. His staccato heartbeat warmed his body. "I might have to keep *you* around."

Was this an invitation for more? Caleb sure hoped so.

"How about Tuesday morning? The pool is getting cleaned so the practices that day are cancelled." Tuesday was few days away, and he wished it was closer. "Are you free then?"

Their feet hit the pavement, leaving the pier behind them. The streetlamps overhead provided enough light on their way back to Hannah's place.

"Sure, Tuesday works." Hannah cocked an eyebrow. "How early is 'early'?"

Caleb cringed. "Four-thirty." He peeked at her with one eye open.

"Four-thirty." Hannah squeezed his bicep with her free hand then removed it. "I thought we were talking like six." Her lips twitched.

"Is this you wanting to back out?" Caleb countered.

"No, no." Hannah shook her head. "I'm not backing out. I want to go with you. Though I must warn you now, I'm not a morning person."

Hannah's place came into view. They stopped at the end of the driveway in front of Caleb's rental car.

He rocked on his heels. "I've been warned."

"You have," said Hannah, moistening her lips.

They stared back at one another. The sound of the ocean became noticeable again. A tension built between them, but Caleb didn't know what any of it meant.

Slowly, Hannah removed his jacket from her body, holding it out to him. "Thanks. I had a wonderful evening." She wrung her hands.

Caleb took his jacket from her, placing it over one of his forearms. "I did too." His hands shook as if he had downed a few shots of espresso. His throat felt dry and restricted. Caleb gulped. Their eyes locked, and the pitter patter of his trusty heartbeat rang in his temples. "I'll see you tomorrow," he finally said.

Opening her purse, Hannah glanced down at it as she dug through it, locating her keys. "Yes, tomorrow—at swim practice." She took a step toward her front door.

He wondered what kissing Hannah would feel like, if her lips were as soft and plush as they looked. Caleb hoped to find out at some point.

Reluctantly, Caleb shoved a hand into his pocket, retrieving his own keys. "Until tomorrow." He waved, making his keys jiggle back and forth.

"Good night, Caleb." Hannah twisted and walked the remaining distance to the front door.

"Good night, Hannah," Caleb said in a small voice.

Caleb waited until she slipped inside, closing the door behind her. Only then, Caleb rounded his car and climbed in.

Fishing?

Really?

What in the world had he been thinking?

He didn't even own one fishing pole.

Starting his car ignition, Caleb drove straight to the local tackle shop to purchase two fishing rods and bait.

CHAPTER 7

Hannah's blaring alarm clock awoke her from a deep sleep. Groggily, she swiped at her eyes with the back of her wrist. Buzz. Buzz. Buzz. She slapped the snooze button. The only thing getting her out of bed at this unreal hour on her one day off was the prospect of spending more time with Caleb.

"Gah." Hannah grumbled as he threw off her covers. Cool air hit her skin, making her shiver. She sat up and swung her feet over the side of the bed. Her feet sank into the extra plush beige carpet as her mind cleared.

Her phone vibrated.

Then it vibrated again.

And again.

Again.

The phone danced on her nightstand. Hannah yanked the charging cord out from it and glanced at the screen.

Just checking to make sure you are awake

You are awake, right?

Hannah are you up? Or do I need to call?

Hannah's fingers zipped across the screen.

Oh, ye of little faith

You are up!

Half up and regretting my life choices

T minus twenty minutes

Oh dear, you're a morning person. I can tell. I AM NOT

I'm not a morning person either, just a person excited to spend the morning with you

Her cheeks splashed with heat, and she used the back of her hand to cool one cheek off at a time.

I always knew you had good taste

The three little dots danced at the bottom of the text chain. Hannah waited for a response. It was fun to flirt with Caleb. And she couldn't remember the last time she felt this excited to see a guy.

I'm picking up the breakfast burritos now. I'll be there soon

There's a place open this early?

I have my sources

Ahh, do you now?

> The Mexican place around the corner from my house is open twenty-four hours a day

> You never know when your desire to wrangle heartburn might kick in

Caleb texted back a laughing and crying emoji. Hannah tossed her phone onto her bed and returned to her suitcase she had still failed to unpack. After a quick scan of her sparse collection of clothing, she selected a pair of jeans, a baby blue hoodie, and black converse shoes.

In the bathroom, she tossed her hair up into a messy bun. Hannah only had time to wash her face and apply a little mascara, blush, and lip gloss before the doorbell rang. Hannah gathered her phone and purse, heading to the front door.

When she swung open the door, Caleb stood on the stoop with a can of Diet Coke dripping with condensation. A grin spread across his face, making her middle flutter. A baseball cap covered his dark locks. He looked at ease in his jeans and grey hoodie. It looked well-loved like it had been washed to a soft comfortable wear. Hannah wanted desperately to run the fabric between her fingertips.

"Good morning, sunshine," greeted Caleb, extending the Diet Coke to her. "Ice cold, as ordered." He stepped closer.

His lips twisted in an incredibly cute way which nearly made Hannah stop breathing for a split second. Were his eyes always that dazzling? Like they had an uncanny ability to push past her many layers right into her soul. There was no way she could fight the half smile slowly growing across her face.

Their fingers grazed as Hannah took the can from him. "Thanks." She popped the top and kept her eyes locked on him as she took a long swig. Once done, she smacked her lips together and glanced down at the can. "I, personally, think it's never too early to have a Diet Coke."

He adjusted the bill of his baseball cap and said, "I'm happy to deliver and don't worry, I have an ice chest full of them." His eyes glinted with amusement.

This day she sensed would go better than she had expected.

Hannah passed through the door, closing it behind her. She nearly pressed herself up against him in the tight space. "I'm glad you're a man of your word." A tremor rolled through her. Hannah held her can out to Caleb without looking at him. "Can you hold this while I lock up?"

Caleb took the can from her. Their fingers brushed one another, again, making an intoxicating thrill skate down her spine. A hint of his cologne filled her lungs, making her dizzy. Oh, boy. She tried her best to brush off the yearning feeling growing inside of her. Hannah locked the front door, shifting back to face him. Caleb handed her back her Diet Coke.

A need to calm herself, Hannah took another swig of soda, letting the bubbles coat her throat. "So," Hannah cocked an eyebrow, "where are you taking me fishing?"

"To Newport Pier, of course." He swiveled and waved for her to follow him. "Come on. I'm willing to bet we'll have fun together."

"Ahh, a bet." Hannah wagged a finger at him as she trailed behind him out to his car. "What will I get if you don't deliver?" she teased.

Opening the passenger side door, Caleb gripped the corner of the door. "Should we make a real one?" Caleb flashed her a challenging stare.

Hannah tried her best to look casual as her back rested against the side of the car.

"Sure." Then she took another sip of her soda.

Caleb raised an eyebrow. "I love a good challenge." He scratched his chin. "What do you think you should owe me when you lose?"

Hannah laughed then shoved him with her free hand. "You seem awful cocky for a guy who I'm about to beat."

"Not a chance." Caleb's gaze narrowed for a split second. "I forgot, what are we even betting on?" He rubbed a thumb over his bottom lip.

"Um." Hannah tapped the bottom of her Diet Coke can against his chest. The condensation on the can darkened the grey of his sweatshirt. "We're betting on if I'll have a good time or not, right?"

Caleb shifted two inches closer. "And how in the world would we judge that?"

Hannah shrugged. "No idea." She pushed her pinky finger into his bicep. "How about we change it to a simple bet of who catches the most fish."

Caleb smirked, leaning a hip against the door of the car. "I don't think that would be a fair bet for you. You've," he ran a finger down her forearm, "never even been fishing before."

"Isn't fishing mainly luck anyways?"

"I like to believe there is some skill involved. But since it's your suggestion—" Caleb's fingers tightened around the corner of the door. "What will you give me when I win?"

Hannah countered, "My, my, my—" She cocked an eyebrow. Her gaze slid down his frame. "How in the world do you manage to walk around with a head growing as big as yours?"

Caleb leaned over the door, making their faces inches from one another. His gaze flickered across her face, making her cheeks splash with heat. Her middle did a jittery jive. Three more inches in and their lips would collide. The thought made her batty.

"I'm not cocky." Caleb swallowed, making his Adam's apple bob up and down. "Just confident I'll win. You can be confident without being cocky."

Her nostrils flared from the mixture of his soap and spicy cologne. "Simmer down." Hannah tried to keep her voice from quivering. "I'm natural at most things, so I should pick up fishing in a flash." She forced herself to straighten her back. A weak attempt to appear bold and confident.

"I'm still winning." Caleb stared back at her. "And when I win, you'll take me to the arcade at Balboa Pier."

"Seems like a decent prize. I think I can handle that." Hannah held up a finger and continued, "But when I win, you owe me dinner at the fancy restaurant at the end of the pier."

Caleb rubbed his jaw and pretended to think over her proposition. "You drive a hard bargain, but I agree to your terms." He removed his hand from the corner of her door. "But only because I have this thing in the bag."

Hannah slid into her seat, setting her empty Diet Coke can in the center console. In between the front seats, the fishing poles took up the entire length of the car.

"Ahh." Peering up at him, she grinned, "Big words from the guy who's about to lose."

Caleb shrugged. "I guess we'll see who's right." Then he shut her door, walking around to his side.

Hannah ran her jittery hands back and forth over her thighs. She wondered if it was the crisp morning dew that had run a chill through her bones or the exhilarating feeling of flirting with Caleb that was making her shaky. Either way, she couldn't fight her building attraction for him. But did Caleb feel anything towards her? Or was he a guy who simply liked to flirt?

Caleb joined her, driving the few blocks toward the pier. A fog surrounded their car, with only the headlights illuminating their way. The sky still twinkled with stars. As they pulled up next to the pier, the streetlamps lit the area. Only a few stray cars peppered the parking lot. Then as they exited the car, the first peek of sunlight skimmed across the top of the water. Black sky faded to a dark blue, pushing away the stars. Hannah admired the quiet serenity of an empty beach.

Caleb rounded the car and popped up the trunk of his car.

Out came the cooler, some camp chairs, and tackle box. Next, he unloaded the two fishing poles from the middle of the car. To be helpful, Hannah strapped one of the chairs to her back. Caleb leaned the fishing poles up against the car.

"We made it before the sunrise," commented Caleb as he strapped the other chair to his back. He picked up the cooler, shifting toward her he asked, "Do you think you can manage carrying the tackle box?" With his other hand, he picked up the tackle box and held it out to her.

"You bet." Hannah took it from him.

Next, Caleb gathered up the two fishing poles with his free hand and motioned with a head nod toward the pier. "Let's go. I promise to feed you as soon as we find a spot to fish."

"A guy after my heart," Hannah teased.

Caleb smiled. "If you mean me, then yes."

The air crackled with energy as they locked their eyes. Hannah's body buzzed with the implications of his words. Caleb broke eye contact first and moved toward the pier. They covered the short distance from the parking lot to the pier. Then they crossed onto the wooden planks of the pier. The sun continued to rise, making it lighter by the minute.

"I think we should walk to the very end of the pier." Caleb squinted. He did a head tilt as his gaze landed on her hand. "Unless that is getting too heavy."

"Nah." Hannah grinned. "I'm stronger than I look."

His eyes narrowed for a split second. "You look pretty strong to me," Caleb replied.

Warmth wiggled its way down her spine. After a few minutes of walking, they made it to the end of the pier. Caleb rested the fishing poles against the wood railing. Hannah set down the tackle box. Next, they set up their chairs side by side, facing the expansive ocean. Some other fishers were on the far side of the pier, but their side was clear.

Caleb squatted down next to the cooler and pulled out a

brown paper bag. He dug inside until he revealed a breakfast burrito wrapped in aluminum foil. Peering up at her, he held it out to her. "Here you go, as promised."

"Thanks." Hannah smiled as she took the burrito from her. "And it's still warm."

Caleb set the bag with his burrito on top of his chair. "I'm going to cast my pole before I eat," said Caleb, gathering up the first pole.

Abruptly, Hannah stood, plopping her burrito on her chair. "Then you need to teach me how to cast my line. I don't want you to win our bet because your line was in the water longer." Her lips twitched against her will.

"Wow." Caleb laughed. His mischievous gaze met hers. "I can see you are taking this very seriously."

Smugly, Hannah countered, "I don't like to lose."

"That makes two of us." Motioning with his hand, Caleb continued, "Come on over. We can cast yours first. I don't need you claiming I cheated when I win this thing."

Hannah came up next to him. Caleb picked up the other fishing pole. He took a minute to point out the simple workings of the reel, showing her how to cast the line and reel it back in. Afterwards, he added some bait to each of their hooks. Then the lines were ready.

"Seems easy enough." Hannah admired the view as Caleb double-checked everything. "I think I'm ready to give it a go."

"Great. Let's cast it from here." With the fishing pole in hand, he shuffled away from their chairs, giving them enough room to cast. "This should be a good spot."

Caleb sidestepped behind her, holding the fishing rod out to her. Hannah took it. Then he came behind her, making his shoulders and arms mirror hers. His hands clasped hers against the rod. And she was done for. Caleb felt so snugly warm and smelled oh so delicious, she practically melted her back against his abdomen. She wanted to live in that perfect delectable moment forever.

Focus.

"Here." Caleb moved her hand over the reel. His large hand cupped hers. Caleb continued to explain the process, but Hannah didn't hear any of it, only the loud thunder of her temples pulsating. Her gaze traced the length of his square jaw. Did he wake up smelling this good? Or had he showered at this unearthly hour? Forcing herself to concentrate, she heard, "Let's try it. Ready?" With his hand guiding hers, they cast out the line. Soon, the baited hook sank deep into the ocean.

Hannah squinted as she glanced up at him. "Was that good?"

"Perfect." Caleb released his grip over her hand, taking a step back. Immediately, she missed the warmth of him against her. "You can leave it leaning against the railing. See this bell," he motioned toward the top of the line, "it'll alert us if the line starts to move. Then we can reel it in if you've caught anything."

Her hands dropped down at her sides. "Okay."

"Let me cast my line." Caleb snatched his rod, tightening the line. After he secured it in place, Caleb swung the pole back then forward, casting it perfectly into the water. He then leaned his pole next to Hannah's against the railing. Then he said, "Now we wait."

Hannah laughed, walking over to her chair. "I might have to get used to this fishing thing." Swiping her breakfast burrito off the chair where she left it, she plopped herself down.

Caleb collected his burrito, sitting down. Next, he fished out a Diet Coke from the cooler, holding it out to her. "Here you go, sunshine." Condensation dripped down his fingers and landed in splats on his pants.

"Sunshine?" Hannah raised an eyebrow. Her fingertips brushed against his as she took the soda. "Is that my new nickname?"

Caleb's cheeks splashed with color. "I don't even know why I'm talking like an eighty-year-old," he muttered.

Hannah nudged her shoulder against his. "Hey, I happen to like hanging out with eighty-year-olds. They eat at four and are in bed by eight. And they understand the importance of wearing stretchy pants whenever they feel like it."

Caleb laughed. "Is this a precursor to how you'll be when you're eighty?" Shifting, he dug into the cooler for a soda for himself. Once obtained it, he placed it in the cupholder of his chair.

"Nah." Hannah took a long swig of her soda then set it down. "Who said anything about waiting? I'm already fully embracing my eighty-year-old-like tendencies." Hannah peeled back the foil from the top of her burrito and bit into it. "This is delicious, Caleb," commented Hannah, glancing down at the burrito.

"I know and I love that they're open twenty-four hours. Oh, I almost forgot the salsa." Caleb retrieved the plastic containers of different colored salsa from the bag. "How hot do you think you can stand?" His brow furrowed as he gave her a challenging stare.

Hannah swallowed her next bite of burrito. Her eyes roamed over the little plastic cups in his hands. "Which one do you usually eat?" she asked.

"I eat the hottest, but it's like flaming hot." Caleb straightened his back and declared, "It's taken me years to work up to the level of heat the salsa offers."

Her hand flew to her heart, "Are you saying you don't think I can't handle a little heat?"

Caleb moistened his lips. "If by little, you mean a salsa that will leave your lips tingling for a long time. Then yes."

With a casual shrug Hannah said, "I mean I like tingly lips, but I usually only experience that while kissing." She boldly met his gaze.

Coyly, he smiled. "We could test your theory." Caleb pointed a finger at his chest. "I, for one, appreciate a good research project."

For a second, they stared back at one another. The air grew thick, and it wasn't from the morning dew. Unconsciously, she wiped her mouth with a napkin. "I'll take the mild." With an almost indistinguishable nod, Caleb handed her a salsa with *M* written on the top. "I'll leave the tingling for another day."

He winked. "Maybe not." Peeling back the top of his burrito wrapper, Caleb took a bite.

Her cheeks burned while her heartrate raced. Then the dinging bell of her fishing rod extinguished the tangible flirty vibe fluttering in the air. Scuttling out of her chair, Hannah placed her burrito down and raced over to her rod.

"It's my rod. My rod!" Hannah jumped up and down as she pumped her arm in the air. "I knew I was going to be good at this fishing thing." Triumphantly, Hannah peered at Caleb who was coming up next to her.

His hand tightened around the rod. "Hannah, come reel it in." She sidestepped next to him. His arms wrapped around her, nudging her closer to him until her back brushed against his abdomen. His breath tickled her neck. "I do think you caught something. Hopefully, it isn't only seaweed." Caleb's hands cupped hers on the reel. "Now when I say go, reel this in as fast as you can."

Hannah gave a small nod.

"Go," he said into her ear. Their fingers gripped the reel, rolling around and around in unison. The line tugged, attempting to pull the rod free from her hands. "Whatever you do, don't stop." Hannah laughed as the pole tried to loosen itself from their grasp. It wasn't any contest against Caleb's strong grip and steady hands. Eventually, the end of the line peeked above the water, revealing a fish, flopping back and forth.

Smiling, Hannah declared, "I've caught something." In her excitement, she stopped reeling the line in.

Caleb tightened his grip around her hands. "Keep going. If you stop, you might lose the fish."

"Ugh, I don't want that to happen," said Hannah as she continued to spin the reel around and around with Caleb's assistance.

After an eternity, they swung the fish over the railing and onto the pier. The fish flapped enthusiastically in every direction. Hannah continued to hold the rod as Caleb bent down and quieted the fish between his hands.

"I believe this is a calico bass." His eyes roamed the fish as Caleb slowly unhooked it. "Should we weigh it?" He peered up at her from his crouched position.

"Yes. Do you have a scale?"

With the fish off the rod, Hannah leaned it up against the wood railing.

The fish flopped back and forth between Caleb's hands. "I have a hanging fishing scale in my tackle box." He nudged his shoulder toward it. "Can you open it up and fetch it out of the top?"

"Sure." Hannah unlatched the top, opening its accordion style box. After she scanned the inside, Hannah selected what she believed was the scale. She flashed it at Caleb. "Is this it?"

"Yep." The fish continued to flap and squirm in Caleb's hands.

Hannah brought it over. Caleb instructed her on how to attach the little hook to the fish's mouth.

"Now, let go," Caleb instructed.

Hannah took a deep breath then let go. The screen lit up with the weight amount. "Two and a half pounds." Hannah read the screen then skidded her attention to Caleb. "How is that size-wise? Is that considered small?"

"For your first fish ever," a huge smile brightened his face, "absolutely incredible."

Hannah couldn't fight her grin. Overly pleased with herself, she asked, "Now what?"

"Now, we throw it back into the ocean." Caleb's nose scrunched up. "You don't eat bass in California." Shifting, he moved his body closer to hers. "Would you like to unhook it from the scale and throw it back into the ocean?"

"Ahh." Hannah peered down at her hands that were still relatively clean though she had touched the fish a tiny bit while inserting the weight hook. "Will my hands get slimy?"

Caleb laughed. "One thousand percent."

She debated whether she'd find the slimy feeling completely repulsive. With a shrug, Hannah said, "Sure, why not."

His lips twitched in response, and Hannah knew she had picked the correct option. Gingerly, Caleb unhooked the scale. "Come closer," he used his head to nudge her near, "I'll hand you the fish."

Hannah obeyed. Caleb slipped the fish into her hands. Only when she had her fingers tightly around the fish did Caleb release his grasp. Her nostrils flared from the salty fish smell. A few times the fish almost bounded out of her hands, and Hannah had to adjust her grip. Caleb removed the fish scale from its mouth.

"I *so* don't like this feeling." Hannah let out a nervous laugh. "Fish are as slimy as I imagined." She moved to the end of the pier and threw the fish over the railing back into the ocean.

"Be free little guy," said Caleb as the fish disappeared into the dark waters.

Hannah climbed the bottom rung of the railing, peering out at the vast majestic view. "And that's it?"

"Yes, we put bait back on the line and cast it again." Caleb trekked to his tackle box, removing his pack of antibacterial wipes. Hannah hopped down from the railing and moved toward him. He tugged out one wipe for himself then held the pack out to her.

"Thanks." Hannah swiped it from his hands, pulling one out. "Can I cast the line myself this time?" She wiped her hands clean then tossed the packed back on top of his tackle box. The used one went into a nearby trash can. "I think I've got it."

"Absolutely," Caleb grinned.

Her body buzzed from his positivity. Then Caleb made quick work of adding new bait to the hook at the end of the fishing rod. Hannah cast the line into the water on her own.

The shimmering sun rose higher, warming her up. Hannah stripped off her sweatshirt. They settled back into their seats, returning to their breakfast burritos. And the rest of the morning passed in a deliciously perfect haze.

CHAPTER 8

Caleb parked his car in Hannah's driveway. For a second, he stared out at the windshield, because his heart was in his throat. "I've had a great time today," Caleb unbuckled his seat, "and it's only ten," he tapped the clock displayed on the dash with his finger, "you still have the entire day left."

With a laugh, Hannah unbuckled her seatbelt too. "Thanks." Her eyes roamed the middle console and fishing poles sticking out between them. "I plan on crawling back into bed and taking a nap."

The car smelled like fish. They both reeked. This didn't exactly scream intimate and romantic, but despite the less-than-ideal setting, Caleb was warm all over.

"You officially won today." Caleb scratched his chin. "Beginner's luck I would say. I was skunked."

"What's skunked?" asked Hannah, running her finger over the cloth armrest.

"It's a fishing term which means you didn't catch anything." Tilting his head toward her, Caleb continued, "But five fish," he whistled, "impressive."

Hannah squeezed his bicep. "I had a great teacher." She jutted her chin and added, "And what can I say? I was the perfect student."

"I'll say."

Their eyes locked, and Caleb wanted desperately to kiss Hannah. His eyes flickered between her eyes and her lips and back again. He wondered what she tasted like, because he absolutely wanted to know. If she tasted anything like how he dreamed, then kissing her would be delectable.

"I guess," Hannah paused, "I'll see you soon." She raised a questioning eyebrow.

Should he lean in and kiss her? Suddenly, Caleb became very unsure of the signals he was reading. More silence followed, making his skin itchy. But the fishing poles in between made it near impossible to get any closer. Kissing at least in here wasn't happening.

"When can I see you again?" Caleb blurted out. "I owe you dinner at the quote 'fancy' restaurant at the end of the pier."

"I'm free tonight," offered Hannah. Then her cheeks splashed with color. It wasn't all in his head. Hannah liked him back. He was almost a hundred percent positive. Hannah bit her bottom lip. "Do you think that place requires reservations far in advance?"

"I'll call and find out." Caleb prayed he could get a reservation. "Then I'll text you."

"Until then." Hannah moved her hand to the door handle.

Caleb opened his door, swinging his legs out. "Can I open your door for you?" At his feet, he peered back into the car.

Hannah paused, hand hovering over the handle. "Sure." She relaxed back into her seat.

He made quick work of rounding the car to her door and opened it.

"Thanks." Hannah's hand grazed his forearm as she climbed out. They meandered together to her front door. When they arrived on the stoop, Hannah searched for her keys in her purse.

"Hopefully, I'll see you tonight." She located them and yanked them out with a jangle.

Caleb took a step toward her. His movement startled Hannah, and she stumbled a step back. Her hip knocked against the front door. Dang, he had zero game. He cringed once again. Hannah made him nervous, and here he went messing everything up.

His courage left him. "I'll text you." Caleb rubbed the back of his neck, forcing himself to smile though nervous energy raced through him. "Have a nice nap."

Hannah inserted her key into the front door. "I will." She pushed it open. "See you soon, Caleb." Then she slipped inside.

Caleb wandered back to his car. He replayed the day's interactions over in his mind. There was no doubt he found Hannah attractive, and he hoped to date her. But what did Hannah want? Did Hannah only see him as a friend? He'd never been good at this relationship thing. His shoulders drooped in defeat as he drove home.

Once home, he emptied his car, putting the fishing supplies into the garage along with the chairs and cooler. Next, he called the restaurant at the end of the pier, but there weren't any available reservations until next Saturday. With so many days in between, Caleb wondered if she'd even want to go.

He texted Hannah.

> The restaurant is booked solid, and they don't take walk ins. But I did snag a reservation for next Saturday night. Does that work for you?

While he waited for a response, Caleb entered his house. His mom lounged on the couch, watching a Hallmark movie.

She glanced up as he entered. "Did you have a good time fishing?" Her hand patted the top of the couch, locating the TV remote. She paused it.

Flopping down on the adjacent loveseat, Caleb removed his baseball cap. He ran a hand through his sweaty hair. "I did," he paused, "but I don't know. Hannah might only want to be friends. I fear she's one of those flirty women, who is overly open, and men mistake it for interest. Men like me." His jaw tightened.

She sat up straight. "What happened?" Her gaze roamed over him. "I'm a woman. Maybe I can give you some insight?"

Caleb cranked his neck side to side. "Nah. I'll figure it out."

"Fine." His mom swiped the remote back off the couch and pressed play. The TV loudly blared. "Have it your way."

His phone buzzed in his pocket. Caleb tugged it free from his pocket.

Bummer. But next Saturday works.

Caleb stared down at his screen with no clue on how to proceed. So, they have something planned for next Saturday. What about the several days in between? He enjoyed being around Hannah, and he didn't want to wait another week and a half to go on an official date. But maybe Hannah wasn't as anxious to see him again as he was to see her. Around and around his mind went like on a Ferris wheel. The summer only had so many weeks. Soon their free time would be gone with the increased swim practices and meets.

His mom interrupted his spiraling thoughts when she asked, "Is that her?" Her gaze fell on his phone in his hands.

"Yes." Caleb scratched his chin and looked back down at his screen.

Hannah's text boldly stared back at him. As much as he loved his mom, he didn't want her getting involved. Most likely this thing between him and Hannah would end when summer ended —perhaps it would end as soon as today. When Caleb didn't elaborate, she leaned against her armrest, tucking her feet under herself. Silence engulfed the space.

She paused the TV again. "So, are you going to see her again?" his mom prodded.

Caleb met her stare. "I want to." He shrugged, desperately faking indifference. She waited. He surprised himself when he continued, "We made a bet. She won. I'm supposed to take her to dinner at the end of the pier which was her restaurant of choice. I called the restaurant, and the earliest reservation I could get is next Saturday. So, I guess I'll see her then."

"Uh." Caleb's mom rolled her eyes then pressed play again on her remote. "Ok," she muttered mostly to herself.

Annoying romantic music played as a couple threw snowballs at each other. Do women really watch this type of stuff?

"What?" asked Caleb, loud enough to be heard over the roaring television.

With her gazed still glued to the television, she said, "You told me to stay out of it."

"I know." Caleb looked back down at his phone. The cursor danced on their text thread. But what was a guy to do? His fear of rejection was pulsating through him. If Hannah enjoyed his company, he didn't want to blow it by waiting to see her again. "Should I find a different restaurant and offer to take her there tonight? I would still take her next Saturday to the place on the pier."

"Are you asking for my opinion or just thinking out loud?" His mom raised an eyebrow.

Caleb regretted acting like a jerk. He knew she had the best intentions but sometimes he wished he could figure out things on his own. Then he reminded himself that taking advice didn't need to lessen his own abilities.

"I'm asking for your advice." Quickly, Caleb added, "Sorry I was acting so touchy."

His mom grinned, clearly satisfied with his apology. "You should offer to take her out tonight. It'll help you to know where she stands. If she says yes, then you know she's at least interested in getting to know you better in a non 'I only want to be friends' way."

"What does it mean if she says no?"

"Then unfortunately, you might be getting put in the dreaded friend zone." Then she held up a finger. "Especially, if she doesn't offer a different time when she could meet up."

"Fair enough." Caleb gazed down at his flashing cursor.

Jenna refocused on her movie. A snowball fight had turned into the couple sipping hot chocolate on a porch with blankets. Caleb stared blankly at the nauseating couple on the TV. They made it seem so easy. It wasn't, but after watching for another minute, Caleb worked up the courage to text Hannah back.

> Would you be up for something more casual tonight for dinner? I still promise to take you to the pier place next week

He hit send.

Caleb rose to his feet and stretched. "I'm going to shower." He smelled like fish.

With her gaze still glued to the TV, she asked, "Has she texted you back?"

"Nah, but I'll keep you posted." He didn't wait for Jenna to respond before leaving.

Even though he hadn't slept much the night before, Caleb felt wide awake. The message changed from delivered to read as he climbed the stairs to his room. The dots danced but then disappeared without a response. Batty with suspense, Caleb opted to plug in his phone and leave to shower. He hoped when he came back a response would be waiting for him.

Only after he had showered and changed did he allow himself to check his phone for messages. His heart sank when there wasn't a response from Hannah. He slumped onto the corner of his bed. Whoa, he misread all the signals from Hannah today. Around and around, he went, analyzing and reanalyzing the entire morning hoping to unpack what each interaction had meant. But he only came up blank.

Finally, an agonizing hour later, his phone buzzed. Yanking the charging cord out of the bottom, Caleb tapped the screen to reveal the message.

Sure. I'm game

Caleb flopped backwards onto his bed. Relief washed over him. His fingers zipped across the screen.

I'll pick you up at six

Wait, where are you taking me?

It's a surprise

I think you just don't know where you're taking me yet

Caleb laughed out loud.

Guilty as charged. But don't worry, I promise to figure something out. Most importantly, I will feed you

You'd better. You know how I can get when I haven't been fed

Adorably cute? And incredibly irresistible?

Smooth. See you tonight

With a wide grin, Caleb let his phone flop face down onto his abdomen. Even though he had zero clue where to take Hannah, it didn't matter, because she'd said yes.

CHAPTER 9

Hannah flipped off the bathroom light then moved into her bedroom to gather up her purse and sweater. Earlier she had taken a leisurely nap and relaxing bath, she had changed into a pair of black slacks and light floral top. The weather could get cold at night, which required Hannah to dig through her sparse clothing to locate a simple cardigan to bring with her.

Then out of nowhere she heard a door creak open followed by some chatter. Was she being robbed? She had parked the rental car in the garage, and maybe someone thought the home wasn't occupied? SOMEONE WAS BREAKING IN! Hannah raced into her bathroom and locked the door. Her heart caused a commotion in her chest. Then Hannah realized she didn't even have her phone with her. What was she going to do now? Hide out in the bathroom and hope they left without finding her?

The noise from downstairs grew louder. Hannah heard several pairs of footsteps march up the stairs. Her body shook. Hannah knew she was defenseless against any intruder, her only hope was they would take what they wanted and leave without discovering her in the home. As an extra measure, she climbed into the bathtub and closed the curtain. A weak attempt to hide herself, but what other choice did she have? Temples pulsating, it made it hard to hear anything, but she swore she heard her name repeated multiple times. How did these people know her name?

Then the footsteps entered her room. She held her breath and clamped her eyes shut, cradling her knees to her chest.

"Hannah, Hannah?" a voice called out. "Are you in there?"

Hannah prayed and hoped they would leave. The voice grew louder then landed directly outside her bathroom door. With a trembling hand, she moved the curtain an inch to peek out. A shadow appeared in the light spilling out of the door crack at the bottom. Her pulse sounded in her ears, making it impossible for her to hear anything else. The doorknob jiggled.

"Hannah, are you in there?" A long pause followed. "It's me. Adam."

Her thundering heartbeat nearly exploded but slowly dropped. "Adam?" She choked out against her labored breath. "Why are you here?"

"It's a long story." Adam knocked on the door. "Can you come on out?"

Once the tremble in her body eased, Hannah climbed out of the bathtub and scurried toward the door. When she swung it open, it revealed Adam, a lingering Trisha, and a scowling Jordyn.

"What are you doing here?" Hannah rescanned the faces staring back at her. "You told me you were staying at some summer house." Her hand flew to her chest. "I was scared you were an intruder."

Adam stepped back. "A pipe burst in Trisha's parents' home. It flooded the entire downstairs. We had no choice but to return home."

"It's a complete nightmare," said Trisha with a huff. Then she inspected her perfect manicure while avoiding eye contact with Hannah. "My parents are going to have to take the place down to the studs. It'll be months, maybe even a year before it's livable again."

On her tiptoes, Jordyn ducked around Trisha and Adam. "Why are you in my room? My dad wouldn't have told you to take my room, " snarled Jordyn.

My dad. Two words, so simple, but they were like a gut punch. Hannah didn't even know how to unpack that statement. So, Adam was willing to be a dad to Jordyn, but not her? Reflexively, her neck tightened.

"This is your room?" Hannah's gaze skidded from Adam, to Trisha, to Jordyn. The room didn't have one trinket, one teen poster, nothing to indicate a teenager lived in it. But from the single minute of being in Trisha's presence, she imagined Trisha didn't allow anything to be out of place. "I apologize. Adam told me to take whatever room I wanted." The small, confined space of the bathroom closed around her. Sweat gathered around her temples. Hannah hated confrontation, even more she hated the feeling of being trapped.

Trisha eyed Adam.

Adam slinked back a foot. "I did tell her that. I thought it didn't matter where she slept, since we were supposed to be gone the entire summer."

"Well, it does matter." Trisha wrapped a protective arm around Jordyn. "You'll need to move your stuff out immediately. I told Adam I wanted you to stay in the workout room." Trisha narrowed her gaze at Adam. He practically shrank into himself. "We can bring in a blow-up mattress from the garage for you to sleep on."

"Trisha," said Adam lowering his voice. "I don't see a problem with her using the guest room."

"I'm sorry—" Trisha's salty voice sent a shiver down Hannah's spine. "Last I checked this was *my* house." Trisha tapped her pointer finger against her chest. "I bought this place long before you came along. So, I'll decide where people sleep."

"It just not very comfortable." His voice was small. Adam's shoulders drooped. "And Hannah is here for the summer. We can't make her sleep on an air mattress for that entire time when there is a perfectly good guest room for her to stay in. Can't you see how unwelcome that would make Hannah feel?"

Hannah's cheeks warmed. Her skin itched. It was like she wasn't even there as they discussed the predicament of where to put her.

Trisha flipped her jet black, perfectly set hair over one shoulder. With a razor-sharp edge, Trisha replied, "My parents might visit and that is where they stay when they come."

Hannah interjected, "It's fine. I can leave. I'll figure something else out." She pushed past them into the bedroom. Her hands shook as she took in her belongings scattered across the room. It wasn't much, and luckily, she still hadn't really unpacked either. Her items were hanging out of her opened suitcase. Her mind tried to play catch up to the entire situation.

Pack your stuff up and get the heck out of Dodge.

Adam came up behind her. "But where will you go?"

Hannah stared down at her opened suitcase and didn't dare turn around to face him. "I don't know. Just give me a minute to think. I'll figure something out. I always do."

Hannah tried to organize her thoughts. She needed a plan. Her stuff was still mainly in the two suitcases she'd brought with her. The rest of her things she had put into storage, with plans to move them when she landed her first real job. It wouldn't take her long to throw everything into her suitcases and zip them closed.

With a twist, Adam tugged on Trisha's arm. "Can we speak privately?" Then Adam pulled Trisha out of the room.

Unfortunately, Jordyn didn't leave. She plopped herself right down on top of the queen size bed. Her hand ran over the top of the silky blue speckled duvet cover. "I'm at least glad to see you haven't damaged my comforter. I spent weeks looking for it," commented Jordyn.

Hannah crouched down in front of her opened suitcase,

grabbing clothing items hanging over the edge. Quickly, she picked up a shirt and folded it, placing it inside. "I wouldn't damage it. On the off chance I had, I would've replaced it," she remarked, without looking up.

Next, Hannah piled up three pairs of jeans, placing them back into the suitcase.

"My mom isn't happy you're here," said Jordyn, matter-of-factly.

"I picked up on that." Hannah folded and shoved more items on top. She zipped the first suitcase closed. "I shouldn't have come. It was a mistake. One I will forever regret. I'm sorry I took your room." She glanced over at a lounging Jordyn. "I wouldn't have taken it if I knew it was yours. It looked like a plain guest room to me."

"My mom hates junk, and she used an interior designer to decorate the space. I didn't get a say in anything except for selecting the bedspread." Jordyn sat up, sitting crossed legged on top of the bed. She studied Hannah for a second then added, "I believe you." Her tone softened a tad. With a head tilt, Jordyn asked, "Why did you come?"

With a sigh, Hannah leaned back on her heels and met Jordyn's inspecting glance. "I thought for some odd reason it would give me a chance to grow closer to Adam. To somehow find a way to repair the big hole in my heart from him leaving me as a kid." Tears tickled the corners of her eyes. Rapidly, she blinked them away. "I can see now it was wishful thinking." She stood, ripping her swimsuit off the hook where she'd left it to dry.

"What are you talking about? There's no way Dad left you. My mom said your mom was a horrible person who kept Dad away from seeing you," said Jordyn.

Hannah didn't need to get into it with Jordyn. After all, Jordyn was only a teenager, a teenager who deserved both a mother and father's love. Just because Hannah never received that didn't mean Jordyn should be denied it, too. Her mistake had been revealing anything personal.

"The details aren't important." Hannah tossed the swimsuit into the remaining open suitcase. "I'm glad you consider Adam your dad. It's nice to know people can manage to get it right the second time around."

"My first dad died when I was a baby. Adam is the only dad I've known." Jordyn continued, "It's been a rough couple of days, so my mom's a little on edge. I wouldn't worry too much about her. Her bark is always worse than her bite." Her lips twitched when she added, "Though Dad and I are completely scared of her."

"Ok," said Hannah. "But I'm not going to stay. I'll finish getting my stuff out."

Then as if the world wanted to throw her into another disastrous loop, the doorbell rang.

"Oh snap," muttered Hannah. Caleb. She'd completely forgotten he was on his way when this entire thing transpired. Quickly, she stumbled toward the door. "That's—" But before she had time to finish, Jordyn ran past her, scurrying down the stairs two at a time.

Hannah swiped her sweater and purse off the bed, racing out of the room after Jordyn. "I'll get it," yelled Hannah at the back of Jordyn's disappearing figure. "It's for me."

But Jordyn, being younger and more agile, was already opening the door as Hannah's feet hit the stairs. Adam and Trisha exited a room to the left of the stairs, checking on the commotion. Hannah froze in place.

Jordyn talked to Caleb, though Hannah couldn't hear what was being said.

"Who's that?" asked Trisha. "All of our friends still think we're out of town. I hope Jordyn didn't open the door for an annoying door-to-door salesperson we can't get rid of. We better go check it out." Trisha tried to push past Hannah.

"No!" said Hannah far too forcefully. "It's for me. I have a date."

Trisha's eyes bugged out. "You've been inviting strangers into our home?" She darted a narrowed gaze at Adam.

Adam's face splashed with red.

"He isn't a stranger," piped up Hannah. "He's the other swim coach that I'm working with for the summer. I've never had him over to hang out. He's never even been inside. Caleb's only here to pick me up."

Hannah hated this entire situation. Here she was a twenty-five-year-old woman trying to justify a simple dinner date. No amount of free rent was worth this level of scrutiny. They say you get what you pay for, and this was the perfect example.

"Well, well, well." Trisha folded her arms against herself. "I can see you've wasted no time making yourself comfortable in *my* home."

Adam wrapped an arm around Trisha's shoulders and squeezed. "I think what Trisha is trying to say is; we don't want our address being given out to people we don't know. And it isn't safe for someone you just met to be picking you up for a date. You should've arranged to meet him in a public place. That's way safer."

"Oh, so now you're worried about my safety?" Hannah gestured wildly with her hands. Anger pumped through her veins, "But not when I was a kid, right?"

Then Hannah brushed past a jaw-dropped Trisha, and a redder-than-red Adam, and bounded down the stairs. Soon, she joined Jordyn at the front door.

Hannah gripped the door. "Thanks Jordyn." She sidestepped her. "I'm here. Caleb and I are heading out." Then she tried to pull the door closed behind her.

Jordyn yanked the door back open, making Hannah release her grip and stumble a step toward Caleb.

Caleb's firm grip on her forearms steadied her. "Umm."

Caleb's gaze skidded between Hannah and Jordyn. "Are you okay?"

"Yes." Hannah snatched Caleb's hand. "Let's go." She tugged him away from the door.

"Oh, okay." Caleb found his footing then twisted to wave goodbye to Jordyn. "It was nice to meet you, Jordyn."

Jordyn beamed back at him, flipping her mousy brown hair over her shoulder. "I hope you come by again. You are *so* cute." She grinned sheepishly.

"Ok. Bye, Jordyn." Then Hannah edged closer to Caleb and muttered, "I need to get out of here. The faster the better."

Trisha and Adam appeared in the doorway, peering over Jordyn's head.

"Hannah, can I talk to you for a second," yelled Adam, moving rapidly from the porch stoop to the walkway.

Hannah paused then waved a hand. "Nah, I'm good." She continued toward Caleb's car.

Adam trotted a few more steps. "You can stay in the guest room." He shoved both his hands into his pockets. "Trisha and I talked. I don't want you to leave. Please stay."

Her heart constricted. Hannah hated how desperately she was willing to accept even the tiniest olive branch from Adam. For so long, she had longed for a father's love. Every daddy-daughter dance, every play, every dance recital, Hannah had held out a sliver of hope that Adam would come through for her and show up. It wasn't something that went away.

"I'll think about it. I'll decide before I get back tonight." Hannah gestured toward Jordyn. "You can move my stuff out. Just put it in the hallway. I'll grab it when I get back."

Hannah and Caleb arrived at his car.

"When will you be back?" Adam called.

"I have no idea," said Hannah through a clenched jaw.

"Well don't stay out too late."

Caleb opened the passenger door and whispered, "Are you okay?"

Hannah gave a small head shake.

"So, they're back." Caleb rubbed his jaw.

Hannah slipped into her seat. Without making eye contact, she replied, "Yep." She sensed several eyes on her and when she glanced toward the porch, Trisha, Adam, and Jordyn stared back at them. She ducked her head back in. "I've got to find another place to live."

"Ahh. I see." Caleb waved to the audience watching them. Then he shut her door and rounded the car, climbing in. He placed the keys in the ignition but didn't start it. "Do you want to talk about it?"

"Yes, but not here. Just drive." Hannah waved her hands in front of herself like she was directing traffic. "I don't care where you go. Just go."

"On it." Caleb started the ignition, backing out of the driveway.

He drove through the neighborhood at a slow pace. Neither spoke, and Hannah appreciated Caleb wasn't bombarding her with an endless stream of questions. She leaned her head against the headrest, closing her eyes for a moment to settle the shaky quiver of her body.

Caleb flipped on the radio. A soothing melody of an artist she couldn't name filled the rattled space in her heart. What in the world was she going to do? With the money she was making from the swim team, Hannah could possibly find a room for rent. But how? And for only two months? That wouldn't work. The entire reason she came to stay at Adam's in the first place was to study and save up money. After years in college, Hannah only had a stack of student loans waiting to be paid.

"A pipe broke in Trisha's parents' summer home." Hannah kept her eyes clamped shut. She felt braver with them closed.

"Apparently, they're back for good, and Trisha doesn't want me here."

A blinker sounded. Caleb changed lanes seconds later. Hannah opened her eyes as he made a left onto the street which paralleled the beach. Sunshine trickled in through the windshield, warming her up. The chill in her bones subsided.

"And something went down with the room you were staying in?" Caleb raised an eyebrow but kept his gaze steady on the road.

"Unfortunately, yes." Hannah shifted, turning to face him. She admired his strong jawline and broad shoulders. "I, accidentally, was staying in Jordyn's room and that blew everything up. Trisha wanted me to move into the workout room and sleep on an air mattress even though they have a spare bedroom." She fiddled with her seatbelt which suddenly felt restrictive against her chest. "I know I can't be picky. I don't have many options. I only came here because I was going to use these few months to figure out what to do next. I need to save up money, and study for my exam. Once I pass, I can find a job as a P.A. But it all takes time." She gnawed on her fingernail.

Caleb pulled over to the curb, turning off the ignition. He gripped the steering wheel with one hand. "Do you think you can stick it out with Adam and his family?" He squeezed her shoulder. "Or should I start texting everyone I know to see if they have an available room?"

His proposition seemed easy. A solution was offered when she thought she was out of them. Everything wasn't doom and gloom. She still had a choice, we always do, even when the path forward can appear to be hard and treacherous, there is always still a choice. Her choice.

Hannah forced her gnawed up fingernail away from her mouth. "I'm not sure." She leaned over the armrest, making her arm graze his. His touch steadied her. "Let me think on this for a second." From her seat, Hannah saw the ocean peeking between the buildings. Blue melted into beige.

Caleb removed the dangling keys, shoving them into his front pocket. He brushed her hair over one shoulder. His hand lingered, but then he shifted and wrapped an arm around her shoulders. Then he waited like he had all the time in the world, and Hannah didn't need to be in a rush.

Her chest heaved. "I don't know what to do," said Hannah in a small, defeated voice.

"I always find it helpful to go over the pros and cons of any sticky situation. Let's hear them." Caleb motioned to give them to him.

Hannah rested her head against his shoulder, inching as close as the restrictive space allowed. "When did you need a pros and cons list?"

With his gaze on the ocean, Caleb replied, "I made one recently when I was trying to decide what residency program to accept. My dad had passed away the week prior. My entire life felt heavy and unimaginable. I didn't know what I was going to do. Should I take the one nearest to Mom? Or did I take the one I wanted and would be the best for my career?"

Hannah tucked some loosened hair behind her ear. "And you chose the one best for your career. Was it hard to make that choice?"

"It felt impossible, selfish really." Caleb tipped his face closer to hers. "But I knew I hadn't worked this hard to not do what I went to medical school to do. I knew I could invite my mom to come with me. I also knew she would have to learn to be on her own too. Her future was up to her, but I had to make my own way, too. But trust me, the situation seemed impossible. Coming home for the summer was a happy medium between the two."

Hannah rubbed her lips back and forth, recoating her lip gloss. "I'd like to stay here in Newport. I like working at the swim club. I'm making good money, and I have time to study for my exam too."

"Yeah, duh." Caleb smiled. "I'm not letting you go anywhere. Even if that means calling every person I know to help you find a room to rent. You belong here in Newport with me."

"I know Trisha doesn't like me, but Jordyn seemed like a nice girl. I wouldn't mind getting to know my stepsister more. As for Adam—"

"Things could end up being better between you," said Caleb.

"Or things could be damaged beyond repair," countered Hannah.

"True." Caleb's hand roamed over her shoulder, distracting her from their conversation. "But you won't know unless you try."

"Maybe I'll give it a few days, see how it goes," Hannah offered.

"How about a week?" Caleb ran a finger down the slope of her cheek to her jaw. Goosebumps smeared across her back. "If you say only a few days, you might be looking for a way out. A week means you're going to give it a fair chance."

"Fine, I'll give it a week," Hannah agreed.

The heaviness in her chest dissipated.

Quickly, Caleb leaned in and kissed her on her temple. "I'm relieved. Now, let's go eat. I'm starving, and I haven't eaten anything since that breakfast burrito this morning." He pulled his arm away from her shoulders.

Unbuckling her seatbelt, Hannah asked, "Are we here?"

"Yes, we're here at one of my favorite places." Caleb climbed out. Once out, he poked his head back into the car. "We're going to the arcade after we eat. I know I lost the bet, but I have a feeling you're good at Dance Dance Revolution," he smirked.

"Dance what?" Hannah asked.

Before he answered, Caleb closed the door and rounded the

car to her side. He continued the conversation as he opened her door and helped her out. "It's a dance competition game."

"Oh dear." Her gaze skidded over him. "I don't like the sound of that."

"You know the one where the squares light up for you to stomp on. It's easy. I promise."

Hannah gave a forced laugh. "Ok. I'll give it a shot."

"I knew you were a good sport." Caleb grasped her hand and tugged her gently in the opposite direction. "This way." They strolled down the street toward Balboa Pier, located next to Newport Beach. "But I have to warn you, I'm good at it."

"You're good at dancing?" she asked.

"No." Caleb shook his head. His eyes sparkled with the sunlight reflecting in them. "I never said I was good at dancing." Soon they arrived at the crosswalk, and Caleb hit the button. Cars passed by in a steady stream. "I'm only good at pretending to dance, where you only must think about stepping on a lit-up square. That, I totally crush."

"I see," said Hannah, unable to fight the grin spreading across her face.

The crosswalk changed to go. They stepped off the curb and entered the crossing walk which led to Balboa Pier.

"I promise it'll be fun," Caleb said.

"Oh dear, is this another bet?" Hannah teased.

Caleb released their hand hold, wrapping an arm about her waist. "I believe it is."

His taunting eyes danced back at her. Hannah let herself imagine kissing that smirk on his face away. "Then I'm game," Hannah said.

"But, first we eat."

CHAPTER 10

"What song should we pick?" Caleb scrolled through the long stream of song selections displayed on the large arcade game screen. "Any suggestions?"

Hannah peered back at him. Without a word, she tapped on *I Knew You Were Trouble.*

"I should've known," Caleb said. "A Taylor Swift fan."

"Who isn't?" Then Hannah shoved Caleb onto the attached square floor.

Caleb smiled. The extended evening was going better than he planned. During dinner, their conversation flowed with an effortless back and forth that Caleb couldn't remember having with anyone else. Plus, Hannah was fun, thus making him fun too. This was what you would call a win, win, win.

"It's already starting." Caleb stomped on the right square then the left as they lit up under his feet. With his gaze firmly on the arcade screen, he added, "I'm winning. If you don't hop in, I'm going to cream you."

"I can see you mean serious business." Hannah wasted no time and hopped on next to him. She attempted to match her step with each square that lit up.

Attempt was the key here, because Hannah was terrible at it. Often her steps were a second off, leading her to miss the step completely then fall further and further behind. Sweat dripped down Caleb's temples as he concentrated to catch every step perfectly. Hannah laughed at her own ineptitude. Caleb encouraged her to keep going, though she continued to fail miserably.

Caleb admired Hannah's lighthearted demeanor. He managed to make her completely forget entirely about the incident earlier with Adam and Trisha. At least, that was his hope when he took her to the arcade to play this ridiculous game; a game he hadn't played since he was a teenager. Hannah stopped jumping around as the song ended.

Triumphantly, Caleb pointed at the arcade screen. "Look. I'm the new high score."

"Congrats." Her breathing was still labored. "Does it let you enter your name next to it?"

"I think only my initials," said Caleb, stepping off the padded squares, moving closer to the arcade screen.

"Ah, bummer." Hannah gathered her unruly hair and swooped it over one shoulder. "How will anyone know it's you?"

Caleb flashed her a wicked grin. "I'll know it's me. We'll have to come back later in the summer together to see if it's still here."

Hannah pursed her lips together and nodded. "What are your initials? I don't even know your middle name."

Caleb's finger zipped across the screen, tapping out his initials. "It's Mark. So, my full name is Caleb Mark Miller."

"C.M.M. not bad. You'd hate to have horrible initials that spell something awful out," said Hannah.

After he hit enter, Caleb stepped back from the arcade screen. "True." With his pointer finger, he swiped at the sweat dripping down his temple. "I guess my parents at least did that for me. How about you?" He raised an eyebrow. "What's your middle name?"

"I'm not telling you." Teasingly, Hannah twirled and moved toward the exit.

"Come on." Caleb jogged to catch up with her. "You know mine now. I want to know yours. What's your middle name, Hannah?"

She went past the marina overlooking the rows of boats without slowing down.

"Nope." Hannah jutted her chin though her lips curled at the corners. "I'm keeping it to myself. I think you must earn that type of intel on me."

Caleb brushed her arm with a single finger. Hannah halted in place, turning to face him.

"Hey, I won the game." Caleb cupped her elbow. "And we never decided what my prize would be for winning. I think you telling me your middle name will do."

"I'm not telling you my middle name." Hannah sidestepped him, walking to the edge of the dock lined with boats. She climbed onto the bottom rung and peered out at the marina.

Caleb came up beside her. "Why not?"

Hannah shifted to face him, leaning her back against the wood railing. "I don't have one. So, there's nothing to tell."

"Oh." Caleb's chest loosened. "I think you're the first person I've met without a middle name."

"My parents wanted my maiden name to become my middle name. So, someday I'll have one, if I ever find Mr. Right and get married."

Married?

The words landed smack dab in the middle of his gut. He let them settle, waiting for the panic and anxiety to set in, but it didn't. Maybe someday if things went well, he could be her Mr. Right?

Whoa, that came out of left field.

Hannah's gaze remained steady on him like a challenging stare. A mounting pressure danced in the space between their bodies. A live crackling wire laced from him to her. Desperately, Caleb wanted to kiss her, and he sensed she desired the same. This challenging stare was becoming his new favorite game.

The wind picked up and flapped Hannah's hair across her forehead. Instinctively, Caleb stepped closer and tucked the flyaways behind her ear. Once the strands were secured, he trailed his hand down a few inches until it cupped her neck. He waited, giving her time to break this spell and end this thing if she wanted. Then Hannah scooted a tad closer. A hope sprung up in his chest as her gaze flickered between his lips and his eyes. His insides did a somersault.

"Are you going to kiss me?" blurted out Hannah, completely bypassing all talk of middle names, bets, and childish banter.

With a laugh, Caleb said, "I was kind of planning on it." He wrapped his arm around her waist, bringing her body up against his.

"Good," Hannah said matter-of-factly. "Because I want you to kiss me."

Then she went for it, making her lips skim across his own. Heat smoldered him as her luscious lips danced with his. Caleb didn't hesitate but tightened his hold around her waist, making their hips touch. He breathed in her sweet perfect fragrance, settling the need to rush. He reminded himself to slow down. To memorize the feelings of her in his arms and their lips against one another's. Their minty breath mingled. Her perfume filled his lungs. He basked in the feeling of her silky hair as it brushed against his cheek and the softness of her lips. He packed every second of it deep inside his heart and promised himself to never let it go.

Slowly, his fingertips trailed the length of her jaw and earlobe. The sun hung low, pushing out the light of the day replacing it with early dusk. A gentle ocean breeze came off the marina, cooling down his ignited body. Caleb couldn't have imagined a better first kiss.

Then their kiss deepened as she parted her lips, allowing him to fully taste her. Her fruity lip gloss mixed with his minty tongue. Somewhere in the distance, Caleb heard the squawking of seagulls, the chatter of people passing them by, and the pounding of sandals as they slapped against the pavement. Though all these sounds competed against the commotion in his chest, the outside world managed to become dimmer as his world orbited only around them.

Hannah palmed his shirt, tugging him nearer. Their kiss spoke of new beginnings and the hope of something more. Caleb dreamed of a way forward with her, despite the many obstacles they faced. Now that he had a taste of her, he knew he could never have enough.

Breathless, Hannah finally pulled away, ending their kiss. His gaze locked with hers, searching for an indication that this meant to her what it had meant to him. She gnawed on her bottom lip as time ticked by without either speaking.

A grin spread across his face, Caleb said, "I really like kissing you." Again, he lightly and gingerly kissed her, wrapping his arms around her waist. "I'd like to do it forever," he smiled.

Hannah leaned her cheek against his chest. "Ditto." Her breath tickled his neck.

He rested his chin on top of her head. "Please don't move away before the summer's over." Loosening herself a tad, Hannah glanced up at him. He continued, "I'd like us to at least have this summer to see where this thing will go."

"I don't think I can promise you that. I don't know how things will go with my dad and stepmom. And if we're being real this might just be a summer thing. Soon, you'll be off to Boston." She dropped her arms from his waist, taking a step back.

The reality of their living situation came roaring back. A heart-stopping kiss, no matter how remarkable, didn't solve everything. This might be a summer romance and nothing more.

The magic of sunshine, sand, and waves dissipated with the sea breeze. His neck tightened making his shoulders ache.

Quietly, Caleb stepped away from the marina and back onto the walkway weaving around the marina out to the parking lot. They didn't touch. Hannah crossed her arms across her chest as she matched his steps.

"I need to know we've at least this summer together," confessed Caleb. "I can't let myself fall for you when the future is so uncertain. You could up and leave on me any second."

Anxiety pumped through him. His worst fears bubbled right to the surface. Falling in love then having it ripped away just wasn't something his heart could take. Why had he been so foolish? *They only had ever had the summer.* Why had he allowed himself to believe in love?

Hannah's back stiffened. "I can't make promises that I know I might not be able to keep. You must at least be able to understand that. If things don't work out living with Adam and Trisha, I'll have to bring forward my move out date. I guess if you can't handle that, then I have no choice but to understand. We can pretend this never happened."

"Whoa, let's back up here a second," Caleb rubbed the back on his neck. "I need a second to think, because I feel like this evening has taken a total turn."

Hannah didn't slow her pace to the car. It wasn't until she was in front of the passenger side door that she stopped and turned to face him.

"I'm sorry we kissed," said Hannah. "We both knew our time together was short, but I decided to look past it. I can see though that isn't going to work for you." She glanced away.

He paused, trying to find the proper words. "I think what I was trying to say was I like you Hannah. I already know I like you, and the more and more I give to you with no promise of a future the harder it will be when things end."

"So, now what?" Hannah blinked. "Do we cut our losses before either of us gets into this thing too deep?"

Her words hit him hard. This wasn't what he wanted, but nothing could change the reality of time and distance. Even if he thought Hannah and him could be great together, it didn't change their circumstances.

"Maybe," he hesitated, "until you know your future better."

"Ok," said Hannah. She yanked open the door and sat down in her seat.

Hannah kept her gaze straight out the windshield. For a moment, Caleb lingered at her door. Why was he putting so much pressure on one kiss? Surely, he could manage to have a little fun with her even if it could only be for a day, week or month. This is what people did at his age. Why couldn't he allow himself a bit of respite from his normal, levelheaded thinking?

Deep down Caleb knew he couldn't do it. He already liked Hannah too much. The more time they spent together the more painful it would be when it ended. It was a story he already knew how it would play out. No, things were better this way. Cut his losses and play it safe. Hannah and Caleb were better off as friends.

Silently, Caleb shut Hannah's door. His shoulders drooped as he went to the driver's side. A dark night sky surrounded his vision without a moon in sight. Heaviness replaced the thrill of kissing Hannah in a snap.

CHAPTER 11

The following Saturday, Caleb carried some boxes from his mom's garage out to his car. When he shoved them into the back, he wondered how many trips it would take him to get everything over to Goodwill. The entire week he'd spent attacking the clutter in Jenna's garage. Luckily, he had made a dent. As he trudged back up the driveway, Jenna appeared, waiting at the opening of the garage.

"What time is your dinner reservation?" His mom put a hand at her hip. "I can run this load over to Goodwill. They usually have workers out to help with the unloading. I don't want you being late on my account."

Caleb paused in front of her. "Say what?" He furrowed his brow.

"Your dinner with Hannah," prompted his mom. "I distinctly, remember you making the reservation last week. You need a shower before you head out. I do appreciate the work you've done getting rid of your dad's stuff, but I'll take over from here."

Shaking his head, Caleb brushed past her. His jaw tightened. Hannah hadn't spoken to him about anything not work-related since last Saturday. He didn't blame her, because he had acted like a complete idiot. At swim practices, Hannah kept their conversations strictly professional, keeping him at arm's length. Turns out it hadn't taken him long to fall for Hannah. She'd buried herself in his heart. He had to cut her loose and had become more miserable than ever.

With his back to his mom, Caleb lifted another box. His arms full, he brushed past her toward his car. "We aren't going to dinner." Caleb shoved the box in the back seat. He forced himself to evaluate the remaining space in the car, he believed he had room for one more box.

Further discussion with her about Hannah was off the table. Caleb didn't want to be reminded of how he'd messed up. His mom marched further out onto the driveway. With the box in place, Caleb whipped back around to head back into the garage, brushing past her in the process.

"Why aren't you going to dinner?" She trailed behind him as he reentered the garage. "Talk to me."

Neck tense, Caleb cranked it back and forth. Aggressively, he picked up another box and headed back to the car. "Because Hannah and I decided we are better off as friends." He shoved the box in and slammed the door. Caleb brushed his dusty hands on the sides of his shorts. "Not that it's any of your business." He moved around the car to the driver's side door. "I'll run this stuff over then come back for another load." He slid into his seat and reached for the door handle.

Before Caleb managed to shut it, she grasped the corner of it. "Nah, I saw you two together." Her gaze roamed over him. "I think you like her way more than you are letting on. So, what happened?"

Caleb attempted to shut the door, but his mom wasn't having it. She stepped in front of it and pressed her back against it, making it impossible to leave. With crossed arms, his mom narrowed her gaze at Caleb and waited.

"I'm not talking to you about this." Caleb tugged at the door handle behind her back. "Now, can you let me go? It's going to take me another load to get everything over to Goodwill, and they close at five."

"Why are you giving up so easily?" Her shoulders stooped. "I saw you light up when you were around her."

"Because," Caleb exhaled and ran a hand down the length of his face. "I can't handle losing one more person that I care about. It just hurts too much."

His mom moved away from the door, stepping to the side to make room for Caleb to close the door. "Then you're more broken than I thought. And I have no idea how to help you." Her eyes misted, and she shook her head.

Clearly defeated, she turned and trudged back into the garage. Against gritted teeth, Caleb slammed the car door and drove to Goodwill.

On her bed cross legged, Hannah adjusted her laptop. Then she hit the apply button on another job listing. The entire week, Hannah had applied to jobs everywhere in the country. The world was her oyster. Truth be told, she'd take the first place that hired her. Unfortunately, none of these places would take her until she passed her exam, although these applications were helping her jump start the process.

Jordyn came bounding into her room and plopped herself down on the space beside her on the bed. "What are you doing? Studying?"

"I should be, but no. I'm applying for jobs." Hannah clicked on another job description. This one was in Boston. Her cursor hovered over the job description. Caleb. He'd be in Boston. Her heart clenched. Luckily, it was a big enough city and the chances of running into each other would be slim to none. "I need a plan. I'm hoping to start as soon as I pass my exam."

"What happens if you fail it?" Jordyn made herself comfortable, tucking her feet under herself.

Hannah laughed. "I sure hope I don't fail it." She scrolled down some more and read the job description further. It looked like a perfect fit for her, because the job didn't start until September. "If on the off chance I failed, I would have to study some more then retake it."

Jordyn clapped her hands together and gleefully said, "Then you could stay here longer."

"I doubt your mom would want that." Hannah shot Jordyn a knowing glance. "Even if I failed, I'm still leaving soon."

The last week with Adam, Trisha and Jordyn had passed without much fanfare. Honestly, Hannah kept her interactions with them to a minimum and tried her best to stay away for most of the day. After swimming practice, she drove to the local library to study. Also, she started teaching some private lessons which filled up even more of her time. This meant she ventured back to Adam and Trisha's late in the evening.

Despite her effort to make herself scarce, Jordyn always wandered into her room shortly after she returned home, no matter the hour. Jordyn and Hannah then spent time chatting while Hannah readied herself for bed. Hannah worried about Jordyn being lonely. Adam and Trisha spent every evening out socializing with friends. Often, they left Jordyn home alone to order takeout. Hannah saw why Jordyn latched onto her so quickly; she didn't have anyone else. From Hannah's observation, Jordyn didn't hang out with anyone her age. Unfortunately, Adam wasn't proving to be a much better parent to Jordyn than he had been to Hannah. His interaction with Jordyn was limited. His time was spent golfing and socializing with friends. He rarely was around. Honestly, Hannah wondered if Adam knew anything about Jordyn's interests.

"Nooo, I like having you in the house. It means I'm not alone, and I hate being alone," Jordyn popped off her bed. "I think my mom and dad have too many friends. I wish they spent more time at home with me."

"Why don't you ever hang out with your friends?" Hannah peered over the top of her laptop. Jordyn wandered around the room, running a finger along the top of the furniture. "Maybe you should invite some of them over?"

Her shoulders drooped. "I don't really have any friends."

Hannah set the laptop beside her on the bed, devoting her attention completely to Jordyn. "I'm sure that isn't true." She tilted her head to the side, studying Jordyn. Jordyn had wonderful silky thick hair along with Trisha's beautiful facial features.

"It is." Jordyn moved to the window, pushing open the curtains. The afternoon sunshine came spilling in. "Mom moved me from my school last year. She claimed she found a better one, and I would like it. It isn't better. In fact, the kids are awful. I don't fit in."

"I'm sorry." Hannah moved her laptop to the nightstand, making more room for Jordyn. She patted the empty space on her bed. "I hope this next school year will be better for you."

Jordyn climbed up, settling next to her. Both leaned their heads against the headboard and crossed their ankles.

"I try not to complain." Jordyn exhaled. "I don't want Mom sending me off to a boarding school. Mom went to one as a kid, and I'm afraid if she thinks this school isn't working then I'll be out of here too. That would be worse, way worse."

Hannah gnawed on her bottom lip as she contemplated how to respond. Where was Adam in all of this? Jordyn called him Dad, but Hannah didn't see how he earned that title. To her, it appeared Adam hadn't learned anything at all. Adam was as selfish as ever. Anger pumped through her veins. Jordyn didn't deserve to be ignored or treated like an inconvenience. Hannah recognized so much in Jordyn that she once saw in herself. It broke her heart.

An idea bounced into her head. "Would you want to join the swim team I'm coaching?" Hannah wished she had invited Jordyn to join sooner. "It might be a good way to meet some nice kids your age."

Jordyn's face lit up. "Do you think they would let me join even though the swim season already started?"

"I'm one of the coaches." Hannah tapped her shoulder against Jordyn's. "I'm pretty sure that gives me the liberty to add my *sister* to the team."

Jordyn beamed back at her. *Gosh, this kid was easy to love.*

"Do you know every stroke?" Hannah inquired.

"Yep." Jordyn nodded. "My favorite is butterfly."

"Really?" Hannah was shocked. Most kids hated the butterfly because it was often the hardest stroke to master and was physically exhausting. "Then I really need you to join the team. I can hardly get anyone to sign up for the butterfly races."

Trisha walked over the threshold into Hannah's room, interrupting their conversation.

Her gaze scrutinized the two of them looking comfortable on the bed together. "My parents are coming this weekend, so I need you to move out of this room and into the workout room," said Trisha without any further explanation.

"Ok." Hannah took a deep settling breath to rid herself of the tight knot in her throat. Her limited interactions with Trisha were less than pleasant. Trisha made it clear her being in their home was a big nuisance. This confirmed it. "For how long?"

Quickly, Hannah's mind sped through the predicament and available options. With Trisha's parents coming, Hannah had to leave. There was no way she'd stay here, but she wondered where she could go. Airbnb? A cheap hotel further inland? She could head out of town, but where? Her exam was a month away, and Hannah only needed to hang on a tad longer.

Trisha examined her perfectly painted red manicure. "It really doesn't matter. They'll stay as long as they want." Then Trisha jutted her chin. "It really isn't your business how long they stay."

"I was only asking, because I don't want to be in the way." Hannah swung her legs over the side of the bed, sitting up. "Maybe I'll get a hotel for a few days."

"No," said Jordyn, gripping Hannah's arm. "I don't want you to leave. Mom and Dad just spend the entire time when my grandparents are here going out to galas, parties or out to eat. I'm left home alone."

"You're too young to attend those with us. It's adults only." Trisha leaned her hip against the door frame. "That isn't all they do when they're here. They like spending time with you, too."

"Yeah, okay." Jordyn rolled her eyes and shot Hannah a knowing glance. "For maybe for like ten minutes, then they are only interested in doing things with you and Dad."

Trisha straightened herself, tugging down her linen blue shirt. "You're exaggerating, and you know it."

"Whatever," Jordyn muttered.

"I'll get my things out." Hannah stood, breaking up the tension. "When do they arrive?" Her mind clicked through workable solutions of how to manage the situation.

"You can stay in my room," said Jordyn, glancing over at Trisha, she added, "Mom, I'll sleep on the air mattress on the floor in my room. Hannah can sleep in my bed. Then you won't get upset when she isn't up by five for you to work out on the treadmill."

"No way," said Trisha. She gestured toward Hannah. "I don't even know her. I'm not letting you share a room with a stranger."

"We're sisters," said Jordyn, scurrying off the bed too.

"*Step*sisters," Trisha said. "There's a *huge* difference."

Hannah held up her hands. "I'll find a place to stay. Please don't fight over me. Just let me know when the guest room is free again." She sidestepped over to her suitcases. Then Hannah picked up a stray piece of clothing hanging over the top. Folding the shirt, she placed it back on top.

"No, Mom!"

"I'm not discussing this with you anymore," said Trisha with a razor-sharp edge.

With another shirt in her hand, Hannah glanced at Jordyn. "It's okay. I'll see you tomorrow at practice."

"What practice?" Trisha questioned.

"Hannah is going to let me join the swim team. She says it might be a clever way for me to make some new friends."

The tight lines across Trisha's forehead loosened. Her tense demeanor softened a smidge. "I, actually, think that's an excellent idea." She shot Hannah a crooked smile. "Thanks, Hannah."

A smile? Could the ice lady have found her heart?

"No problem," said Hannah, zipping her first suitcase closed.

Luckily, Hannah knew not to get too comfortable at the house. Most of her things were packed, and it would only take her a few minutes to grab her items out of the bathroom.

"What time are the practices?" Trisha asked.

"There's two a day, one in the morning and one in the afternoon. Jordyn can come to one or the other or both," Hannah said.

Jordyn glanced at Trisha then over at Hannah. "Can I start today?"

Hannah maneuvered her suitcase upward so she could roll it out of the room. "I don't see why not." She grappled her other suitcase upright too. "The afternoon practice starts in an hour."

"Mom, can you take me right now to go buy a new swimsuit?" With a pleading look, Jordyn clasped her hands together. "None of mine will work for a swim workout."

Suddenly, Hannah remembered she needed to doublecheck with Caleb about Jordyn joining the swim team. She knew he'd say yes, because it was Caleb. Hannah tugged her phone out of her pocket and shot Caleb a text while Jordyn and Trisha discussed shopping details.

> Can Jordyn, my stepsister, join the swim team? I already told her she could. Sorry. But I think it would be good for her to meet some new kids her age. So please say it's okay

Her attention went back to Jordyn and Trisha.

Trisha said, "I think Dad might have time to run you there. I need to get things ready for Grandma and Grandpa."

Her phone dinged. Hannah glanced down and swiped at the screen to reveal the message.

> Sure thing. No problem

Rapidly, her fingers zipped across the screen.

> Ok, great. She's coming to the afternoon practice today

The dots at the bottom of their text exchange danced back at her.

> Then I'll see you both then

For a split second, Hannah contemplated telling Caleb about her lack of housing. Then she thought better of it and slipped her phone back into her pocket. She'd figure something out, even if it meant checking into a one-star motel outside of town.

"I'll get out of your hair." Hannah dragged her roller suitcase across the bedroom.

Trisha took a step out of the way to clear her path to the door.

"You aren't really leaving, are you?" Jordyn flashed her gaze to Trisha. "Mom, do something. I don't want Hannah to leave."

Through tightly pursed lips Trisha replied, "You're welcome to stay in the exercise room."

Hannah left the first suitcase right outside the door then brushed past Jordyn and Trisha a second time to retrieve her other one. "Nah, I'm good." Hannah trekked by with her bag to the hallway. "You enjoy the time with your parents."

"But you'll come back once they're gone, right?" Jordyn wandered into the hallway behind Hannah. "I want you to come back. Please."

Honestly, she didn't know if she would be back. Trisha seemed happy to finally be free of her. Hannah flashed her gaze to Trisha. Trisha picked a stray piece of lint off her blouse. The woman clearly wasn't jumping at the opportunity to invite her back. There was her answer, no matter how bleak her bank account balance might be, Hannah knew there wasn't a place for her here.

"I can't make you any promises." Hannah seized a roller suitcase in each hand. "But I'll see you in an hour at practice." Hannah directed her attention to Trisha. "Do you know where the swim club is located? Or do you need me to text you the address?"

"I've lived here my entire life, and Adam got you your job." Trisha gave her a dismissive wave. "I know where it is."

"Of course." Hannah herself to keep her voice even and undeterred. "Then I'm off. Tell Adam I said goodbye."

CHAPTER 12

At the edge of the pool, Caleb crouched down and hooked the lane line into place. Once secure, he stood up, shuffling a few feet to adjust the next lane line. Swimmers were arriving. He flashed his glance at the huge clock on the gate opposite him. Caleb wondered when Hannah would make an appearance.

Earlier, he'd spotted her rental car in the parking lot. Most likely she was in the lounge, avoiding him until practice started. Ever since their kiss, things had been awkward. Avoidance became the fragile dance they both engaged in. Nothing too unpleasant, mainly a slight coldness from her when they had to interact.

With the last lane line attached, Caleb stood, wiping his wet hands on the sides of his khaki shorts. Hannah walked out of the lounge. *Dang, she looked cute.* Caleb turned away when some swimmers came up to her, chatting with her. Here they went, another practice where Hannah only spoke to him when necessary. It stung, but he only had himself to blame. You shouldn't kiss someone then back off.

To appear busy, Caleb trekked to the other side of the pool, snatching his clipboard off a chair where he'd left it. It listed every swimmer along with their practice times for the various strokes and lengths. Hannah broke from the swimmers surrounding her and proceeded around the pool toward him. Caleb pretended to make notes next to swimmer names as she neared.

"Hey—" Hannah shuffled her feet then shoved a hand into her back pocket. "Caleb—"

Caleb glanced up at her while he clipped his pen at the top of his clipboard. "Hey, what's up?" He brought the clipboard to his hip.

Hannah didn't chat casually with him. He wondered why she was now. So, he waited.

Hannah bit her bottom lip. "I wanted to thank you for allowing Jordyn to join the swim team this late in the season. I really appreciate it."

As if on cue, Jordyn strolled through the pool gate with Adam in tow.

"No problem." Caleb pointed toward them. "It looks like she's here."

"She is?" Hannah swiveled on her feet, peering over her shoulder. Her shoulders drooped. "I don't want to talk to Adam," she muttered under her breath.

"Is everything okay?" Caleb inquired.

"Um." Hannah shifted back to face him. "Besides not having a place to stay tonight—everything is just dandy."

Caleb wanted to inquire further. Was Hannah leaving tonight? He panicked. His heartrate galloped. Hannah couldn't leave, even if they weren't on the best terms, he at least got to see her every day. He wasn't ready to say goodbye, not before he made things right between them, if such a thing was even possible.

Jordyn and Adam rounded the pool, nearing them.

When they arrived, Hannah said, "Hey, there. I'm glad you made it, Jordyn." She didn't address Adam's presence. Instead,

Hannah flung her hair forward, gathering it up. She repositioned it on top of her head in a bun, using the hair tie from her wrist. "I love the suit."

Jordyn's face lit up. "You do?" She glanced down at her blue-green speedo.

"Definitely." Hannah folded her arms. "I think that is your color. It makes your eyes pop."

Adam didn't attempt to speak to Hannah. For a few awkward seconds, they stood and stared at each other.

Then Hannah clapped her hands together, shifting toward Caleb, she caught his gaze and said, "I guess we'd better start."

With a nod, Caleb picked up the whistle around his neck and blew it. Cupping his mouth, he then yelled, "Time to start stretches!" He stepped toward the corner where the team gathered. "Come on." He motioned for Jordyn to follow him. "I'm with the older swimmers. I'll get you put into the right group."

Enthusiastically, Jordyn joined him. Caleb glanced back to see if Hannah was coming. She said something to Adam. Adam shook his head. Hannah made a big gesture with her hand then jogged to catch up with them.

"Do you know the four strokes?" Caleb asked Jordyn, trying to gauge Hannah's mood at the same time.

Jordyn nodded. "Yes, I've done lots of swim lessons, but I've never been on a swim team."

With Jordyn sandwiched between them, Hannah asked, "How about flip turns and diving off the block? Are you comfortable with those things?"

They arrived in front of the group of swimmers gathered to stretch.

"I can do flip turns," said Jordyn. "And I'm getting better at diving off the block."

"No problem." Caleb made some notes on his clipboard about Jordyn. "I'm sure we'll get you caught up in no time, and we have private sessions too."

Caleb found the swim captains and asked them to get the group started on the stretches. Jordyn joined in. Hannah shuffled around the back of the circle, checking on each swimmer. Caleb took the roll. Once the stretches were completed, Caleb announced it was time to jump into the water. The swimmers scattered to their assigned lane. Jordyn didn't move, but instead timidly froze in place as the others jumped into their lanes.

"Come on Jordyn, you're with me." He motioned toward Hannah and continued, "Hannah works with our youngest swimmers."

With a bounce in her step, Jordyn smiled, "Ok, sounds good."

"Good luck," said Hannah encouragingly. Then she mouthed to Caleb, "Thank you."

Caleb smiled, finding himself overly pleased to be helping Hannah in a small way. Hannah went to her end of the pool. Caleb moved in the opposite direction. The swimmers waited in his three lanes for his instructions.

He stopped in front of the lanes. "Listen up, we have a new swimmer." He motioned his clipboard toward Jordyn. "This is Jordyn."

Jordyn gave a wave then added with a smile, "I'm Hannah's stepsister."

"Really?" asked one swimmer.

Nodding, Jordyn said, "Yep."

Another swimmer said, "You're lucky. Hannah is so nice."

"Okay," said Caleb ending the chatter among the swimmers. "Jordyn, join this lane." He motioned to the middle of the three lanes. If he found Jordyn was better than he expected, Caleb could move her up a lane at the next practice.

Jordyn jumped into the water, joining the other swimmers in the lane. Then she popped her head out of the water and tugged her goggles over her eyes. Caleb instructed them to start doing hundreds of each stroke. The first set of swimmers pushed off the wall. Seconds later, the next group of swimmers began, then the next. Eventually, every swimmer was swimming, including Jordyn. Caleb studied her for a while. Her strokes were good, and she kept up with the other swimmers her age. She'd be a terrific addition to the team.

His gaze trailed to Hannah like it always did during practices. He regretted his rash choice to end things. If Hannah didn't have a place to stay then she'd probably leave, for good. The thought made his throat grow tight. Hannah leaving? No, that wasn't going to work. After practice, he'd find a solution to help her stay. Among Jenna's many friends, he knew at least one of them might need a house sitter for the week or have a room to rent out.

Practice ended. Jordyn left with the rest of the swimmers. Soon, it was only Caleb and Hannah at the pool. They worked together in silence to get everything put away. Then Hannah proceeded toward the lounge without so much as a word.

"Hannah, wait up!" Caleb jogged to catch up with her.

Halting in place, Hannah twisted to face him.

"Jordyn did great today," said Caleb as he stopped next to her. "I think she's going to fit right in, and I want to add her to the relay races too."

Hannah smiled for the first time since practice started. "I'm happy to hear it. Thanks for being so understanding about her joining."

For a second, they stared back at one another. "So, what's this about you needing a place to stay?" Caleb readjusted his baseball cap.

Her chest heaved. "Jordyn's grandparents are in town. Trisha has made it clear I'm not wanted in her house." Hannah peered away toward the empty pool. "I said I would leave for the weekend, but I have no plans on going back. I can't go back, but I don't have anywhere to go either. I called a few places listed on a rental website, but I haven't heard yet." She shuffled her feet. Sadness and defeat stared back at him.

"Ok." Caleb placed a hand at his waist. "Where are you going to stay tonight?"

Hannah shrugged. "I was going to head to the lounge and book a hotel on my phone for the night."

Gosh, the woman looked like she needed a hug. He almost moved to give her one but forced himself to remain in place. His gesture would be unwanted.

"Why don't you come over for dinner?" offered Caleb. "Mom will be there. I think she might be able to help you find a place to stay amongst her friends. We'll both work together to help you figure it out."

Hannah shook her head. "I can't let you do that." She folded her arms around her middle.

"Please let me help you." Caleb stepped closer. He lightly gripped her elbow. "I want to."

Hannah hesitated.

Caleb dropped his hand, freeing his phone from his pocket. "I'm texting Mom." He tapped on the text thread with his mom. "And you know she won't take no for an answer." He shot the text, putting his phone back into his pocket.

A single tear ran down the side of her face. Hannah nodded, swiping the tear away with her pointer finger. "Okay," she whispered.

Hannah appeared so defeated; Caleb could no longer resist the urge to comfort her. Caleb wrapped an arm around her shoulders. "Do you remember the address to my house?"

Hannah nodded and blinked her tears away. "I do." She sniffled then straightened her back and squared her shoulders.

"Great." Caleb squeezed her shoulders once before dropping his arm. "Once you're ready, just head on over. I'll go straight there."

"Thanks." Hannah shot him a crooked smile. "I appreciate it."

Caleb nodded. Hannah disappeared into the lounge. He double checked with the pool manager to make sure he hadn't forgotten any items to attend to. With his tasks completed, he left the pool area toward the exit, finding Alyssa stationed behind the check-in desk. His neck tightened.

"See you tomorrow, Alyssa."

Caleb briskly walked to exit through the gate. He hoped Alyssa would take the hint.

"Hey, wait up," she called.

Inwardly, Caleb groaned. Alyssa tended to get a little handsy when she spoke to him. He hated it. Reluctantly, he swiveled on his heels.

With a raised eyebrow, he forced himself to keep his voice level when he replied, "Yeah?"

Alyssa ducked around the desk, jogging toward him. "Did you give any thought to that concert I mentioned?" She landed a foot from him. Caleb stumbled a step back to get out of her sphere of influence. "I need to buy the tickets this week, and so far, I have three other lifeguards who are going to come too."

"I don't know—" Caleb rubbed his jaw as he attempted to find a proper excuse. Anything that let Alyssa down gently but also helped her receive the message that he wasn't interested in her. As luck would have it, Hannah strolled by. Their eyes caught. "Hey," he motioned toward her, "Alyssa is arranging for a group of people to go to this summer concert next week. Do you want to come?"

Hannah halted. Her gaze skidded between Caleb and Alyssa. "Nah," she shuffled her feet. "I don't want to spend any extra money right now."

"That's understandable. I should skip it too, based on my lack of finances." Caleb turned back to Alyssa. "Sorry, count me out. It sounds fun, but I need to save up money, too."

"Ahh," choked Alyssa. "Are you sure? It's going to be fun."

"I'm sure. Thanks anyways."

Hannah slipped through the gate without further interaction.

Caleb bade Alyssa goodbye and ran to catch up with Hannah.

Once beside her, Caleb pointed toward her rental car. "Any word on when you'll get your car back?" They strolled to their respective vehicles.

Hannah adjusted her purse strap. "Next week, which is good, because if I need to head out of town earlier than expected, I don't want to have to come back to pick up my car. How about you? Any update?"

"I get mine back tomorrow." Caleb used his thumb to point toward his rental car. "But, I've grown rather fond of my rental. My car is going to feel like I'm driving around a piece of junk."

"I know the feeling." Hannah crinkled her nose and continued, "Mine has a working AC, a luxury I haven't enjoyed in a long time."

Caleb felt his lips twitch into an unfightable smile. Dang, Hannah was cute. Her hair glistened under the rays of the sun, and Caleb allowed himself to admire her beauty for a smidge of a second. He missed her, even though he saw her every day, he missed *this*. Why had he panicked and pushed her away? He wished he could work to repair what they had started.

Bam, and there it was again, *hope*. Something he hadn't had since the night he kissed her.

"I hear you." Caleb tugged his keys free from his pocket. Hannah's car was parked two spots down. "My first order of business when I start making enough money is to buy a new car. It won't be until after my residency, so maybe in four years, I'll finally enjoy the luxuries of windows that roll down, seats that aren't stained, and AC that works."

Hannah lingered, halfway between his car and hers. "Do you even need a car in Boston? I thought it was a city where you can take the subway everywhere."

"True." Caleb fidgeted with his keys, finding the correct one. "Mainly, I'm keeping it to drive home for holidays, since I won't have the money to fly. My apartment has an underground parking space included with the rent."

"I see. I'm sure that's very sought after in Boston. I've heard the parking is horrible. I had a college roommate from there. She told me in the winter after a snowstorm, people dug their cars out, then put a chair in the space to claim it when they weren't parked in it."

"For real?" Caleb questioned.

Hannah made an X motion over her heart. "True story."

Caleb shook his head and muttered, "I have so much to learn."

The conversation lulled, and Caleb stared back at her. A crackle of chemistry buzzed in the air. Caleb missed this. He missed her.

"So," Hannah twisted on her feet, "Should I'll follow you to your house?"

"Right." Caleb snapped back into gear, shaking his keys. "Yes, let's go."

Hannah ambled the few remaining feet to her car. Caleb climbed into his own and backed out of his space. He waited until he saw Hannah cued up behind him before he drove home.

CHAPTER 13

Hannah followed Caleb up to the front door of his house.

When they arrived, Caleb shifted to face her. "As a warning, the house is packed up." His hand hovered over the door handle. "There are boxes everywhere. Half of the furniture has been sold. Sorry for the mess." He rubbed his lips back and forth.

She remembered how those lips felt against her own. Geez, Hannah needed to get their kiss out of her head, but she found it impossible to shake.

"I don't care one bit." Hannah was thankful she had a place to spend the evening until she figured out where to stay for the night. "Are you getting close to putting it on the market?"

"It's getting listed this weekend." Caleb exhaled. "I'm moving everything in boxes into storage before then so the house will be show ready."

"Can I help with the moving?" asked Hannah. "I'm stronger than I look."

"Umm—you might be volunteering for more than you bargained for." Caleb's eyes twinkled back at her. "It's a ton of stuff. I have an old friend from high school coming over, but I'm sure it would be faster with one more person." He rubbed the back of his neck.

"Then count me in," said Hannah. "Besides, I'd *love* to meet someone who knew you in high school." She winked at him then gave his bicep a playful whack.

"Oh dear. I'm sure you would," muttered Caleb under his breath. He opened the front door and pushed it open, revealing a packed hallway lined with boxes. "Mom," Caleb continued into the house. "Hannah and I are here."

Jenna appeared at the end of the cluttered space with a dish towel in her hands. "Wonderful." She waved them in. "Come on back here." She pivoted on her feet, disappearing back into the kitchen.

"After you." Caleb scooted over enough for Hannah to enter and for him to close the door behind them. He tilted his head toward the kitchen. "Just follow the path of boxes."

"I think I can handle that."

Hannah weaved her way around the stacks of boxes as Caleb trailed behind her. He was close enough for her to smell a mixture of spicy shampoo and sunscreen. It drove her batty. They entered the kitchen. Jenna had pulled out various containers of food and spread them out of the counter.

With the fridge open, Jenna glanced over her shoulder at them. "Tonight is called eat whatever is left in the fridge night."

"Sounds fantastic." Hannah smiled, leaning against the high-top counter. "Thanks for having me last minute."

After Jenna selected a stray container of food, she bumped the fridge closed with her hip. Then she stretched to place the food on the counter. "We have left over Chinese food from two nights ago, some roast meat from yesterday that would be good on sandwiches." Jenna popped off the top of one plastic container, revealing some cut vegetables. She swiped a baby carrot and took a bite. "I even have chopped up veggies. So, there's your vegetable."

Caleb moved closer, examining the food. "What looks good to you?" He raised an eyebrow at Hannah.

"Oh," Hannah shrugged. "I'll have whatever the two of you don't want."

"Chinese food." Jenna collected the containers of Chinese food, walking them to the microwave. She placed them inside the microwave. "Let's start with this. It's the oldest thing that's still edible in the fridge." Jenna closed the microwave and punched in three minutes, hitting start. The microwave lit up, churning the food around in a circle. Munching on another carrot, Jenna continued, "Caleb texted me earlier from work, when he asked if you could come over for dinner. He says you need a new place to stay."

Hannah climbed onto the bar stool in front of the counter, taking a seat. "I do." She propped her elbow on the counter, cradling her chin. "Do you happen to know of anyone who would be willing to rent out a room to me for a month or so?" She tried her best to keep her voice light and upbeat.

"I've texted my friends." Jenna eyed the microwave, watching the countdown. "I'm waiting to hear back, but I'm sure between one of them, we can find you a place to stay."

"Thanks." Hannah ran her finger over the top of the quartz countertop. "I really appreciate it." Then Hannah's phone rang. Caleb tracked her as she dug it out of her purse. "It's Adam. I need to take this. Give me a second." She slid off her bar stool. "Can I take it out on the patio?" She gnawed the inside of her cheek so hard she tasted blood.

"Of course." Caleb walked to the sliding patio door and opened it. "Take as long as you need."

"Thanks." Hannah hit accept on her phone, placing the phone up to her ear. "Hello, Adam." She closed the door behind her.

Her pulse quickened. Whatever Adam had to say to her, she really didn't want an audience. Caleb left her alone for the dreaded conversation.

In the kitchen, the microwave dinged. Jenna opened the door and fetched out the container of Chinese food. Promptly, she plopped another one inside and pressed start. Caleb's gaze flickered to the outside patio. Hannah paced the small length back and forth. He commanded himself to stop staring, so he opened the fridge and swiped a Diet Coke. He flat palmed the door closed. Without consent, his attention shuffled back to the patio. Inwardly, he groaned, popped the top of his Diet Coke and took a long swig. The bubbly mixture coated the back of his throat.

"I feel sorry for Hannah." His mom opened a cupboard, revealing a small stack of plates. "I don't think she has much support in her life."

Everything else in the kitchen was packed up besides the essentials of plates, cups, and silverware. After the walk-through with the realtor, Caleb was hopeful about his mom being able to stay in Newport Beach. The realtor believed with the equity in the home, she could pay off the left-over debts and find a small one-bedroom condo in the area. It wouldn't be as close to the beach but would still be in Newport. This lifted his mom's spirits immensely and lowered Caleb's constant level of stress. His mom would be okay. And he'd be able to go to Boston guilt-free. Things were looking up, too bad he couldn't get Hannah out of his mind.

As he sat down on a bar stool, Caleb glanced over his shoulder again. Hannah had moved to the far corner of the patio and was using big arm gestures. The conversation didn't appear to be going well.

"I do too." Caleb took another sip of his soda and faced Jenna. "I don't want her to leave early this summer. The swim team still has four weeks left. Our four biggest meets of the season are coming up." The tension in his shoulders made his neck ache.

His mom folded her arms against herself. "Is that the only

reason you don't want her to leave early? You're worried about the swim team?"

Caleb set his soda on the counter. He swiped at the dripping condensation. "No." He hesitated.

Caleb never talked to his mom about the women he liked or dated. It became way too messy when things ended, but Hannah was different. She'd waltzed in and burrowed herself deep into his heart, he needed all the advice he could get. Even if it meant involving his mom.

Scratching his chin, Caleb continued, "You know I like her. But I messed that up too when I became scared. I'm going to end up alone, because I can't allow myself to take a risk. And going for Hannah is a risk, I mean look at her." He traced his gaze to the patio.

"Ahh." His mom plodded to the fridge, opening it. She obtained a water bottle and shut it with her hip. "You've never been one to do anything rash. As a child you were always cautious, which is probably why you and your dad never saw eye to eye. He was all risk. I was the cautious one. You take after me in that way. But sometimes, people like us must learn to stretch a little to get the things we want."

Caleb knew his mom was right. In every aspect of his life, he constantly weighed out the pros and cons, trying to make good sound decisions. It worked in medicine, if anything it made him better at what he did, but not in relationships. Rarely did Caleb allow himself to open to someone enough to get hurt. Then with Hannah—he backed away too.

"I know you're right." Caleb fiddled with the top of the soda can, moving the metal top back and forth until it broke off. He set it down on the counter. "Hannah would've been worth the risk."

The microwave dinged again then went dark. Jenna fished out the warmed-up container of food. "You still have time to fix it. I know Cindy has a little casita in her backyard." Opening one of the containers, she served herself some of the fried rice onto a plate. "That woman loves to spend. I'm sure she'd take the extra money since it's only for a month. Would you try again with Hannah if you knew you still had a month together? A lot can happen in a month. A month was all it took for me to fall in love with your dad."

"I don't know," Caleb ran a hand down the length of his face, "because nothing changes the fact, I'm leaving for Boston at the end of the summer."

His mom scooped up some fried rice with a fork and blew on it lightly before taking a bite. "There you go again, acting with your head and not your heart."

"Maybe. This is the only way I know how to be."

She waved her fork at him. "I don't believe that for one second. When you're in love, you can be someone entirely different."

"Who said anything about love?" Caleb mumbled.

Instead of a reply, she shot him a knowing look and took another bite of her fried rice.

CHAPTER 14

Hannah tasted blood as it seeped out of the side of her raw cheek. A knot between her shoulder blades made her neck ache. From her seat on the patio, she peered through the sliding door back into Jenna's kitchen. Caleb and Jenna sat chatting. This conversation needed to end. Adam didn't get it, nor would he ever.

"Adam, it's done. I'm not coming back." Hannah pinched the bridge of her nose, "I don't know what I had been thinking by coming to Newport Beach."

Radio silence. Hannah's shoulders slumped. This is where she wanted Adam to jump in and say he was glad she came, but nothing. The vast quiet made her feel so empty inside. Adam never cared for a relationship with her. This summer only proved what she already knew. Now, she could close the door on this chapter of her life. If she managed to do that, then the summer wasn't a total wash. In addition, meeting Caleb had been a fun distraction, even though it blew up in her face. She'd forever have that heart-stopping kiss tucked safely away in her memories.

"Umm." Adam paused. "I probably should've done a better job discussing you coming with Trisha."

Exasperated, Hannah asked, "You think?"

"I am sorry," said Adam. "But do you have someone where to stay tonight?"

His words made her gut grind against itself. Her jaw clenched. Skipping his question, Hannah said, "You and Trisha need to spend more time with Jordyn. She's lonely, and you two gallivant around Newport without a thought about your daughter spending every night by herself. That's right Adam, she's your daughter. You married someone with a kid. You don't get to only have Trisha. Jordyn was part of the deal."

Dang, Hannah was letting it all out. And it felt so good.

No response, more silence greeted her. Hannah feared Adam had hung up on her, but when she checked the connection, it was still good.

A fire raged in her, and Hannah pushed forward. "Jordyn is a good kid. You might have messed up with me, but you still have time to get things right with her. Please Adam, be a dad to her. She's desperate for a little love and attention."

Adam cleared his throat. "So, I'll see you at the swim meet on Friday."

Well, Friday was at least a start. "I guess so."

Then she ended the conversation without giving Adam a chance to say anything else. Once her racing heartbeat settled, Hannah stood and made her way back inside through the sliding glass door.

Jenna and Caleb stopped talking and peered over at her as she entered. Hannah must have looked like a train wreck, because Caleb's brow furrowed as his gaze slid down the length of her. Instinctively, Hannah ran a hand over the top of her hair to smooth it out. Slowly, Hannah crossed the room to the kitchen.

Caleb studied her. "Everything okay?"

Jenna fiddled with her fork. Hannah nodded slightly and

slumped into the empty bar stool next to Caleb. Every ounce of energy was zapped right out of her.

"Can I dish you up some of this warmed Chinese food?" Jenna asked as she set her fork down on her half-eaten plate of food.

"Sure." Hannah forced herself to smile. "Sounds perfect. Thank you."

Caleb tapped his shoulder against hers. "Things will get better." He ran one finger down the length of her arm and leaned in closer. "They always do." Caleb straightened his back. "And it's become my personal mission to make sure you're okay."

A tightness grew in her throat. "Thanks, I appreciate your help." Hannah glanced away as tears tickled the corners of her eyes.

Caleb scooted closer. His lips hovered an inch from her ear. "I'm sure glad you're here tonight. I've missed you." The words sent a tickle down her spine.

"Despite everything," Hannah found his gaze. Her lips curled into a smile. "I'm glad I'm here too."

For a second, it was only the two of them. Hannah forgot Jenna was even in the kitchen. A beep broke their stare. Jenna scuttled to the microwave, removing a plate of food. Caleb picked back up his fork, taking a bite of his orange chicken.

"Here, you go." Jenna placed the warmed plate of food in front of Hannah.

"Thanks." The intoxicating scent made her stomach rumble. Her previous woes drifted away for a minute, enough for her to appreciate the hospitality of Jenna and Caleb. "I'm starving."

Jenna leaned up against the counter on the other side of the bar. Caleb slid a Diet Coke toward her. They ate in contented silence.

While they finished eating, Jenna asked, "Do you think the Dolphins have a shot at winning the meet on Friday?"

Hannah took a sip of her Diet Coke. "I think they have a good chance." Hannah nudged Caleb. "What do you think?"

"I'm not sure." Caleb leaned back in his seat, cupping the back of his neck with his hands. "We didn't do so hot last week, but the kids sure had a fun time."

"Have the Dolphins beat Laguna Beach before?" Hannah asked.

"Yes, but they always go back and forth." Caleb shrugged. "I don't worry too much about it. If the kids are improving, learning to be on a team, and working together, the rest is icing on the cake."

Hannah admired how Caleb approached coaching. He preferred to help the swimmers develop confidence, trusting everything else would come too. Jenna tossed the leftover food into the trash. Caleb went to the sink and rinsed the plates and forks. Afterwards, he placed them in the dishwasher. Hannah checked her phone, wondering what her next move would be. It was getting late, and she needed to go before she overstayed her welcome.

As Jenna yanked the full trash bag out of the can, she said, "So, I haven't heard back from anyone of my friends yet. I'm sorry."

Hannah slipped out of her seat, pushing her phone into her back pocket. "No worries. Thank you for trying. I appreciate it." Her stomach lurched, but Hannah faked a confidence she didn't have. "And thanks for dinner." She moved to exit the kitchen. "I can let myself out."

"What?" Jenna dropped the full trash bag from her hands onto the grey tile floor. "Where do you think you're going?"

Hannah halted. "I'm going to get a hotel room for the night."

Jenna tsked. "I know how much they're paying you at the swim club." She raised a knowing eyebrow. "I can't let you waste your hard-earned money on a hotel room. You can stay here tonight if you don't mind sleeping on the couch."

Hannah hesitated. "I—I—" She shot a glance at Caleb, trying to gauge his reaction to Jenna's offer.

Caleb stepped closer to her. "Please stay here for the night."

His arm brushed against hers. "I'm sure by morning Jenna will have heard from one of her friends."

Hannah fiddled with the loosened wisps of her hair. "Are you sure you don't mind?"

"Not at all." Jenna picked back up the trash bag, shuffling toward the door leading to the garage. "Come Monday, that couch will be gone, so we need to put it to good use one more time." Jenna opened the door to the garage and disappeared.

"Do you think Jenna's telling the truth?" Hannah searched Caleb's face for an indication that the offer was sincere. "I didn't come over trying to beg for an offer to stay."

"I know you didn't, but accept Jenna's offer. It's only for the night." Caleb glanced at his watch then tapped the glass screen. "And it's late. I know you've been working all day. There's no need to have you rushing off trying to figure something out. I'll only worry. At least if you stay here, I can relax knowing you're safe. Please."

Hannah gnawed on the raw inside of her cheek. "Umm," she ran a hand over the top of her hair.

Caleb's face brightened. "Hey," He cupped her elbow with his hand. "You can consider it payment for the free labor you're offering me. Remember, you agreed to help me move Jenna's stuff into storage."

Well, when he phrased it like that, how could a girl refuse?

"Okay." Hannah's cheeks warmed. His hand on her elbow was making it hard for her to concentrate on anything else. Their kiss flitted through her mind. "I'll stay." She gulped. "Thank you."

Caleb grinned.

Jenna returned from the garage, trash free. "So, are you staying, right?"

Staring straight at her, Caleb moistened his lips and said, "She's staying."

"Hooray." Jenna clapped. Then she went next to her and

linked elbows with Hannah. "Now, what chick flick should we make Caleb watch?" Jenna flashed Caleb a toothy grin.

Caleb groaned. "Please no." He scratched his chin while shaking his head.

"Nonsense." Jenna rolled her eyes. "Come on." Tugging Hannah into the living room, Caleb meandered behind them. "I'm picking something Hannah and I will like." She swiped the remote off the side table, plopping herself down on the loveseat.

Hannah lowered herself onto one end of the sofa. Once in place, Caleb took the other end, leaving the middle cushion between them.

"I can't remember the last time I watched an entire movie." Hannah rested an elbow on her armrest. "So, I don't have any idea. What do you suggest, Jenna? Do you have a favorite chick flick?"

"Too many to count." Jenna pressed buttons on the remote, bringing up a streaming service with a ton of movie selections. She hit the romance category and started scrolling through the titles. "Let me see. Have you seen *While You Were Sleeping* or *Sleepless in Seattle*?" Jenna peeled her gaze from the TV to Hannah.

"Are those part of a series?" asked Hannah.

"Oh, sweet little one." Jenna tilted her head toward her. "They are not. I think a marathon watching party is in order."

"I'll probably fall asleep." As if on cue, Hannah yawned. After her yawn ended, she added, "I'm notorious for not lasting through a movie."

"As long as you don't snore too loudly." Caleb's eyes twinkled back at her. "I promise to not say anything if you drool."

"Hey," Hannah picked up a throw pillow and whacked Caleb's arm. "I don't snore."

Caleb jostled the pillow out of her hands, tossing it onto the floor. "I guess we're about to find out." He shot her a challenging stare.

"Shh," interrupted Jenna. She waved an exaggerated arm. "It's starting."

"Which one did you pick to watch first?" inquired Hannah, peering up at the TV.

Jenna rested an elbow on her armrest. *While You Were Sleeping.*

"Let's go." Hannah rubbed her hands together. "I'm ready."

"I'm flipping off the lights." Caleb stood, walking across the room to the light switch. "There is a huge glare across the TV." He hit the light switch, and the room instantly darkened.

Hannah's eyes slowly adjusted.

"Much better." Jenna stretched out her legs on the loveseat, grabbing a blanket off the armrest, she threw it over her legs. "Thanks." She turned up the volume even louder.

Then Caleb returned to the sofa, but this time he took the seat right next to Hannah. He leaned in close. "I hope you don't mind me sitting here." His breath tickled her neck. Warmth smoldered her insides. "I can see much better from this angle."

Hannah cleared her throat, and whispered back, "I don't mind."

The movie started. Hannah forced herself to not think about Caleb's body being so close to hers. Soon the movie captured her attention, and she found it funny and entertaining. Caleb was the one who fell asleep halfway through it. His head rested against Hannah's shoulder, and soon it ached from the weight. Without waking him, Hannah snatched a throw pillow and placed it on her lap and finagled Caleb's head to it.

Caleb responded by kicking up his feet onto the empty cushion, tucking them under his back side. Hannah couldn't resist his nearness. Soon, she ran a hand through his hair in a soothing continuous motion. He smelled delectable with a perfect combination of spice and musk. In a daze, Hannah watched the rest of the movie contentedly and found herself disappointed when the credits played across the screen. Even then, Caleb failed to wake up.

Jenna sat up, flinging the blanket off herself. "Are you ready for the next one?" she excitedly asked.

Hannah could tell that Jenna wanted her to say yes. "Absolutely." Hannah grinned though her eyes stung from lack of sleep and an extra-long day. She pointed down at Caleb sound asleep. "Though Caleb might use this time to nap more."

Their voices awakened Caleb, making him stir. Shifting around, he stretched his arms high above his head, nearly knocking her in the jaw. Hannah removed her hands from him.

Swinging his legs in front of himself, Caleb sat up. "What did I miss?" he asked through sleepy eyes.

"Only the best chick flick ever." Jenna stood. "No worries *Sleepless in Seattle* is up next and is a classic too. You'll love it. I'm going to go pop some popcorn."

Caleb gripped the sofa on both sides of himself. "How long was I out?" He tilted his head toward her.

His cheeks had long red sleeping creases across them, making him look one hundred percent adorable. The familiar pitter patter of her heartrate increased.

Hannah yawned, stretching her arms herself. "Maybe an hour."

"I thought it was only like fifteen minutes." His eyes crinkled around the edges as they slowly adjusted to the dim lighting.

"Nah, it was long." Hannah teasingly shoved his shoulder. "My legs fell asleep from you resting your big head on my lap."

Caleb seized the throw pillow, tossing it at her. Hannah moved in time to block the blow with both her hands.

Hannah faked a hand injury. "Hey, what was that for?"

Caleb leaned in his closer. "That was for making me self-conscious about my big head." His breath tickled her neck. A tantalizing zing swooped down her spine.

Hannah tipped her chin. "Maybe you do have a big head, and I'm not referring to it physically."

"But," Caleb ran a hand down the side of her arm, leaving a long trail of goosebumps. "I know you still love me and my big head." Their gaze locked. His nearness made her mind run rampant with possibilities, possibilities of them, together, kissing.

Was he going to kiss her? A ridiculous notion. There would be no kissing with Jenna's expected return any moment. Besides, when they'd kissed the first time, everything had hit the fan, making Caleb bolt faster than a racehorse. Kissing? Was. Out. Of. The. Question.

Still, Hannah couldn't shake how much she desired it. Nor could she fight how much she hoped they could stumble their way back to each other. Being this close to Caleb was perfectly intoxicating, like a steroid that made you stronger and braver than you ever thought possible.

"Ahh," Hannah brought her hand to his face, cradling his chin. "You wish." She flashed him her most wicked smile.

"I do wish," he said slowly and deliberately.

Zap.

Zing.

Was it hot in here or was it just her?

Somebody needed to crank up the AC.

Please.

Perspiration pooled at her back. With her hand still cupped around his chin, her palm sizzled from the touch of his skin. Heat crawled its way up from her neck and splashed across her cheeks. Luckily, the room remained dark. Only the glow of the TV provided light. Ever so slightly, his gaze flickered between her lips and her eyes. This was happening, and she had zero plans to stop it. Caleb moved his face closer to hers. Without hesitation, Hannah slid her hand from his chin to his neck. Seconds passed or maybe it was minutes. *Kiss me already.*

Then boom, the lights flipped on.

Jenna barreled into the room.

Hannah flinched, quickly pulling her hand away from Caleb. Caleb jumped a half foot, scooting his body back onto his seat cushion. With popcorn in hand, Jenna returned to her spot on the loveseat.

As she shoved a handful of popcorn into her mouth, Jenna said, "If you want some, you need to go pop it yourself. There is a box on the shelf closest to the microwave." She munched on her mouthful of popcorn.

Caleb scratched his chin. His cheeks were branded red. Guess it wasn't all one sided. The realization gave her heart a smidge of hope.

"I think I'll go pop some." Caleb scooted forward on his cushion, motioning to her. "Do you want some too?"

With trembling hands, Hannah gathered her hair up and tossed it over her left shoulder. "Sure." Her voice shook. She cleared her throat and hoped it sounded stronger when she said, "I'll take some."

"I'll be back." Caleb stood and left for the kitchen. "Feel free to start that thing without me."

Jenna cued the TV for the next movie. As she pressed play, Jenna asked, "Hannah, can you flip back off the light?" The opening credits sprawled across the screen. "There's a glare."

"Yep." Hannah jumped up and flicked off the lights. Instantly the room darkened, and the soft glow of the TV filled the room. Hannah sat back down, tucking her legs underneath her. "What's this movie called again?" Hannah whispered loudly.

"*Sleepless in Seattle.*" Jenna picked up the remote again, turning up the volume. She set it on the cushion next to her and spoke loudly over the sound. "Tom Hanks and Meg Ryan. So, you know it's going to be good with those two together."

Romcoms to Jenna were serious business. Hannah propped her elbow up on the armrest, cradling her chin. A few minutes later, Caleb came back with a big bowl of popcorn in one hand

and two Diet Cokes in the other. When he stopped in front of her, he held one can out to her. Hannah took it from him. Caleb lowered himself next to her.

He placed the bowl between them, balancing it in the place between their thighs. Caleb whispered, "Sorry, we have extremely limited bowls. Everything is packed up. I hope you don't mind sharing." He set his Diet Coke down on the ground near his feet.

"I don't mind."

After Hannah took a swig of her soda, she set it on the side table next to her. Then she dove her hand into the bowl, snagging a handful of popcorn. From her side eye, she caught Caleb studying her. It made her hand tremble as she tossed the popcorn into her mouth. The music from the TV blared, and Hannah forced herself to concentrate.

Every so often their hands grazed while they dug into the bowl for more popcorn. Jenna fell asleep halfway through the movie. Her light snoring competed against the sound of the TV. Hannah didn't register any of it, not with Caleb's thigh resting against hers. Heat ignited her skin while her nerve endings tingled.

After an extra loud snore from Jenna, Caleb asked, "Do you think we should call it a night?"

The glow of the TV outlined the strong features of Caleb's chin. To settle the pounding of her temples, Hannah took a sip of her soda.

With a shrug, Hannah replied, "It's up to you." She set her soda back down. "I mean, I know how much you like your romcoms. I wouldn't want you to have to miss the ending."

Caleb grinned then rubbed a thumb along the stubble on his jaw, placing the almost empty popcorn bowl on the sofa beside him. Shifting closer, he draped his arm along the back of the sofa. They weren't touching, but Hannah swore her skin sizzled from the simple possibility of his arm grazing her shoulder.

His eyes shone with the lights from the TV. "These all end the same way. So, we don't have to keep watching on my account."

Crossing her arms, Hannah jutted her chin. "And how do they end?" She raised a skeptical eyebrow.

Two inches down, his arm moved. *Praise be.* His fingers wrapped around her shoulder, giving it a squeeze. "Come on." Caleb shot her a pointed look.

Her lips twitched. "No, really. I'd love to hear a guy's perspective on how you think romcom movies end."

He paused, tipping his head closer to hers. He smelled like buttery popcorn, and she could only imagine how good he tasted. "Well, first off the guy has messed everything up."

"Naturally," Hannah interjected. "Go on. I'm listening."

"Then he realizes he's messed up, and he's going to lose her. So, he either runs or bikes or flies, you name it, but he has to do it in a hurry, or it doesn't count."

Hannah laughed. "I'm loving this. You may continue."

Caleb smoothed Hannah's hair down. The strands weaved through his fingertips until he pulled away. Goosebumps swooped down her spine. "He makes a huge romantic gesture by tracking her down before she moves, heads out of town, or changes jobs. The important part is he confesses to her before she moves or whatever that he is in love with her."

Their eyes caught. Hannah wondered if Caleb spoke about the romcom or about them.

Unconsciously, Hannah moistened her lips. "And what happens when he catches up with her and confesses his feelings?" Her pulse quickened.

His fingertips tightened around her shoulder. Flushed, a trickle of sweat traced the outline of her spine.

Caleb shifted even closer. "Then," his gaze roamed between her lips and eyes, "the woman confesses her mutual love for the guy, and they kiss."

"They kiss?" Throat dry, Hannah forced herself to swallow. "What about her moving or changing jobs?"

"Ahh," Caleb ran a finger along her jaw. "It's never addressed. They figure it out or at least nobody cares, because the couple is kissing," he smirked.

Hannah fidgeted with the hem of her shirt. "This sounds eerily familiar."

Caleb cupped her chin between his thumb and pointer finger. "It does, doesn't it?" His lips hovering inches from hers.

Crinkling her nose, Hannah asked, "So, maybe I'm living in a romcom right now?"

Caleb shrugged. "You can be if you want. It's up to you."

"Is the movie over?" Jenna abruptly sat up.

Hannah flinched. Caleb dropped his hand from her chin. Heat crawled up her chest and neck. Their moment or almost-kiss flitted away as quickly as it came, and Hannah snapped out of her love-sick haze.

Jenna rubbed her eyes. "How long have I been sleeping?"

"Um," Caleb scratched his head. "I'm not sure."

"Let's call it a night." Jenna patted the top of the sofa cushion, locating the remote. "We can finish it up tomorrow night." She turned off the TV.

Wiggling his way off the couch, Caleb took the popcorn bowl with him as he stood. "I'll go grab you some sheets and blanket for the sofa." He moved toward the kitchen, flipping back on the lights on his way out.

"Great," said Hannah with a shaky voice. "I appreciate it."

"Good night," said Jenna as she stood and exited the room.

As Hannah sat in the empty room waiting for Caleb to return, she tried to shake off the feeling of almost kissing Caleb again, and how much she wanted it to happen. Then she remembered why she was couch crashing. Another kiss? That wouldn't fix anything. It would only make things a thousand times worse.

CHAPTER 15

Lightly, Caleb knocked on his mom's bedroom door the next morning, waiting for a reply to come in. He hadn't slept a wink, not after his flirty encounter with Hannah on the sofa. If he paused for a moment, he could still feel her hands running through his hair while he faked sleeping. No doubt Caleb had been drifting off, he found romcoms boring and predictable, but the minute Hannah pushed her fingertips through his hair, he was wide awake. Every single sweep of her fingers he experienced down to his last cell. So he went on fake sleeping, enjoying every single minute of her hands on him.

"Come in. I'm up," bellowed his mom through the closed door. When Caleb pushed open the door, he found her tossing her pillows back onto her white duvet bedspread. She paused at his entrance. "What's up?" She took the last pillow from the ground then set it properly on the bed.

After he peeked out the door, Caleb decided to shut it behind him. "Any update from your friends on a room for Hannah?" He strode across the room.

His mom put a hand on her hip and tilted her head to the side. "Are you that anxious for her to leave? You two seemed to be getting nice and cozy on the sofa last night." She wagged a finger at him. Then swiped her phone off the bed stand, yanking the charging cord from it. She tapped a few things on her screen. Without looking up, she continued, "And don't you think for one second I didn't know what was going on."

"You were asleep during the second movie. We could hear you snoring," countered Caleb. Jenna tapped and scrolled without answering him. He took a step closer to her. "Anything?" He tried to peer at her text message thread she had pulled up.

Abruptly, his mom slid the phone into the pocket of her sweatpants. "Nada." She brushed past him, flipping on the light on her way to her attached bathroom. "But she can stay here again tonight." She turned to face him. "As long as you promise to behave."

Caleb sighed and rolled his eyes. "I'm going to pretend you aren't inferring what you just inferred."

With a nod, his mom went to her vanity. After she opened and closed a few drawers, Jenna removed a clean washcloth and face cleaner. "I like Hannah." Flipping on the faucet, Jenna wet her washcloth then squeezed face wash onto it. "I think you two could be really great together." She closed her eyes and scrubbed her face with the washcloth.

Inwardly, Caleb groaned then decided to feign indifference by leaning his back against the door frame of the bathroom. "Liking Hannah isn't the problem. The problem is she'll be gone soon, pretty much whenever she finds a permanent place to land, and I'm heading to Boston. I'm not into getting my heart broken."

With her eyes still closed, his mom flipped back on the faucet, rinsing her face off. Once clean, she turned the faucet off and snagged a towel from the towel rack. "It's too late for that. You already like her." When she finished wiping her face dry, she opened her eyes and stared back at Caleb. "I say have a little fun, see where it goes for as long as you have."

"This is coming from a lady who categorizes her canned food by expiration date?" Caleb jested.

"Hey," Jenna tossed the wet towel into the laundry basket. "Watch it."

Caleb held up his hands in defeat. "I'll let Hannah know she can stay here tonight too. We have the swim meet today. We'd better get going."

"Are you still moving all of my packed-up things into storage this weekend?" she asked as she opened a drawer, tugging out her makeup bag.

"Yep." Caleb scratched his head. "Damien is helping. Hannah offered her services too. I imagine it'll take the better part of the day."

"I appreciate it." She unzipped the top of her makeup bag, removing her face lotion. After she removed the cap and squirted some onto her hands, she continued, "I'm ready to have this chapter behind me. I think moving is going to be the best thing for me. This home has too many memories. Your dad is lurking at every corner. I need a fresh start." She patted the lotion onto her face.

Caleb bit his tongue to prevent himself from bashing his dad. His mom was always optimistic, and it didn't surprise him she found the silver lining in a very difficult situation. Even after finding out how much debt his dad had left behind, his mom remarked he must have had a good reason to keep it from her. It wasn't the way he'd want his relationship to be. He'd hope for a marriage built on mutual trust and honesty.

"I understand. Let's hope the house sells for what the realtor mentioned." Caleb pivoted to leave. "If it does, then you'll be fine to purchase a condo in Newport. See you tonight."

"Bye," his mom said.

After he exited her room, Caleb went downstairs and quietly peeked into the living room. The blankets and sheets were carefully folded into a tight pile and placed on the armrest.

"Hannah," Caleb called. "Are you around here somewhere?" He paced the downstairs rooms.

When he spotted her small suitcase in the corner, Caleb knew she hadn't left permanently. He blew out a ragged breath he didn't know he held in.

The front door creaked open and closed. A few seconds later, Hannah entered with a box of donuts in her hands. "Good morning." She greeted him brightly. "I walked to the donut shop and bought some for everyone." Flipping open the box, Hannah asked, "Would you like one?"

Hannah's hair was still wet, and she had on her swim team polo shirt and shorts. He resisted the urge to kiss her right then and there.

"Um," Caleb stepped closer, close enough he was hit with a mixture of sugar and citrus scented shampoo. His head spun. As he eyed the box of donuts, he spotted a chocolate glazed and plucked it out. "Thanks. This was certainly nice of you." He took a big bite and chewed.

Hannah sauntered further into the kitchen, setting the box down on the counter. "It's the least I could do after Jenna allowed me to stay here for the night." With a twist, she faced him and leaned her back against the counter. "So," her voice grew serious, "I saw the email that Riley and Zach can swim today. They are two of our top swimmers. I'm glad their plans changed. Do you think that increases our chances of winning?"

After he finished his next bite of donut, he replied, "It will help. Considering there are four teams competing today, I think we at least have a good chance of not coming in last."

"Ahh," Hannah laughed. She snatched a chocolate sprinkle donut for herself. "That's not exactly a glowing measure of confidence in the team."

Caleb shrugged, taking another bite. "The kids have an enjoyable time. By the end of the summer, they will have improved a tremendous amount. That's what matters to me, and quite frankly to the parents too. If they were cutthroat, they would've signed their swimmers up for one of the year-round swim teams."

Hannah tasted a bite of her donut. Sugar flakes clung to Hannah's bottom lip, and she swiped at them with her tongue. Caleb stared on, mesmerized by her casual demeanor. How did a person make eating a donut look so ... sexy? With her donut an inch from her lips, their eyes locked. He was caught red handed. Caleb darted his gaze away and rubbed the back of his neck.

"I like your coaching style." Hannah took another bite. Then once she chewed and swallowed, she continued, "You're firm but fair, tough but compassionate. I believe the swimmers on the team respect you."

His ears perked up, pleasing Hannah and receiving compliments from her was his new favorite thing. "But it doesn't mean you have a winning team, and for some winning is all that matters." With his donut finished, he snagged a paper towel from the roll on the counter to wipe his face.

"True." Hannah licked her lips again and polished off the rest of her donut. "Though you help build the confidence in the swimmers you coach, and that is priceless."

Jenna arrived in the kitchen. "Good morning," she announced cheerfully. Her gaze landed on the open box of donuts. "Yum. Donuts." After picking out a glazed one, her gaze traveled between them. "Thanks. Who bought these?"

Caleb nudged Hannah with his shoulder. "Hannah did."

"Thanks." Jenna licked some glaze from her finger. "How thoughtful of you."

Red splashed Hannah's cheeks, and she tucked her damp hair behind one ear. "Thanks for letting me stay here last night." Shoving a hand into her back pocket, Hannah inquired, "Did you happen to hear back from any of your friends about renting me a room for the month?"

"No, sorry." Jenna took another bite of her donut. "But you

can stay here tonight. Caleb told me you're helping him, and Damien move my things into storage."

"I am helping." Hannah gnawed on her bottom lip and fidgeted with the hem of her polo shirt. "Are you positive it's okay to stay another night?"

"Absolutely." Jenna set her half-eaten donut on the open lid of the donut box. She puttered into the kitchen then opened the cabinet and removed a glass. She set it on the counter then opened the fridge and peered inside. "Besides, we need to finish *Sleepless in Seattle.* If you leave now, there's zero chance Caleb will watch the rest of it with me. I'm not nearly as cute as you." The fridge was nearly bare, especially only after their leftovers raid last night. She selected the orange juice, shutting the fridge door with her hip.

"Hey, I live to watch romcoms," Caleb teased.

His mom shot him a look over her shoulder as she twisted off the top of the carton and filled her glass. "He's lying," she wagged a finger at Caleb, "don't believe these lies for one second."

Hannah laughed. "You mean to tell me this guy," Hannah gestured with her thumb at Caleb, "doesn't watch romcoms with you in his free time?"

"Unfortunately, no." She flat palmed the kitchen counter with both her hands. "You're special though Hannah, when you're here he'll mysteriously put up with them. For that reason alone, I'm holding you hostage until I finish it."

"I'm happy to help." Hannah bumped her hip against Caleb's. "I'll make sure we watch it tonight."

Caleb cleared his throat. "Do you want to ride to the swim club together?" He checked his watch. "We probably need to get there in an hour or so to get everything set up for the meet."

"Sure. I'm just going to send out a few more applications before we leave, though." Hannah moved toward the living room sofa. Caleb spotted a backpack leaning up against the side of it.

"I've everything ready to go, so just tell me when you want to head out." Hannah removed the hairband from around her wrist, gathered her hair up and secured it into a ponytail.

"Where are you applying?" Jenna tossed the empty orange juice carton into the trash can. "Do any happen to be in Boston?" She found Caleb's gaze and winked.

Inwardly, Caleb cringed and hoped Hannah didn't see the exchange. Luckily, when he swung his gaze over to Hannah, she wasn't looking but instead had settled onto the sofa with her laptop.

Hannah opened the top of her laptop, wiggling her finger across the touch pad. "I'm applying all over." Her screen lit up, illuminating her face. "Mainly on the east coast, it seems like the jobs there pay a bit better, especially the ones in bigger cities."

"Like Boston," his mom chirped.

There she went again.

"Like Boston." Hannah typed rapidly on her keyboard. Without looking over, she added, "But also New York, Chicago, and DC."

Caleb shot his mom a *cool it* look.

His mom pushed up her chin and brushed past him. "I'll see you both tonight for the conclusion of our viewing party. I hope the swim meet goes well."

"Thanks." Hannah glanced up from her laptop and added, "I'm looking forward to finishing our movie together."

Once his mom exited, Caleb scratched his chin. Hannah appeared enthralled by her job applications. "I guess," Caleb took a step toward the garage, "I'm going to do a bit of organizing in the garage. I'll be back in an hour."

Without looking up from her laptop, Hannah replied, "Sounds good."

Caleb forced himself to leave, to quit staring with admiring eyes at Hannah. Not dating had been his idea, and he fully regretted it. Once he made it to the garage, Caleb went to work, trying his absolute best to not think about Hannah comfy and cozy on his sofa.

CHAPTER 16

Instinctively, Hannah's back stiffened the minute she proceeded through the pool gate. Her body knew. A split second later her gaze landed on Trisha, Adam, and Jordyn on the far corner of the pool. Her stomach lurched. Though she tried to prepare herself before arriving, but nothing made the sting of rejection quite as fresh as seeing them in the flesh. Hannah hesitated, slowing her pace to a dragged-out crawl.

Then out of nowhere, Caleb was by her side. "You, okay?" His gaze searched her face. "I'm sorry I ran ahead to unlock the pool supply closet. The pool manager left a to-do list for me. It left you bringing up the rear." He shifted his weight, throwing a fast glance at her family in the corner. "I won't let it happen again."

For an odd reason, tears tickled the corners of her eyes. "It's not that," said Hannah, making her voice trail off. Adam hadn't attended one of her sports events ever. Old wounds ripped at the seams. Hannah hated how seeing them here made her a mixed-up jumbled mess. "Adam's here." She tilted her head in their direction. "He never came to one thing for me. I did rail into him last night and tell him he needed to step up and be a better dad to Jordyn than he was to me."

Caleb cupped Hannah's elbow. "It looks like he listened."

"Apparently." Hannah blinked back at the tears and pushed away the emotion. "I guess I should be happy about that." She peeled her eyes away from them and pivoted to face him. "What do you need me to do to get the pool and team ready?"

"Um." Caleb stared at her for a moment then continued, "Let's hook up the lane lines. Then we can start taking roll and figure out who's here."

Jordyn spotted Hannah and waved enthusiastically at her.

"On it," replied Hannah, her mind elsewhere.

Hannah forced herself to wave back at Jordyn. Adam and Trisha tracked Jordyn's wave. Neither waved their hands in acknowledgement. Even from way across the pool, she picked up on how Adam's posture changed from relaxed to rigid. Trisha primly smoothed down her hair as her lips tightened into a straight line.

"And Hannah," Caleb leaned in and said, "Just let me know if you need back up."

Startled, Hannah questioned, "What?"

Caleb nodded toward where her family sat. "If things are getting too hot to handle, just give me the code word or gesture and I'll come to your aid."

"I'll be fine." Hannah blew out a shaky breath. "Let's get to work. I plan on ignoring Adam and Trisha during the swim meet."

Caleb tipped up his baseball cap, rubbing his hands together. "Still, we need a code word." His eyes were full of mischievousness like the two of them were co-conspirators in some major coup.

"A code word?" Hannah shook her head. "Nah, I'll be fine."

"Okay, have it your way," said Caleb, his voice clearly trying to hide some level of disappointment.

She hated seeing Caleb disappointed, he only wanted to help.

"Burritos." Hannah's lips twitched. "That's the code word. When I want out, I'll say I'm ready to go eat a burrito."

"Alright," said Caleb. "I can work with that."

Hannah shifted, staring out at the clear water of the pool. "What end of the pool should I take?"

"This one." Caleb pointed to the one closest to them and furthest away from where her family lingered. "I can take the other end."

"Thanks."

Hannah made her way over to the big storage reel. Caleb went to the opposite end. Hannah tugged the first line free from it and sidestepped toward the pool. Once in the proper place, Hannah then bent down and hooked it in. The sun peeked out from the clouds, pushing away the morning dew. A trickle of sweat ran down her temple, reminding her of how hot she was going to be in an hour. Ryker, one of her swimmers, passed by with his parents.

"Ryker, can you help me out with the lane lines?" Hannah smiled and waved at his parents. "I need you to jump in and swim this end over to Coach Caleb."

"Me?" Ryker grinned, pointing at to his chest. "Do you think I'm old enough to help?"

"Yep," nodded Hannah. "You've become one of my best swimmers."

Without hesitation, Ryker jumped in feet first. A few seconds later he popped his head out of the water. Hannah tossed the end of the lane line to him. Once he had it in his hand, Ryker swam it down to Caleb on the other end. Caleb wasn't paying attention but was in deep conversation with Jordyn who had joined him.

Hannah cupped her mouth. "Caleb, can you grab the lane line from Ryker?"

Both Jordyn and Caleb stopped talking and shifted toward Ryker. Caleb gave a thumbs up. Then he crouched down, taking the lane line from Ryker. Quickly, Caleb fastened it into place.

Ryker swam back toward Hannah. Caleb sidestepped to the next lane ready for when Ryker returned with the next one. Jordyn left Caleb and headed around the pool toward Hannah. Hannah unwove the next lane line. When Ryker arrived at her end of the pool, Hannah handed him the line. Immediately, Ryker set off down the pool, swimming with the lane line trailing behind him.

Smiling, Jordyn arrived next to Hannah and said excitedly, "I'm so nervous. I hope I do well at the swim meet. Especially, because my mom and dad are here to cheer me on."

"I'm sure you'll do fantastic." Hannah tried her best to sound equally thrilled. She moved back to the lane line holder, yanking the next one free. She crouched down and hooked it into place. "Are your grandparents coming too?" asked Hannah, glancing up at Jordyn from her crouched position.

"Oh," Jordyn shook her head. "They didn't end up coming into town. Something came up at the last minute. But that's how they always are. They break plans at the last second." Jordyn glanced across the pool toward her parents. "I guess you didn't need to move out after all." She pursed her lips together.

The morning sun blinded her, and Hannah placed a hand above her eyes to see. "I'm sorry." Hannah's heart thawed a bit as compassion wiggled its way into her. Jordyn knew too much about people letting her down, too. Hannah wanted to help change that. "I bet that was disappointing for you to not see them."

Jordyn shrugged. "I little bit, but at the same time, I don't care. They tend to ignore me and spend their time going to parties with my parents. Them not coming meant my parents could come watch me today." Her lips curled fighting back a smile.

Ryker returned, taking the lane line from Hannah. Hannah stood. The sun further pushed out the clouds and sunshine cascaded down her back. Hannah still needed to apply sunscreen. She moved a few feet, swiping her baseball cap from behind the lifeguard station where she last stored it.

"I'm glad they are here to watch you too." Hannah placed the cap on her head, adjusting the bill until it felt comfortable.

"Um," Jordyn pointed in the direction of her parents who were now walking around the side of the pool directly toward them. "I think they are headed this way to say hello."

A brick landed in Hannah's stomach, and she tried her best to ignore it. "I need to grab my clipboard from the lounge with the list of the swimmers and racers." Quickly, Hannah swiveled in the opposite direction. "The swim meet starts in five minutes. You'd better go start stretching." Hannah gestured toward Caleb who was yelling for the team to gather.

"Oh, you're right." Jordyn took off at a brisk walk toward her parents. Over her shoulder, Jordyn added, "I'll tell them you can chat afterwards."

Hannah was grateful to not have to chat with them before the swim meet. Her mind was not in the right head space to be gracious. Some more swimmers trickled in through the gate, she knew she really did need her clipboard, so she went to fetch it from the lounge. As she pushed open the lounge door, it nearly whacked Alyssa in the face.

"Hey!" shrieked Alyssa, grasping the door an inch from her face with one hand. "Watch it."

"I'm sorry." Fresh heat splashed Hannah's cheeks. "I didn't mean—I'm in a bit of a hurry. I need to be out there for the start of the meet." She sidestepped and spotted her clipboard. After she snatched it off the table, Hannah turned to face a glaring Alyssa. "Sorry about that. I'll be more careful next time." She moved toward the exit. "But Caleb really needs my help."

Alyssa stood in the doorway, blocking the exit. Crossing her arms, Alyssa made an aggressive head nod. "What's up with you two anyways? Are you dating or is Caleb still free game?"

The clipboard dug into Hannah's hands as she tightened her grip around it. "Does it matter?" asked Hannah.

With narrowed eyes, Alyssa replied, "I guess not." Alyssa moved enough for Hannah to pass through the door.

A chill ran down Hannah's spine, but she chose to brush it aside. Alyssa liked Caleb, and Hannah didn't blame her. Caleb was a great guy. One of the best. Bottom line, Caleb could date whomever he wanted. Maybe it would be Alyssa. When Hannah made it back to the pool deck, the swimmers had completed their stretches. Caleb ambled over with an airhorn.

Hannah shook the clipboard she held. "Sorry." Then she pointed at it for good measure. "I had to grab this. Where do you want me?" The pool was crowded with parents and swimmers from the various teams.

"Why don't you take the airhorn? You can do the start line. I'll take the times at the other end with my parent volunteers." Caleb leaned in a tad. Hannah could feel his breath tickle her neck. His gaze found hers. "I figured you'd prefer that, seeing your family is hanging out at the other end of the pool."

"I appreciate it." Hannah handed Caleb the clipboard. He handed her the bull horn in return. "An interaction with them is the last thing I need right now."

For a second their eyes locked, and unflinchingly, Caleb said, "I'm buying you a burrito tonight." He winked. "It is our code word after all."

"As long as we make it home in time to watch the rest of that movie with Jenna. I think she's looking forward to it." The tension trapped in her chest loosened. "But burritos actually sound fantastic."

"I know they do." Caleb brushed his body against hers and leaned in close enough his woodsy scent filled her lungs. "And as for the movie, I wouldn't miss it. I mean your hands in my hair— let's just say I'm there."

Warmth crept up from her toes, pooling in her middle. Caleb hadn't been sleeping in her lap. A million scenarios of reconnecting ran rampantly through her mind.

With his gaze directly on her, Caleb blew his whistle. Then he cupped his hand and yelled, "Swimmers, time to line up." Quietly, Caleb whispered, "Until then." He stepped away.

Swimmers came from every direction, filling in the widening gap between Caleb and Hannah. Heat furthered smeared across her chest and neck. Hannah didn't have time to unpack the meaning, because the pool was abuzz. Instead, she went to her station, swiping the megaphone she needed, waiting for things to settle in the staging area.

First, Hannah announced for the first swimmers to get in place. Those in the first heat climbed onto the starting blocks. Every swim meet began their heats with the youngest swimmers then continued up to the older swimmers. Ryker climbed onto the starting block nearest Hannah.

Hannah gave Ryker a thumbs up then brought the megaphone to her mouth. "Swimmers, take your mark."

Hannah glanced across the pool to confirm Caleb was set to time. He gave her a nod. Raising her arm above her head, Hannah squeezed the blow horn. The young swimmers dove off the blocks, some weren't as smooth into the water as others, but it was okay. They were still young and learning. The whole point was for them to make progress. Ryker ended up winning the heat and came out of the water beaming.

Many heats of swimmers came and went. The summer sun blazed down. Hannah remembered once again that she had forgotten to put sunscreen on. When they took a short break between heats, Hannah ran to the lounge to snag a bottle of sunscreen. In a rush, Hannah liberally applied the lotion. Her face was already tinged pink, and Hannah knew by the evening her skin would be tingling with a sunburn.

Jordyn swam in several races, including one relay. To Adam and Trisha's credit, they did stay the entire meet which ran notoriously long. Sometimes they lasted for three to four hours due to the substantial number of swimmers and events. And today was no different. The last heat of swimmers climbed out of the pool. After Hannah set the airhorn and megaphone behind the lifeguard station, she went and joined Caleb who was next to the other team's coach tallying up the results to see what team won.

When the tallying was completed, Caleb swiftly pivoted around.

"So?" asked Hannah, bringing a hand to her hip. "Do we have something to celebrate?"

Caleb gave a quick nod confirming the win without revealing it to others loitering around. "Where is the megaphone?"

"Behind the lifeguard station, I'll grab it."

Hannah went and fetched the megaphone, handing it to Caleb. Their fingers brushed as he took it from her.

Caleb raised the megaphone to his mouth. "Listen up swimmers. I have the results." The previous light chatter stopped. Many of the swimmers moved closer to listen. "It was remarkably close this year. But the winner of today's meet is the Newport Dolphins, winning by four points."

A thunder of applause followed with a mix of groans from the opposing team. Caleb lowered his megaphone and gave Hannah a quick hug before they were bombarded with swimmers high fiving them. Caleb and Hannah were separated from one another in the mist of the celebration. Jordyn joined Hannah with Trisha and Adam in tow.

"Congrats." Hannah leaned in and gave Jordyn a quick hug. Jordyn was already dressed in her parka, ready to head home. "You did terrific. You should be proud of yourself."

Beaming, Jordyn clapped her hands together and said, "I am. I love being a part of this team. I wish I had joined last year."

"Ahh," Hannah brought a hand to her hip. "But I wasn't coaching last summer, and I'd like to believe I have something to do with you enjoying the team." She scrunched up her nose in a teasing expression.

Adam and Trisha stood stiffly in the wings. Hannah didn't know if Trisha appreciated her interest in Jordyn or not.

Jordyn replied, "You're right. I'm glad you're here too."

"Only a few more meets," said Hannah.

Adam interjected, wrapping an arm around Trisha. "You said there are only a few more meets." He shuffled closer. "When are they?"

"Next week is a bye week." Hannah forced herself to stand tall and meet Adam's gaze. She tried her best to keep her voice even and undeterred, even though speaking to Adam again rocked Hannah more than she cared to admit. A fresh sting of rejection slapped her, but she continued, "So in two weeks."

"When do you leave again?" asked Trisha, adjusting the bangles on her wrist.

"I'm not positive." Hannah scanned the pool area, hoping for a parent or swimmer who might need her help. "I'm applying for jobs all over. I will take my exam to be a Physician Assistant in two weeks. Hopefully, I'll have a job lined up by then. Once I find something, then I'll have a better idea of my departure date."

Nobody needed her attention, bummer. A long stretched out silence gathered in the space between them, making the gap widen with each passing second. This was where a parent might ask a follow up question but not Adam or Trisha.

Sweat gathered on her brow, and Hannah swiped at it with the back of her wrist. "I'm going to go find Caleb." She mustered up a smile for Jordyn then gave her arm a reassuring squeeze before she shuffled her feet. "You have a nice evening." Then she left in search of Caleb. The code word from earlier taunted the tip of her tongue.

After she spotted him, Hannah beelined it to him. Caleb was crouched down next to the pool, readjusting one of the lane lines. They were leaving the pool open for lap swimming, so they didn't have to roll the lines back up. Hannah arrived beside him, but before she talked to him she was interrupted.

"Hannah," said Adam from behind.

Her back stiffened. Hannah closed her eyes for a moment to gain her composure. Slowly, she pivoted to face him. "Adam."

"I wanted to speak to you for a moment," said Adam.

Caleb stood and wrapped a protective arm around her waist, tugging her gently to his side until they were hip to hip.

"Alone," said Adam. Then as if an afterthought, he added, "If you don't mind."

"I do mind." Hannah gave him a pointed look. "Besides, Caleb and I are headed out to get burritos. We haven't eaten all day and are hungry." Caleb wrapped a comforting arm around her shoulders. "So, I don't have time to talk."

Adam blinked. "Well then—" He shifted, glancing over his shoulder. Hannah looked in the direction too. Trisha and Jordyn were nowhere in sight. Hannah guessed they had gone to the car to wait for him. He faced her again and wrung his hands. "I want to apologize for everything. For inviting you to stay with us, not being there when you arrived, and then making you feel uncomfortable enough to leave." He exhaled, glancing down at his feet. "I'm bad at this parenting thing. I think some of us just aren't meant to be parents, and I'm one of them."

Hannah interjected. "It doesn't matter if you think you're cut out to be a parent or not. It's too late. You married Trisha knowing she was a widow and had a daughter. You signed up for that. Now, you may have gotten it entirely wrong with me, but you have a chance to make it right with her." She tilted her head and pleaded, "Please don't mess this up twice. Jordyn needs you. She needs Trisha. Adam, you have a shot to get this thing right with her. We might not have time, but you still have time with her. Please."

Adam cranked his neck back and forth. "I'm sorry I got it so wrong with you."

"I know," said Hannah, though it didn't change anything.

"I'm going to make more of an effort with Jordyn."

"Good," replied Hannah. "I'm happy to hear it."

"Can you come home?" Adam asked. "Trisha's parents didn't end up coming into town."

"No, that isn't my home." Hannah placed a hand over her chest. "I made the mistake of thinking I could rebuild something between us when we didn't even have a foundation to begin with. I'd like to get to know you Adam, but I won't be staying with you again."

Hannah's chest felt lighter. Like she was strong enough to only take what she deserved. A relationship with Adam would have to be repaired before it could be added to. It didn't mean it was impossible, but she wasn't going to be desperate enough to only take the crumbs thrown at her either.

With a nod, Adam said, "I understand. Maybe we could all go out to dinner sometime before you leave Newport, as a start." He shifted his gaze to Caleb. "You'd be welcome to come too, Caleb."

"Thanks. I appreciate the invitation," Caleb replied.

Hannah smiled. "I think dinner would be a great place to start."

Adam glanced at Caleb. "Take care of her, okay?"

"It would be my pleasure," Caleb said.

Then Adam said goodbye and left. Hannah exhaled once he was out of sight. The pool had completely emptied while they talked.

Caleb squeezed her shoulders. "I wasn't lying about the burritos." She leaned her head against his shoulder. "I'm starving."

"Me too." Caleb dropped his arm from her shoulders and interlaced his hand with hers. Then he led her toward the exit. "See, I knew our code word would come in handy."

Hannah laughed. "Touché."

CHAPTER 17

Horns honked. Caleb shuffled his foot from the brake pedal to the gas pedal as he passed through the light, entering the freeway. Hannah sat where she belonged, in the seat next to him.

"Where did you say this burrito place is?" Hannah peered out the passenger side window.

Caleb changed lanes, leaving the city of Newport Beach behind them. "It's only like ten more minutes." He flashed his gaze from her then back to his lane. "I promise it'll be worth it." As a second thought, he tugged his cell phone free from his side pocket, holding it out to Hannah. "Do you mind texting Jenna to see what type of burrito she wants?"

"Sure." Hannah took the cell phone from him and swiped at the screen. "It's locked."

"Hold it up to my face, and it'll unlock it."

He double checked his rear-view mirror as he increased his speed and changed lanes.

"Gotcha." Hannah held it out in front of him, but enough out of the way that it wouldn't be a distraction. The phone unlocked. She brought it back to her lap. His phone dinged. Then it dinged again. "You are getting text messages from Damien. What should I do?"

Caleb's stomach tightened. Earlier, he had been texting Damien about him coming tomorrow to help move his mom's things into storage. The last texts they exchanged were entirely about Hannah. He'd told Damien he had the hots for her. It wasn't anything Caleb was ashamed of, but Damien wasn't exactly known to mince words. More likely than not, Damien would text some idiotic message that could be interpreted the wrong way if Hannah saw it.

"Umm." Caleb flashed his gaze from the road to Hannah. "Ignore it. He's helping us with the move tomorrow. Damien is my old friend from high school."

Hannah didn't glance up or respond right away.

"Hannah?" Caleb asked. "Can you ignore it and find the text thread I have with Jenna?"

Hannah's cheeks grew red. "Sorry." Her fingers stumbled across the screen. "I'll text Jenna right now." She tapped again then glanced over at him. "What am I asking again?"

"What type of burrito does my mom want us to bring home for her." Caleb's back stiffened.

He only could imagine what Hannah read. Why did things like this always happen to him? Caleb took the next exit, barreling down it toward the light at the end of the off ramp.

"I'll ask her." Hannah hunched over the phone, and her fingers danced across the screen. Once done, she palmed the phone between her hands. "Okay, it's sent. What should I do with this?" Hannah held up the phone.

It dinged again. Then again. Both of their gazes landed on the screen. He swiped it from Hannah's hand, but he knew she saw Damien's text.

Send me a pic. ASAP

His pulse hammered in his ears.

The light turned green. He tossed the phone into the middle console. He could only imagine the text messages Damien had sent prior to that one. Once through the intersection, Caleb made a hard right into the parking lot of the little strip mall where the hole-in-the-wall Mexican place was located. After he parked, Caleb turned off the ignition.

Hannah unbuckled her seatbelt and shifted to face him.

Before Hannah said anything, Caleb blurted, "I have no excuse for Damien. He's an idiot. A helpful idiot willing to help me move my mom's stuff for free, but still an idiot. I apologize for anything he may or may not have texted. I don't even want to read what he wrote, because then I'll have to crawl into a cave and hide."

Hannah raised an eyebrow as her lips did the cute twitching thing. "Do you think we should humor him? Maybe send a photo?"

"How are you being chill about this?" Caleb rubbed the back of his neck before he picked up his cell phone. He tapped on the screen, illuminating it. His mom had responded that she wanted a carne asada burrito. "What did the guy say?" He scrolled through the text thread with Damien next, looking for any incriminating texts.

"Damien did say, my mind can't unknow this, that you said I was gorgeous and smart, a truly lethal combination." Playfully, Hannah shoved him. "How could I possibly be upset by that? Embarrassed, sure, but not upset."

Caleb lowered his phone. "I do stand by that." A string of crackling energy made his heart pound. He gulped at his candor and added, "If we send Damien a photo then he's going to believe we are together, together." Slowly, he unbuckled his seatbelt, waiting for Hannah's response.

"Exactly. This will be fun." Hannah swiped the phone out of his hand, tapping on the camera icon. Before he had time to process the consequences of the photo, Hannah held up the phone and leaned into his arm. "Smile." She paused for him to move a tad closer.

Caleb wrapped his arm around her shoulders, bringing her tighter against his body. Dang, she felt good pressed up against him. He'd forgotten how much. Hannah snapped the photo then toggled back to the image for them to examine.

"What do you think?" Hannah peered at the photo then held it up for his approval.

Caleb took the phone from her, staring at the image of them looking happy and perfectly content in each other's embrace. He couldn't remember the last time his smile really looked like a smile. A smile which touched his eyes. Hannah made him happy. Now he wondered why he had spent the entire summer denying what he always knew. They belonged together, end of story. Unfortunately, he had acted like a complete fool by pushing her away when he thought he'd get hurt. News flash, he hurt because he wanted her and nobody else.

Like a grinning fool, Caleb replied, "It's perfect. Let's send it. You'll meet him tomorrow." He texted the photo to Damien knowing the bazillion questions coming his way. "Let's grab the burritos to go." He opened his car door, pushing it open. Hannah mirrored his movements. "Then we can bring Jenna hers. We have no food in the house, and I know she's banking on us watching the rest of that movie with her."

They plodded across the parking lot to the hole-in-the-wall Mexican place. When they entered, they found it empty. After they placed their order, they sat at one of the four tables to wait for their food. Caleb's phone dinged and instinctively, he tugged it free from his pocket. Damien had simply texted a winking eye emoji and stated they looked good together.

Caught in a trance of gleeful happiness, Hannah interrupted his thoughts. "Did your friend Damien already text you back about our picture?" She tilted her head toward his phone, eyeing his cell phone.

"Um." Caleb shoved the phone back into his pocket. "He said we look good together." A fresh sprinkle of red splashed her cheeks, making her even more adorable. "I'm sure Damien will have lots of things to say about it tomorrow. Damien is one of my oldest friends. We did swimming and water polo together, and Damien has really been there for me since my dad's death."

"Then I can't wait to meet him." Hannah smiled but then her eyes glinted with mischievousness. "I'm ready to grill him for dirt about you as a teenager. Though I doubt there's much dirt, you strike me as someone who bypassed the terrible choices teenagers make and skated right into responsible adult."

With a shrug, Caleb replied, "Damien used to call me President, because I was always the levelheaded one in our friend group."

"I can see that." Hannah leaned forward, cradling her chin. "What about me? What do you think I was like in high school?"

Caleb studied her for a moment. "I think you were a good kid too." Hannah was everything that was right in the world, and he couldn't imagine she was vastly different as a teenager. "Because I think you are pure goodness now."

"Yikes." Hannah cringed. "I don't know if I can live up to that. I'm not pure goodness. I have so many flaws, and even more that I need to work on and change."

Caleb covered her hand with his own. "You're wrong. I think you believe in people. I think you give people the benefit of the doubt. Look at how many times you've tried to make things work with your family. You are generous and kind with your compliments. You opened your heart up to Jordyn, and she immediately changed her sour disposition toward you because she couldn't help but love you." He almost added he loved her too, but he kept the words from tumbling out.

"Jordyn's only a child." Hannah shook her head. "That's different. I still have hang ups with Adam and Trisha."

Instinctively, Caleb squeezed her hand. "But maybe someday you won't, because you're willing to give them a second chance."

"I think you've overestimated my ability to forgive," said Hannah.

"I don't think I have, because Hannah—" Caleb tried desperately to spit it out, to ask Hannah to forgive him and give him a second shot. Even if they had to do long distance, even if they were separated for long stretches of time, Caleb no longer cared, because a life without Hannah in it seemed unfathomable.

"Order's ready," announced the worker behind the counter. They both turned, glancing in the direction. The worker read the name on the receipt attached to the brown paper bag. "Caleb?"

"That's me." Reluctantly, Caleb slid out of his seat.

Their conversation ended. They took the food and drove back to his house. When they arrived, they found his mom in the living room with the movie cued up to where they'd left off the night before.

"Hey, you two." She removed the blanket from her lap and stood, walking toward them. "Thanks for getting me something for dinner. It smells delicious."

"No problem." Caleb set the brown paper bag with their burritos at the kitchen table. "Do you want to eat while we watch the movie or eat first then watch the movie?"

"Let's eat first."

They sat down at the table. Hannah took the seat next to Caleb and across from Jenna. Caleb tugged the burritos out of the bag, handing them each theirs. The tight foil wrapped around each one kept them toasty warm.

Jenna took a bite first then said, "Hannah, one of my friends needs a house and pet sitter for the next few weeks." She paused with her burrito midair. "She was going to take her dog to a place to board it, but if you are willing to watch the dog, she said you could stay at her house for free."

Excitedly, Hannah asked, "Are you serious?" She nearly

dropped her burrito but straightened it in time. She nodded. "That would be amazing." Hannah squeezed Jenna's shoulder. "Thank you. I really appreciate it. It'll give me enough time to take my exam and hopefully line up a job." She smiled brightly.

"No problem. I was happy to help." Jenna shifted toward Caleb. "Do you mind grabbing us something to drink?"

"Duh. I should've gotten drinks to begin with." Caleb slid out of his chair and went to the fridge to grab a few sodas.

When he glanced over his shoulder toward the kitchen table, his mom and Hannah's heads were touching. To him, it looked like his mom was doing all the talking. Caleb couldn't hear their conversation, but by the way they were huddled together he knew it was on purpose. Then Hannah nodded and straightened herself.

With sodas in hand, Caleb returned to the table, setting them on the table before sitting down again. As he scooted his chair in, Caleb asked, "What were you two whispering about?" He raised a skeptical eyebrow.

His mom smirked. Hannah's cheeks splashed with red, and she didn't meet his gaze.

"Nothing." Jenna straightened her shoulders. "We were only chatting."

"About what?" Caleb asked.

"Nothing you need to worry about." His mom gave a dismissive wave. "Now, tell me about the swim meet."

"Are you wanting the highlight reel?" Hannah doused her burrito with salsa. "Or the lengthy explanation?"

"Lengthy," she snapped and said, "Go. I've been holed up in this house packing all day."

Hannah exhaled, wiping her face with her napkin. "Well, my dad, Trisha, and Jordyn were there."

"Um," Jenna paused, waiting for Hannah to give more details. "That was probably a bit awkward."

"You have no idea," Hannah said.

Hannah then continued to retell the entire exchange. Caleb sat back and listened, wondering if these type of conversations between his mom and Hannah would become a regular thing. The thought struck him that he wanted Hannah to be a part of his life. She fit it so well. The big question now was, how did he bridge the gap between friends and something more?

CHAPTER 18

When Hannah arrived at Caleb's, a truck was already backed in and facing the retracted garage door. As she trudged up the driveway, she spotted Caleb with who she assumed was Damien, in the corner of the garage with boxes in their arms.

"Good morning," she announced as she came near them.

A smile slid across Caleb's face, warming her to the core. Even though Hannah was beyond exhausted from studying late into the night at Jenna's friend's house, she wouldn't miss another opportunity to spend the entire day with Caleb.

"Hi, Hannah." Caleb threw a head nod toward the other guy. "This is my friend Damien."

"Hello," smiled Hannah. "It's nice to officially meet you, Damien."

Damien's gaze slid down Hannah's frame. He laughed to himself then shook his head, weaving around the piles of stuff toward the back of the truck. "No wonder I haven't heard from this guy all summer." He loaded up the cardboard box into the back of the truck. Caleb came to the truck and slid his box into the back. Playfully, Damien shoved Caleb. "Hannah, you're way better to look at than me."

Heat splashed her cheeks, and Hannah fidgeted with her hair before shoving it behind her ear.

"Stop flirting with Hannah." Caleb readjusted his baseball cap and shot Damien a pointed look. "We need to get this stuff loaded up. Let's start with these boxes." Caleb pointed at a tall stack of boxes, retrieving one.

Damien selected a box after Caleb moved out of the way. Hannah came up behind them, selecting a box herself. Soon, they roamed back and forth in tandem loading things into the back of the truck until it was full to the brim. Caleb closed the truck hatch.

"I think this will take us a few trips." Caleb swiped at his brow with the back of his wrist. "Mom has so much stuff."

Damien rested his forearms on the back of the truck hatch. "Do you think she will even have enough space to move this into her new place?"

"There's zero chance." Caleb readjusted his baseball cap. "Most likely she'll only be able to afford a one-to-two-bedroom condo, but it's baby steps. I know she's not ready to part with most of these things."

"Is some of this your dad's stuff?" Hannah asked.

"I'm sure most of it is his stuff, and I already took several trips to Goodwill to donate. Dad and Mom lived in this home forever. I guess over a lifetime you accumulate more than you realize," said Caleb.

They stared at the back of the packed truck. Caleb's eyes misted. Hannah wondered what would happen to her things when she passed away. Currently, everything she owned was stuffed into a few suitcases and a couple of things in storage. Someday she hoped to have a home and someone to share with it. Someone like Caleb wouldn't be half bad.

Caleb slid his hand across the top of the slick paint of the truck. "Come on. Let's head out." He cleared his throat. "I know Damien doesn't have all day."

"That's right, I've got way better things than to do than play chaperone for you two," Damien teased.

Caleb rounded the truck to the opposite side. Hannah trailed behind him. Opening the door, Caleb said, "I'll sit in the middle." He climbed in and slid down the truck bench. "I don't want you to feel uncomfortable crammed up against Damien."

"Instead, I can be pressed up against you?" Hannah smirked.

Caleb rubbed the back of his neck while Hannah joined him. Damien had taken his spot at the wheel. As he turned on the ignition, a Taylor Swift song blasted out of the speakers.

Hannah laughed, leaning forward to peer at Damien. "Damien, you're a Swiftie?"

Damien put his arm along the back of the seat, glancing over his shoulder. "Guilty." He backed out of the driveway then headed down the street.

Leaning back into her seat, Hannah commented, "Then I like you already."

For a few minutes, they listened to the lyrics as the residential neighborhood passed by them in a blur. Hannah couldn't resist and started to sing along to the lyrics of the song. Damien joined in, singing along while his fingers tapped on the steering wheel to the beat. Caleb sat stiffly in his seat.

Hannah nudged him. "Aren't you a fan?" She cocked an eyebrow.

Caleb shook his head. "It isn't that. I've nothing against Taylor Swift."

He gulped, staring directly out the windshield. The song changed to another song by Taylor Swift. Apparently, Damien had cued it to a playlist of her songs. They listened for a while. Hannah knew there was more to the songs, and she hoped he'd divulge what had soured his mood.

Finally, Caleb said, "My parents," Damien turned down the music. Even Damien appeared to know this was something big Caleb wanted to share. "They used to dance around in the kitchen to her songs when they cooked together." He bit down on his quivering lip. "I do think they were happy together. Dad had his flaws, but he had made Mom happy. I need to remind myself he wasn't horrible, just terrible with money. I think I hurt him so much when I didn't want his business. I think he thought I was rejecting him, thinking I was too good for him because I wanted to be a doctor instead. But I wish he knew it wasn't that at all. I didn't have the knack for it, and medicine was what made me come alive. There are so many things I wish I could tell him." His voice faded away.

Hannah wrapped her hand around the crook of his arm and leaned into him. "What a beautiful memory of your parents. I'm sorry you didn't get the chance to tell him what was in your heart when he was alive."

Caleb patted the top of Hannah's hand. She rested her head on his shoulder. Her body felt warm and comfortable next to him, and she soaked up every second of feeling him so close to her. Suddenly, Damien changed lanes, making her flinch and straighten herself.

"Sorry," muttered Damien. He flashed a knowing look at them then quickly returned his attention to the road. "I didn't mean to interrupt the little love fest you are having over there." Caleb punched Damien in the arm. "Ouch. What did I ever do to you?"

"Did you need a list?" Caleb wrapped an arm around Hannah's shoulders "How about we start with when you ditched me in tenth grade at the football game to go make out with Ellie under the bleachers. Should I start there?"

Damien chuckled. "I can't believe you're still hung up about that."

"I had to walk home alone in the rain, because you were my ride home," countered Caleb.

This made Damien laugh even harder. "I'm sorry. It was a complete jerk move, but you knew how hung up I had been on Ellie since middle school."

"Did you and Ellie at least date after that?" Hannah interjected.

"No." Damien shook his head. "The next day Ellie texted me and said she just wanted to be friends. So, I had Caleb mad at me for a week and no girlfriend to speak of." He pulled into the parking lot in front of the storage facility.

Hannah laughed and Caleb joined in too.

"I did forgive you eventually," Caleb offered.

"Only after I brought you McDonald's breakfast every day for a week," Damien said.

"I do think Damien has a point." Both guys turned and stared at her. "A week," tsked Hannah. "I didn't realize you were such a baby, Caleb."

Damien half choked and half laughed. "I like this one, Caleb."

Caleb swung a finger between Damien and Hannah. "You two can't be friends," he teased.

Nonchalantly, Hannah shrugged. "Too late. I think we're already friends. Aren't we?"

"Yeah, we are." Damien opened his door, climbing out of the truck. Once he stood, he popped his head back inside. "And don't forget who's helping you with free labor for the day."

"I know. You're the best." Caleb held his hands up in defeat. "Fine, you and Hannah can be friends."

Caleb and Hannah piled out of the truck. They rounded the truck to Damien's side.

"Let me go grab the key from the office," said Caleb.

Then he left them, wandering over to the office. Neither spoke as he slipped inside. A minute ticked on by.

"Caleb is way into you," Damien remarked.

Startled, Hannah shuffled her feet. "How can you even know that?"

"I can tell." Damien kicked some loosened gravel in front of himself. "So, what's up with you two?" He skeptically searched Hannah's face.

"Honestly," Hannah leaned her back against the truck and crossed her ankles. "I'm not sure. He's all over the place. One minute he's into me, the next minute he backs off and goes cold on me. We kissed then he said he didn't think it was a good idea for us to date since I was leaving soon." Through the glass wall of the storage office, Hannah spotted Caleb speaking to the worker behind the desk. "Now, I have no idea where his head is at."

Damien rolled his eyes. "Sounds like Caleb to me." His gaze traveled to the office too. When he continued, he kept his glance on Caleb. "But I've never seen him talk about someone like he's talked about you. And I haven't seen him this happy since before his dad died."

Hannah gnawed on her bottom lip. "I'm leaving in a few weeks."

"And Caleb is off to Boston," stated Damien, like he'd already heard it. Damien shifted, facing her. "I understand a relationship with Caleb could be a challenge, but Hannah, Caleb is one of the good ones. I've known him my entire life and he was always the guy to offer his seat, his food, or whatever. When my girlfriend dumped me in college, Caleb brought me Taco Bell and slept on my floor in my dorm room so I wouldn't be alone."

The door to the office swung open. Caleb exited with the keys in his hands.

"You'd be a fool if you let him go," muttered Damien under his breath.

Hannah wanted to add, it wasn't her. She hadn't let him go. It was Caleb. After spending only a few hours with Caleb, she knew he was different, better and of a higher caliber than most guys she met. If only Caleb chose to like her back. Hannah wanted to believe Caleb was letting her in, but bottom line, the ball was in his court. He'd have to make the first move, or it wasn't happening. And she hated how much power that gave him and how little control she had of the whole thing.

The keys jingled in his hands as Caleb approached. "I've got the keys. I told them we'll be back and forth for a while, and then I'll turn them in after the last trip."

Damien clapped his hands together then rubbed them back and forth. "Let's do this. I'm ready to show Hannah how much stronger I am than you. I bet I can unpack my half of the truck faster than you."

Caleb tipped up the bill of his baseball cap. "Is that a challenge?" he questioned.

"Hey," piped in Hannah. "I might be smaller, but I'm strong too." She straightened herself, putting a hand on her hip.

"Really?" Damien flashed her a skeptical glance. "You want in on this little competition?"

Hannah squared her shoulders. "I sure do. I live for a little bit of healthy competition. Especially, when I have the potential to beat out two strapping men."

Damien slapped Caleb on the chest. "I, for one, fully champion equal opportunities for all."

"Me too," Caleb interjected.

"Thanks." Hannah laughed. "What does the winner get?"

"Bragging rights, duh," Damien said.

Caleb scratched his chin and appeared to be thinking. Finally, he suggested, "How about the loser buys the other two dinner."

"Nah." Playfully, Hannah shoved Caleb. He pretended to stumble a few steps. Hannah added, "You still owe me dinner on the pier." She raised an eyebrow. "Remember?"

Caleb met her stare. "I do. And I'm looking forward to it."

Bang, zing, sizzle. The air pulsated with their combustible flirty vibe. After a few moments of them staring at one another, Damien stepped in between them, cutting the invisible string of desire.

"Ok. I've got it—" Damien held both his arms out between them. Then he swung his gaze left then right. "Loser has to sing a Taylor Swift song at the top of their lungs on the way home."

"Deal." Hannah held her hand up to high five Damien.

Damien high fived her back.

"Hey," Caleb wagged a finger at them. "I don't like you two ganging up on me."

"Is that what we were doing?" Damien asked.

Hannah added, "I thought we were only having a little fun." She tilted her head toward Caleb. "Why? Are you afraid you're going to lose?"

"Of course not," said Caleb defensively. "I just don't know the lyrics to any of the songs."

Shaking a finger at him, Hannah said, "Nah, no excuses. You can display the lyrics on your phone while the song plays. Everyone knows that."

Caleb's jaw tightened but his eyes were playful. "Fine." He held up a finger and added, "I agree to your terms, but only because I know I'm going to win."

"Yeah, yeah, yeah. Those are fighting words." Damien climbed back into the truck so they could drive to the appropriate storage unit.

Hannah shifted to face Caleb. "You've asked for it," she smirked.

Caleb shrugged. "I suppose I have." He opened the passenger door and held it open.

As she brushed past him to get into the truck, Hannah ran a finger down his Adam's apple. Then she tapped on his bobbing Adam's apple. "You better start warming this thing up." Their eyes locked as her finger trailed further down to the concave place between his collar bone.

"I guess I'd better." Caleb swallowed, making his Adam's apple bob back and forth in a tantalizing manner.

With weak knees, Hannah removed her hand. All she could think about was the feel of his skin under the pad of her finger.

CHAPTER 19

After returning the storage keys, Caleb climbed back into the truck where Damien and Hannah waited. Hannah scooted to the middle seat.

Caleb grumbled, "Ok, you two. What Taylor Swift song do I have to sing?" He scratched his jaw.

"We haven't decided yet. We're leaning towards *Shake It Off*, but we're going to see where our mood takes us." Hannah held up a finger, wiggling her cell phone out of her pocket with her other hand. "But we did decide on what karaoke place to go to." Hannah tapped a few times on her cell phone screen then held it out for him to see the place displayed on her phone.

Caleb groaned, swiping the phone from Hannah's hands. "You can't be serious. I never agreed to karaoke. I agreed to singing out loud in the truck." He shifted closer to her and double glanced at her. Gazing back down at the screen, he continued, "What are you trying to arm wrestle me to do? Do people go to karaoke places for fun?" Suddenly, his skin itched. Caleb looped his finger around his collar and tugged.

"People love karaoke places." Damien started the ignition,

pulling out of the storage place and onto the street. He continued, "I, for one, think this is going to be a ton of fun."

As she swiped her phone back, Hannah grinned. "Me too."

Caleb rubbed the back of his neck. Then he leaned in closer to Hannah and said, "I think you're enjoying this too much." Her gaze skidded up to his, making his pulse jackhammer. Dang, he wanted to kiss those twitching lips of hers. "Just wait until you both endure four minutes of me singing off key in nails on a chalkboard voice."

Damien chuckled. "There's no enduring involved on our part just pure listening bliss. I can guarantee it."

Hannah linked her hands around his elbow. "Ahh." The pads of her fingers tightened against his skin. "Are you going to bow out because you're scared?"

"Never." Caleb flashed Damien a pointed look, though Damien couldn't clock it since he was focused on driving. "I wouldn't dream of backing out of it." Then Caleb gave Hannah the toothiest smile he could muster.

Inside his middle churned. Caleb was a terrible singer, and not in a he's so bad it's kind of cute way. No, he was awful enough that his church choir leader asked him to stop attending, because he threw everyone off key. Supposedly the choir took everyone, at least that was what they advertised when he went.

"I'm glad to see," Hannah moved her other hand to his chest, giving it a quick pat, "you're being a good sport."

His mood lightened a tad from having Hannah cuddled up close to him. "You did just do manual labor for several hours for free." He weaved his fingers through the hand on his chest, bringing it down to his lap. "So, thank you. I appreciate it, and I think this is a small price to pay."

Hannah nodded and gave his hand a squeeze.

"You can say that again." Damien made a hard left into a parking lot. "You owe us this."

"I guess I do." Caleb unbuckled his seatbelt. "Just get ready for your ears to bleed."

Damien laughed, opening his truck door. "By the way, you're buying us food too. Hannah and I are starving. We looked up the menu while you were returning the storage key. I've heard this place has incredible nachos." After Damien climbed out, he glanced back into the truck at Hannah and Caleb. "Show him the pictures we were looking at Hannah."

Hannah fidgeted with her phone until she found the photo she wanted. She held it up for Caleb to see the image. "See look at those," her finger grazed the screen, "they serve the nachos on a platter the size of a pizza pan. Don't those nachos look delicious?" Her eyes sparkled with childlike wonder.

Caleb couldn't fight his attraction even if he wanted to. He had an irresistible urge to lean in and kiss Hannah on the temple, so he did. "They look great." Afterwards, he pulled away, opening his door. "Let's go get them."

With a smile, Caleb climbed out of the truck, offering Hannah a hand to help her unload. Hannah took it, climbing out of the truck. Caleb didn't let go of her hand after he closed the truck door. Instead, he weaved his fingers with hers as they crossed the parking lot to the karaoke place. Being late afternoon, when they entered it, they found the place basically empty. The tension between his shoulder blades loosened a tad. If he was singing, at least it was only to a few random people.

They waited for the host to seat them.

Damien slugged Caleb's arm. "See, we're going easy on you."

Caleb dramatically rubbed his arm. "Would you quit hitting me?"

"Like I could ever hurt you. You've got thirty pounds of muscle on me," replied Damien.

"Do you want to sing first or eat first?" interjected Hannah.

"Let's get this thing over with," muttered Caleb, rubbing the back of his neck.

With her gaze directed at Damien, Hannah asked like they were co-conspirators, "Are we still going with *Shake It Off?*"

"Yep." Damien looped his thumb through his empty belt loop. "I believe you can't sing that song and *not* dance."

Cold sweat gathered at his temples. Caleb couldn't believe he was doing this. The only reason he was even entertaining the idea was because Hannah looked pleased with him for playing along. He reminded himself it was one song and was playful fun. Though his mounting blood pressure begged to differ.

"I want dancing too." Hannah went up on her tiptoes and kissed him rapidly on the cheek. "I know you've got moves. I saw them at the arcade."

"The arcade was different. I stomped on some squares that lit up. It wasn't real dancing." Why was it so hot in here? Sweat trickled down his temples, and Caleb swiped at it with the back of his wrist. "I never said I would dance."

"Dancing is one hundred percent required," smirked Damien. "The song is about shaking it off."

His jaw tightened. "Fine." Then Caleb brought up his hand into air quotes. "I'll try my best to, quote, *shake it off.*"

Hannah gleefully clasped her hands together and grinned brightly. A host interrupted them and led them to a table. After the host set the menus down, they slid into their chairs.

Before the host left them, Damien said, "Our friend here is ready to sing. How does it work?"

"Nobody is here," the host motioned around the room, "just walk up to the stage, search for the song you want, select it, and start singing into the microphone."

"Sounds easy enough. Thanks," Hannah warmly replied. Then she wrapped her arm around his shoulders. "You can do this." She gave his bicep a squeeze then removed her arm.

As he rubbed the back of his neck, Caleb asked, "Can you promise not to make fun of my terrible singing voice?"

Tilting her head to the side, the lines on Hannah's face

softened. Her voice took on a serious tone when she said, "I wouldn't dare."

They perused the menu for a minute. When the server came by, they put in an order of nachos to share. Music played in the background, because nobody was singing.

After Caleb's jittery knee hit the table one too many times, he slapped his hand on the top of it. "I'm ready." He slid out of his seat and made his way to the small stage.

Damien cupped his mouth and yelled, "Woohoo!"

The sound of Hannah's overly dramatic slow clap rang in his ears. Though his hands shook, Caleb forced himself to find the song on the machine and hit play. He took a deep cleansing breath. Then he brought the microphone up to his mouth and began to sing the lit-up lyrics on the screen. It wasn't terribly hard, but it was embarrassing and completely out of his comfort zone.

After he sang a few lines of the song, Damien and Hannah jumped to their feet and danced along to his terrible voice. His shoulders loosened. Eventually to his surprise, a laugh escaped him as he continued to butcher the song. But when he peered over at Damien and Hannah fully enjoying his pathetic attempt to karaoke, Caleb knew it was a small price to pay to see Hannah so happy and alive. By the time the chorus came around, his hips naturally started to sway to the beat.

Hannah clapped then pointed at him. "He's dancing!" She gave Damien a high five.

Damien cupped his mouth. "Look at those moves. This guy could be a backup dancer."

Finally, the song ended. Caleb took a dramatic bow and wandered back to the table.

"You've been holding out on us." Hannah shoved him as he sat down next to her. "I didn't know you had such great dance moves." Her eyes glimmered as she peered over at him, and Caleb couldn't remember a time when he found someone more beautiful.

The server came and plopped down a huge platter of nachos in the middle of their table. "Let me know if you want to order anything else." Then they disappeared without further explanation.

Damien's eyes dilated as he stared at the big platter. "These look amazing." He swiped a chip covered in cheese and guacamole. After Damien took a bite, he pointed at his mouth and said, "These are amazing. It makes having to sit through your awful performance worth it."

"You know you loved it," said Caleb, pulling a chip free from the pile.

Hannah took one too. They sat in contented silence for a few minutes eating the nachos and listening to the background music. Nobody else had tried to karaoke since him, but then again it wasn't even five.

"So, Hannah," Damien wiped his face with a napkin, "when do you leave Newport and where are you headed next?"

"Um." Hannah fumbled with the napkin dispenser on the table, yanking one free, she wiped her face then continued, "I leave in a few weeks give or take. As to where I'm headed, it'll depend on where I get a job."

"Where did you apply?" Damien tossed another cheesy chip into his mouth.

"Everywhere," Hannah rubbed her hands back and forth over her thighs, "but mainly on the east coast."

"Boston?" Damien asked.

"Yes," Hannah selected another chip with extra guacamole on it, "Boston is on my list." She shoved the chip into her mouth and chewed. Then licked her lips clean.

Damien further inquired, "Have you ever been there before?"

"Nope." Hannah shook her head, taking a sip of her water. "But I've heard it's great."

"Caleb will be there, so that would make Boston even better." Then Damien wagged a finger between Hannah and Caleb. "You two need to keep whatever this thing is between you going, because the fact you were able to get Caleb to sing means he's really into you."

Heat rose up his neck. "Hey," said Caleb with a pointed glare.

Innocently, Damien held up his hands. "I speak the truth."

Meekly, Hannah tucked her hair behind her ears. "I think he sang for you, Damien," she said quietly.

"Nah," said Damien. "I can't get him to do things like that. He did that just for you."

Caleb leaned in and whispered, "He's right. You're the only one I'll ever sing for." Then he gave her thigh a quick squeeze.

They finished the nachos.

Damien drove them back to Caleb's house to drop them off.

"It was nice meeting you," said Hannah as she slipped out of the truck.

"Likewise," replied Damien. He pointed at Caleb. "Call me later."

"I will," said Caleb, closing the truck door.

They stood in the driveway together watching the truck disappear down the road.

Once his truck was out of sight, Hannah swiveled to her feet. "I should go." She wrung her hands together. "I have some studying to do. My exam is close."

Caleb didn't want her to go. If anything, he cared to whittle away the remaining hours of the evening together. Hannah's exam had to come first. "I know you have to go." Caleb couldn't resist, he grasped her hand and gently tugged her body closer to his. "But I didn't want you to leave without me confessing something." He paused. Her gaze flickered across his face, warming his insides. His pulse thundered behind his ears.

"And what would that be?" asked Hannah, her perfect eyebrows went up.

"I wish I had handled everything differently this summer," confessed Caleb. He pushed some of her loosened strands of hair from her forehead. "I wish I hadn't freaked out and pushed you away. I wasted so much time, when we could've been together."

Hannah shifted closer. Her body brushed up against his chest. "Maybe it was for the best." But her hand went up and cupped his neck around the collar of his shirt. "You're off to Boston, and I don't know where I'll be. It was less messy this way to prevent our lives becoming too intertwined. You can go off and be a free man."

"But I don't want to be a free man." Caleb gulped. His skin ignited where her fingertips lingered at his neck. "Hannah, I want to be with you."

There he said it. He showed her every card in his deck, and it was terrifying. For a second, Hannah locked eyes with Caleb. His pulse raced. She had him hook, line and sinker. It didn't matter where Hannah went, a part of her would be firmly planted in his heart, forever.

"That's well and good, but now what?" A single car drove by the house, and Hannah glanced toward it as she continued, "I must make the best choice for me." She paused. Then found his gaze again but when she continued, her voice was smaller, "I'm not wandering to Boston to chase after you. It's absurd. There are no promises between us. A few dates, one kiss, that isn't enough to rewrite one's life."

"But what if you visited Boston and saw what a fantastic place it was. Maybe you'd fall in love with it. Then you wouldn't be going there only for me. You'd be going there for you too. Plus, Boston is a huge city. It's not like we'll run into each other randomly if things didn't work out between us," said Caleb.

Hannah exhaled. "You've given me a lot to think about." She swung her gaze back to Caleb. "Because if I'm being honest, I'd like to give us another chance too." His heart soared. He wrapped an arm around her waist and brought her toward his body until their hips collided. Her other hand flat palmed his chest, "Especially, after you showcased your brilliant singing voice. I mean, a lady can't resist that."

Caleb laughed. He cupped both sides of her neck between his hands. "I know I'm super impressive. How can the ladies resist when I'm singing?"

"Ladies?" Hannah raised an eyebrow while she smirked.

Caleb chimed in, "I mean, you're the only lady I care about."

"That's better." Hannah peered up and him with a scrunched nose. "Though you are terrible at singing, in an adorable, *how can you not love him* kind of way."

His words were music to his ears. "I warned you." Caleb leaned in closer. Their faces an inch apart.

"You did," Hannah's gaze skidded between his lips and his eyes then back again, "warn me."

The air cackled causing an addicting thrill to race through him. His nerve endings tingled as he anticipated their lips dancing with one another. How much he had missed holding her, kissing her, being with her. His biggest regret was it took him this long to open himself up to the possibility of them.

Slowly, Caleb said, "I'm going to kiss you." He paused, waiting for her approval.

Hannah nearly covered the inch of ground left between their lips. "I'm counting on it," she whispered.

Her cool minty breath tickled his cheek. Not waiting a second longer, Caleb skimmed his lips lightly across hers. She tasted even better than from that day in Balboa. Hannah rose on her tiptoes as her hand plunged into his hair. Caleb's thumb glided down the length of her jaw. Hannah fisted a handful of his shirt while she deepened their kiss. He brushed his tongue along her bottom lip, and they parted, allowing his mouth to fully taste her. Her sweet scent radiated in the air he breathed, making his head spin and mind blank.

Why had he forced himself to wait this long? To have Hannah, to be with her. Because, kissing Hannah, Caleb knew he'd do whatever it took to make this thing work. He didn't know the future, but he knew his heart. It only beat for her. Caleb lost track of time, and his worries whisked away with the salty summer air. With Hannah in his arms, he knew everything would work out, the universe would align, and they'd end up with each other. He was being completely optimistic, because for once, he believed in the magic of love.

Finally, Caleb forced his lips away from hers. He kissed her gently on the temple, wrapping his arms around her waist in a tight embrace. Hannah snuggled her head against his chest as his galloping heartrate slowly returned to its trusty beat.

With her head still buried against him, Hannah said, "Will you go with me to dinner with my parents and Jordyn? I don't think I can face it alone. I know Adam wants to do it before I leave. I'll probably put it off until the night before I'm out of here." She tilted her head back, finding his gaze.

Caleb brought his hand to her hair. With his pointer finger, he swiped the loosened strands of hair across her forehead to behind her ear. "I'd love to go."

A smile spread across Hannah's face, a smile he felt down to his toes. "Thank you," she whispered.

"Anytime," said Caleb.

Once again, Hannah snuggled her head against his chest, and Caleb held her until the darkness of the evening made them say goodnight.

CHAPTER 20

The next few weeks passed with Hannah in her own little love bubble with Caleb. They coached the rest of the swim season together. In between practices, she studied like crazy for her P.A. exam, usually with Caleb next to her, reading a book or surfing the internet.

Once they officially started dating, they couldn't get enough of each other. Every available minute they spent together. She tried her best not to worry about what things would look like at the end of summer. Instead, she poured her entire anxious energy into preparing for her P.A. exam.

Hannah believed it paid off, because when she left the exam, she felt like she aced it. Unfortunately, her self-doubt crept in. So, when the results for her exam ended up in her inbox, her courage faltered. She called Caleb for support.

"Caleb," Hannah readjusted her phone in the crook of her neck, "Can you stay on the phone with me while I check if I passed my P.A. exam?"

"Absolutely," replied Caleb.

A swirling whirl of self-doubt and anxiety made it seem

impossible to face the results. Caleb always knew what to say to make her feel better.

Her heart rate rose to a staccato beat. "What if I don't pass?" Hannah asked.

"Then you'll take it again, but I think you nailed it. If I learned anything about you, it's that you don't give up on anything. Besides, I know the long hours you've put into studying for it. Plus, you felt good after you left the exam. Remember?"

Caleb sounded so reasonable.

"True. I did leave the exam thinking I aced it," Hannah said.

"See. You might as well open it."

"Okay." Hannah held her breath and clicked open. Her eyes scanned the page and read the beautiful word; pass. "I passed!"

"Congratulations! I never doubt it."

Hannah exhaled, and her blood pressure lowered. "I'm so relieved."

"I bet."

"Now, I just have to find a job," Hannah said.

"And you will."

"Can we go out to dinner tonight to celebrate?"

"Duh. It's not every day I get to take my girlfriend out after she passes her P.A. exam."

Her heart melted. "I love it when you call me that."

"My girlfriend?"

"Yep." Hannah smiled. "It never gets old."

"Well, my girlfriend, be ready at seven dressed in your finest attire, because we are celebrating."

"I can't wait." Hannah ran a hand over the top of her head. "Oh, I almost forgot to ask. How did the open house go for Jenna?"

Caleb and Hannah had worked together over the past few weeks to get the home completely ready for the open house. Beachfront homes with gorgeous views didn't go on the market every day. The realtor had told them Jenna shouldn't have a problem selling it.

"Great, even better than we expected. Mom received a few offers."

"Already?" questioned Hannah.

"Yep, so I think she is going to put in an offer on that condo we went and looked at with her last week."

"The one with the gym and rooftop patio?" asked Hannah.

If it was the place Hannah remembered, she believed it would be a perfect place for Jenna.

"Yes, that's the one."

"Ah, I'm so happy for the both of you. I'm sure you're relieved." Hannah scooted off her bed and went to her suitcase to find something to wear to dinner.

"I am. I can't believe I accomplished everything I set out to do this summer," Caleb said.

"I can, because you're you." Hannah shuffled through the contents of her suitcase.

"Thanks. I'll see you tonight."

"Tonight," said Hannah.

~

Three weeks later, Hannah pounded a fist against the AC button. "Dang, AC." She'd forgotten how good she'd had it with her rental car. Having her car back from the repair shop only made her starkly aware of how desperately she needed a new vehicle.

Caleb pressed the lower button on the window. The window went down halfway. "Sorry, that you have this thing back." He glanced around it. "It's still in better condition than my hunk of junk. I hope my car will make it across the country. Once I get to Boston, I'm selling it for parts. I figure with the subway system as good as it is there, I won't need to have a car."

"Really?" Hannah cocked an eyebrow and changed lanes. "No

car? I thought you said you were keeping it, because you won't be able to fly back for holidays."

Suddenly, she wished she hadn't insisted on picking up Caleb. He'd offered to drive her to dinner with Adam, Trisha, and Jordyn. But she was too anxious to sit in the passenger seat, so when she pulled up to Caleb's house, she had told him to hop in. Her mind was reeling, and she knew it wouldn't slow down until the dinner was over.

Besides seeing Jordyn at swim practice, Hannah hadn't spoken to Adam or Trisha since the swim meet. Though they had made an effort to come watch Jordyn compete, this made Hannah happy. Maybe her chat with Adam had made a difference. Maybe he'd get it right this time around when he still had time to correct the course.

"Yeah, my hunk of junk, I need to ditch it. And I don't have the money to replace it. I talked to the mechanic that did my repairs from the accident, and he had a lengthy list of things that were wrong with the engine," said Caleb.

Hannah still didn't know where she was headed after the summer ended. So far, she'd applied for jobs in most major cities on the east coast.

When she didn't reply, Caleb shifted in his seat and faced her. "Have you given any thought about making the road trip with me for your job interviews while I head to Boston?"

Caleb was headed across country himself to move to Boston permanently. Hannah had interviews lined up along the east coast, but who knew what city she would land in. Her heart told her to take a job in Boston if she landed one, the logical part of her brain told her to hold her horses and weigh out every job offer.

"It's the car situation." Hannah made a hard left into the parking lot of the restaurant and parked. "I'll need my car to get me to the different cities. I have my first interview in Boston, but then I'll need to drive to Washington DC and New York."

"What if we took your car? I could sell my car before we leave. You could drop me off in Boston then venture on to your other places," said Caleb, unbuckling his seatbelt.

"My car doesn't have AC." Hannah flipped down the visor and scrutinized her makeup a second time.

"Mine isn't in great shape either. It sputters a bit, but no real cool air comes out. I had forgotten how broken everything was until I got it back from the repair shop," said Caleb.

"Ahh." Hannah dug her lip gloss out of her purse and reapplied some to her lips. "Do you think we can handle driving across country together with no AC?" She raised a skeptical eyebrow. "It might be a recipe for disaster. We might hate each other by the end."

"I could never hate you." Caleb leaned closer.

"I think you don't know what heat with full humidity can do to a person," Hannah said.

Caleb laughed. "Maybe it would be the perfect thing to test our true feelings for one another?"

"True." Hannah smacked her lips together then tossed her lip gloss back into her purse. For a moment, she hesitated. It wasn't like they hadn't discussed this numerous times over the past weeks. Their time together had only solidified her feelings for Caleb, but traveling across the country together was an entirely different animal. Without analyzing it any further she said, "Sure. Let's do it."

Caleb smiled. "Perfect. I have the entire route mapped out. I think we could do it in three days. Mom has an aunt in Oklahoma we can stop at for a night, and my dad's brother in Ohio said we could stay there for a night. You'd save on gas and not be driving alone across the country. It's a win win."

"Are you sure your family won't mind me staying with them too?"

"Of course not, I've already spoken to them about you."

"You have?" Hannah slammed the visor shut and unbuckled her seatbelt.

Caleb nodded then leaned in and kissed her on the lips. "I told them my girlfriend was thinking of moving to Boston too."

Hannah shoved Caleb and opened her door with her other hand "Hey, I don't want them getting the wrong idea about us." She climbed out. Caleb did too. He rounded the car to meet her on the other side.

Once in front of her, Caleb stopped and shoved one hand into his pocket. "And what idea about us would that be?"

"I don't want them thinking I'm moving in with you," said Hannah. "I'm not moving in with anyone until I'm married."

Caleb shook his head. "No, I was very specific that you'd be looking for your own place."

Hannah spotted Adam as he pulled up to the front of the restaurant. He parked the car. Trisha opened her door, and Jordyn climbed out from the back seat. Tightness pinched her chest.

Caleb tracked her gaze, spotting them too, he wrapped an arm around her. "It's going to be okay. I'll play referee. I won't leave you, even if I'm bursting for the toilet."

With her gaze still on them, Hannah rested her head against his shoulder. "I'm holding you to that."

Halted in place, Hannah's heart seized as their family of three wandered into the restaurant. Her heart ached a tad for what she'd never have. She wondered if in the future if Adam would be in her life or if once, she left Newport, they'd go back to no contact. She was hopeful for something more. Hannah remembered how much Jordyn had grown to like her. At least she was leaving Newport with a new sister. A sister was one more person in her life than she had before summer started. With Caleb, that made two. Sometimes you had to be grateful for what you were given and not fixate on what you'd never have.

Hannah straightened herself and found Caleb's hand. "I

suppose we'd better go in." They trudged across the parking lot to the restaurant.

They arrived at the front of the restaurant. Caleb's hand hovered over the door handle. He found her gaze and asked, "Are you ready?"

Hannah nodded. "Let's do this."

Somehow with Caleb by her side, even an awkward dinner seemed doable.

Caleb opened the door to the restaurant, and they entered the lobby. Hannah peered over the tops of people's heads in the tight restrictive space. She spotted Jordyn and made eye contact with her and waved. Jordyn jumped up from her seat and raced over to them, throwing her arms around Hannah in a big hug.

"I'm so glad you're here." Jordyn dropped her arms, breaking their embrace. "Come on. We're in the back."

They moved to follow.

Caleb leaned into Hannah's ear and whispered, "You've got this." He kissed her on the temple.

Hannah straightened her back and found her equilibrium.

She and Caleb took the seats across the table from Trisha, Adam, and Jordyn.

For a moment, nobody spoke. Hannah wondered if the entire evening would be filled with awkward and forced conversation. Jordyn elbowed Adam.

Adam cleared his throat and asked, "So, I heard from Jordyn that you passed your P.A. exam. Congratulations."

"Thanks." Hannah snagged the menu in front of her and opened it. "I've already set up some job interviews."

"Are any of the jobs for around here?" asked Jordyn hopefully.

Hannah scrunched her nose. "Unfortunately, no. But I promise once I'm settled, I'll fly you out to visit me." Then Hannah darted her glance to Trisha. "That is only if you're okay with it."

Trisha fluffed her hair. "I think that could work. What do you think, Adam?" She shifted toward him.

"Or maybe we'll have to make a vacation out of it." Adam looked to Hannah for approval. "Then we'll all come to visit you."

"I'd love that," said Hannah.

Then the server came by and took their order.

So, she and Adam would most likely never be close. But she could create something with him, even if it was different than what she imagined. She knew she and Jordyn would stay in touch, which was more than she had at the beginning of the summer.

Then there was Caleb. She had him too.

And it was more than enough.

CHAPTER 21

Summer ended. Caleb said goodbye to his childhood home, and his mom moved to a new two-bedroom condo in Newport Beach. Caleb and Hannah drove across the country together. A few days after arriving in Boston, Caleb anxiously waited outside of the medical facility where Hannah was inside interviewing for a job. He double checked his watch. Hannah's interview started an hour ago, and she still wasn't finished. Caleb chose to believe the lengthy interview time was a good sign. If Hannah received an offer of employment, Caleb was one step closer to getting her to stay in Boston.

Next week, Caleb started his residency. Hannah had lined up interviews in New York and Washington DC. The plan was for her to decide where she wanted to be once she saw those places too. Caleb selfishly hoped today's interview was a success, and Hannah would stay without needing to venture on to those other places. A man could dream. He cared far too much for the woman he met in Newport Beach only a few months prior.

When he checked his watch a third time, Caleb knew he needed to stop. With a bench a few feet away, Caleb forced himself to sit down to wait. Cars honked. The summer air was sticky like cotton candy. Sweat trickled down his temples. Despite the stifling heat, he knew once they reentered the subway tunnel, the outside would feel heavenly.

The automatic glass sliding doors of the facility opened. With her hands filled with papers, Hannah spilled out to the street. Quickly, Caleb rose to meet her. "So, how did it go?" He forced his shaky hand into the pocket of his shorts.

Hannah gnawed on her bottom lip. "Well, they offered me the job on the spot."

Relief washed over him. "They did?" he asked excitedly.

"Yes." Hannah shook the papers in her hands. "But I'm not making a decision until I go to New York and DC."

His heart plummeted, but with courage he replied, "I wouldn't expect anything less. You need to make the best choice for you." There that sounded normal and reasonable.

Hannah folded the papers in her hand in half and shoved them into her purse. After she readjusted her purse, Hannah said, "Thanks for being so supportive."

"No problem." Caleb wrapped an arm around her shoulders, bringing her closer to him. "Besides you don't have to leave for two days, and that gives me plenty of time to help you fall in love with Boston."

Hannah cocked an eyebrow. "Oh, is that your plan?" She swiped at the sweat tickling her brow. "This humidity isn't helping to win me over."

"It's summer. New York will be miserable too. I'm not sure about DC but I imagine it's terrible there too."

"I'd still have to find an apartment that I can afford," Hannah said.

"I'm already on that," said Caleb matter-of-factly. "There are two women who are in my residency program. Their third roommate took a different placement than originally planned. They need someone to fill that vacancy. The room is yours if you want it, and it's within your price range."

"Wow. You've managed to think of everything." Hannah motioned toward the subway stop a few blocks up the street. "Should we go to lunch?"

Caleb nodded. They meandered down the street holding hands. By the time they entered the subway station, Caleb's shirt stuck to his skin. They swiped their metro cards at the entrance and continued to the proper track.

A few subway trains came and went, but they were waiting for the green line. Somewhere someone was playing the saxophone. The long drawn out notes vibrated down the tunnel. Hannah glanced over her shoulder in what appeared an attempt to locate the musician.

"I've always enjoyed a good saxophone solo," commented Hannah.

"Guitar for me," added Caleb. "I regret I never learned to play. In thirty years, when I retire, I'm going to finally take lessons."

"Maybe you could learn now?" Hannah patted down her hair. "Why wait?"

His chest felt tight. Caleb didn't want Hannah to take a job in New York or DC. He wanted her here in Boston. After their road trip together, Caleb knew Hannah was the one for him. The days on end of driving in a hotter than hot vehicle had only solidified Caleb's feelings.

During the trip, Hannah had entertained him with stories from her childhood and college years. Caleb soaked up every little bit of information she revealed like he was seeing her for the very first time. The woman fascinated him, enraptured him, and more importantly Caleb knew he loved her. Loved her enough that if Hannah chose him, chose Boston, Caleb knew it was only a matter of time before he proposed.

"Please stay here in Boston with me," Caleb sputtered out. "Please don't go to New York, DC, Chicago or wherever else you might go. I must live here for the next four years, after that I'll go wherever you want when I finish my residency. You can pick. I don't care where, because if I'm with you, I know it will be home to me."

Hannah stared back. She blinked. Caleb's courage faltered. A long pause landed smack dab in the middle of them. The worry he had been fighting the entire summer was staring him dead in the face.

The green line train finally arrived. Caleb interlaced his fingers with hers. He guided her to the sliding doors. They climbed in. Luckily, it wasn't as crowded as rush hour. When he spotted two seats next to each other, Caleb led them over to them and sat. Abruptly, the train bolted forward. Hannah squeezed on Caleb's forearm to keep herself from crashing forward.

"Say something." Caleb scanned her face for an indication of how she'd respond. A sinking feeling spread across his gut. "Anything." His voice was small.

Hannah's gaze flickered to him then to the window which only had long stretches of tunnel and nothing to see. After an eternity, she shifted back to face him. "I'm scared. Scared that I'll rewrite my entire life for the simple hope of something. It's a lot to ask of a person." She closed her eyes briefly and exhaled.

"I know I'm asking a lot. If circumstances were different, I wish I could be the one following you, but I can't, I'm locked in here. But Hannah," Caleb found her hand, "I love you. This thing between us is better than anything I've experienced with anyone else. I don't want to rush you. And you don't have to say it back, but Hannah someday in the future when the time is right, and you feel comfortable, I plan on marrying you. Because you're it for me. You're the person I've spent my entire life trying to find."

"Do you," Hannah pushed her hair over shoulder, "really mean all of that? You love me?"

"I do." Caleb smiled. "Rear ending your car was the best thing that ever happened to me."

Hannah laughed. "I'm glad you hit me too, as weird as that sounds."

The train slowed down and stopped. People brushed past them, getting off and getting on. A few seconds later, the train lurched forward again. It barreled down the track.

"And, Caleb," Hannah wove her fingers through his and gave them a reassuring squeeze.

"Yeah." Caleb waited.

"I'll stay." Hannah's eyes sparkled back at him. "I'll give Boston a try, because I love you too. And they say go big or go home."

Caleb beamed, leaning closer. "Now that," he brought his lips to her ear and whispered, "is music to my ears."

Then Caleb cupped her neck with one hand. His hand weaved through the silky strands of her hair. Slowly, he brought his lips to hers until they brushed against one another. Hannah dissipated the dull ache in his heart. She had fit herself perfectly into the spot he didn't know needed to be filled. As their lips skated with one another, Caleb knew they were going to be fine. Even better than fine, they'd be magic.

Soon, the train filled with more people as they climbed on at the next stop. The crowded space around him became dimmer until it was only him and her, kissing like today was a promise, tomorrow was a gift, and the future with Hannah was the only thing that mattered. Together in Boston, he had it all.

EPILOGUE

The heat of summer faded into fall. Leaves changed with the season. Winter came with its blustery bone chilling cold. Then after a never-ending winter, spring arrived. On a rare Saturday off in the springtime, Hannah and Caleb drove out of the city to Walden Pond. Walden Pond had been on Hannah's bucket list since she had moved to Boston last summer. With their busy schedules, a planned visit had taken the back seat. Finally, Caleb took the initiative and finagled a way for their schedules to line up to go.

Tall trees older than a century lined both sides of the road. Hannah peered up at the soaring, long branches. She wondered if transcendentalists like Emerson and Thoreau had meandered down these same shady roads during their time here. Caleb turned down the path which led to the parking lot in front of the pond. After he parked, they both climbed out and went to the trunk of the car. A morning dew chilled Hannah a tad.

"I think I'll put on my jacket over my sweatshirt," remarked Hannah, pulling it out of the trunk where she had left it

After she put it on, they shut the trunk of the car. Caleb appeared distracted as he patted his pocket. "I think I misplaced the keys.

Um," Caleb's glance skidded around the parking lot, pond, and her, "can you unlock the car with your set so I can look for them. I think they slipped out of my pocket." She dug her set out of her pocket and pressed the unlock button. Then he disappeared to the driver's side.

While he looked for his keys, Hannah yelled back toward Caleb, "Hey, should we leave the picnic stuff in here? Or take it?" She waited for a reply.

Right when she was about to round the car to find Caleb, she heard him say, "Let's leave it. I thought we could go for a walk on the path around the pond then come back to gather our things for a picnic. I found them." He held them out of the car for her to see.

"Good." Hannah closed the trunk, leaving the picnic basket in the back.

Caleb shoved his keys into his side jacket pocket and straightened himself. He closed his door and locked it. "Are you ready to go?" He neared her.

"I'm ready." Hannah peered out at the woods taking in a deep cleansing breath. The air smelled like dirt and dew, but it beat the urine-ridden subway any day. "This place is beautiful. No wonder it was the inspiration for Thoreau and so many other writers."

"I agree." Caleb took Hannah's hand walking toward the path at the end of the parking lot.

Their feet hit the dirt path. They roamed further down. Soon, they entered the thickly dense woods and as if on cue the sounds of nature became louder. Birds chirped. Insects buzzed. Beauty of nature surrounded them.

"I forget how loud the city is," remarked Hannah. "The silence here is something dreams are made of."

"It is quiet here," agreed Caleb. "I'm not sure if I find it soothing or terrifying."

They continued for a while, enjoying the silence. Since they entered the path, they hadn't seen a single other person. It was vastly different from the everyday hustle and bustle of Boston, a city she had grown to love.

A little path cut toward the pond. "I read this leads to a nice view of the pond," said Caleb.

Caleb veered down it. Hannah followed. Soon the trees broke and gave way to the pond. The sight was spectacular.

A hand flew to Hannah's chest. "This is beautiful." She wistfully sighed. "Like magical things really happen here." When Caleb didn't respond, Hannah shifted to face him. His brow was furrowed and slick with sweat. "Everything, okay?"

Caleb nodded. "Sorry, I'm super nervous." He exhaled.

Hannah tilted her head to the side. "Why?"

"Because—" Caleb glanced out at the pond then back her. "Because, Hannah, I love you. And I want to ask you to marry me."

She gasped as her hands flew to her mouth. Caleb kneeled, removing a ring from his pocket. He held the ring up. "This was what I was looking for in the car. This ring was Jenna's. I almost flipped out earlier when it slid out of my pocket. I didn't want you to spot a big bulky box." He shook his head. "Sorry, I'm rambling, but Jenna wants this to be yours. More importantly, I want this to be yours." Caleb locked eyes with Hannah. "Since the day I crashed into you, I have fallen more in love with you than I ever thought possible. You make everything better. You make me want to believe and trust. You make me want to be a better person. I love you more every day. Hannah, what do you say? Will you marry me?"

Tears tickled the corners of her eyes. Hannah didn't have the words, they were caught in her throat, so she enthusiastically nodded. Caleb jumped up and pushed the ring on her finger. Once the ring was secure, Caleb spun her around. Hannah laughed with delight.

"I can't believe I'm getting married," yelled Hannah. Her voice echoed around her, rippling across the dazzling water.

When her feet touched the ground, Hannah wrapped her arms around Caleb's waist. "Thank you. I love you." She peered down at the sparkly diamond on her finger then back up at Caleb.

Caleb kissed her and said, "I love you, back."

Hannah gazed at her ringed finger again. "So, Jenna already knows—"

"Jordyn does too." Caleb kissed her on the cheek. "She made me promise that you would make her a bridesmaid."

"I think that sounds perfect," replied Hannah. "And Adam?"

"He knows." Caleb wrapped his arms around her. "He said Trisha and him wouldn't miss it."

"But I'm walking myself down the aisle," said Hannah.

"Of course, you're the only one I want to look at."

Hannah kissed Caleb again. "You've thought of everything."

"I wanted you to say yes," said Caleb casually.

"And I did," confirmed Hannah. "And I'll continue to say yes for the rest of my life."

"Me too." Caleb rested his chin on top of her head. They stared out at the beautiful lake. "I love you, Hannah."

"I love you back."

MEET THE AUTHOR

Emi Hilton is a California native who was born at March Airforce Base, to an Officer in the US Army Combat Engineer Battalion father and an English Professor mother. Emi followed in her mother's footsteps and graduated from Brigham Young University in English. While in college, she took a year and a half break from her studies to serve as a full-time missionary for her church in the Canary Islands. Emi writes sweet contemporary romance novels. Both her debut novel, Memories in Morro Bay, and second novel, Bluebird Sky, were nominated for Whitney Awards. When Emi isn't writing, she enjoys training for marathons, fishing off local piers with her husband and three sons, or visiting her other love, Spain.

OTHER TITLES FROM

5 PRINCE PUBLISHING

225

www.ingramcontent.com/pod-product-compliance
Lightning Source LLC
Chambersburg PA
CBHW020834260626
47169CB00003B/978